This book should be returned to any branch of the
Lancashire County Library on or before the date

D0297618

1/16

Lancashire County Library
Bowran Street
Preston PR1 2UX

Lancashire
County Council

www.lancashire.gov.uk/libraries

WHEN SOMEBODY KILLS YOU

WHEN SOMEBODY KILLS YOU

A Rat Pack Mystery
Robert J. Randisi

Severn House Large Print
London & New York

This first large print edition published 2016
in Great Britain and the USA by
SEVERN HOUSE PUBLISHERS LTD of
19 Cedar Road, Sutton, Surrey, England, SM2 5DA.
First world regular print edition published 2015 by
Severn House Publishers Ltd., London and New York.

British Library Cataloguing in Publication Data

Randisi, Robert J. author.
    When somebody kills you. – (A Rat Pack mystery)
    1. Gianelli, Eddie (Fictitious character)–Fiction. 2. Rat
    Pack (Entertainers)–Fiction. 3. Garland, Judy–Fiction.
    4. Murder for hire–Fiction. 5. Los Angeles (Calif.)–
    Fiction. 6. Detective and mystery stories. 7. Large type
    books.
    I. Title II. Series
    813.6-dc23

    ISBN-13: 9780727871749

Severn House Publishers support the Forest Stewardship Council™
[FSC™], the leading international forest certification organisation. All
our titles that are printed on FSC certified paper carry the FSC logo.

MIX
Paper from
responsible sources
FSC® C013056

Typeset by Palimpsest Book Production Ltd.,
Falkirk, Stirlingshire, Scotland.
Printed and bound in Great Britain by
T J International, Padstow, Cornwall.

To Marthayn,
You kill me – but what a way to go.

Prologue

March, 2008

I was reading an article on mob ties, which had appeared in that morning's edition of the *Las Vegas Sun*, when the doorbell rang. I put the paper down next to my morning coffee, took off my glasses and went to the door.

'Hey, Mr Gianelli,' my mailman said.

''Mornin', Dennis.'

'Got an express package for ya,' he said, holding a flat envelope out to me. 'Ya gotta sign.'

I signed the small pink slip he gave me and handed it back.

'Thanks,' he said.

'Thank you, Dennis.'

As he went back down the hall to the elevator, I closed the door and looked at the front of the flat, cardboard envelope. There was a return address – a PO Box in New York – but no one's name.

I sat back down on my sofa, picked up my glasses, perched them on my nose and took another look. Nope, no name, just the PO Box.

I tore the envelope open and drew out a regular office-sized white envelope. It wasn't sealed so I opened it easily. Inside was a ticket to a show – a tribute show to Judy Garland, which was taking place the next night.

I had been hearing about this production over the past few weeks, and had considered going, but the date had gotten away from me. If some anonymous someone hadn't sent me this ticket, I would've missed it.

There was something else in the envelope. It was a plain white card, and on it was written: 'See you there.'

Obviously, my mysterious benefactor intended to be there, maybe in a seat next to me.

I set the card and ticket down on the coffee table in front of me, next to the newspaper. The article covered the history of the mob in Las Vegas. It referred to the mob's 'heyday' as being from 1950 to the early eighties, but there was stuff going on before and after that. It covered personalities such as Kenny Roselli, Tony Spilotro, Lefty Rosenthal and Momo Giancana – all men I had known very well.

Looking at the newspaper next to the tickets reminded me of the time when the mob and Judy Garland were both a big part of my life – a very specific part at a very specific time . . .

One

'How do you like your new job?' Dean Martin asked.

'I'm not sure.'

'Why not?' Dean flicked some ash from his ever-present cigarette into a glass ashtray on the bar.

'Well, look at me,' I said. 'It's the middle of the day and I'm sittin' at the bar in the lounge not doin' anythin'.'

'And getting paid for it,' Dino pointed out. 'Sounds like a cushy gig to me.'

'You work harder than anybody I know,' I said. 'This would drive you crazy.'

'No,' he said, with a grin, 'it would drive me to the golf course – which, by the way, is where I'm headed.'

Dean Martin was one of the few golfers I knew who wasn't out on the links and ready to play at six a.m. That was because when you're Dean Martin you can get any old tee time you want.

He was dressed in his golf clothes – a striped, collared polo shirt, white pants and shoes, all of which cost more than my mortgage payment for the month.

Dean had played the Sands in January, with Francis Brunn, the German juggler, opening for

3

him. He'd made a bet with a friend that Brunn wouldn't make one mistake on stage. Although the German never dropped anything, he did make a minor flub. The audience didn't catch it, but Dino's buddy did. And so Dean had to get his friend some time on the golf course, and this week was the first opportunity they had to get together to honor his wager. Dean would be playing the Sands on November twenty-third – with the Half Brothers – so coming in a few days early had been no hardship. Golfers were notorious for paying off their bets. He'd be going home to spend Thanksgiving with Jeannie and the kids after his show.

'So tell Jack you don't like the job,' Dean said. 'You want to go back in the pit.'

'Ah, I can't do that,' I said. 'He thinks of this as a promotion, a reward. Not takin' it would be a slap in the face. Besides, I'm not sayin' I don't like it. I'm just sayin' I'm kind of antsy just sittin' here.'

'Well, I gotta go,' he said, finishing his coffee and setting the cup down on the bar. 'We on for dinner tonight?'

'We are,' I said. 'I'll come to your suite to pick you up, say, eight.'

'See you then, pally.' He slapped me on the back and headed for the door. All eyes followed him until he was gone, and then they looked at me, probably wondering how I rated having a drink with Dean Martin.

I vaguely heard a phone ring, and then somebody poked me in the arm. 'Yeah?'

'It's for you, Eddie,' the bartender said, holding the receiver out. 'It's the boss.'

4

'Thanks.' I took the phone. 'Jack?'

'Where the hell are you?' Jack Entratter barked.

'At the bar,' I said. 'You called me here.'

'I didn't give you this new job because of your good looks, you know,' he said. 'And I don't pay you to sit at the bar.'

'Whoa, whoa, hold your horses. What's this about?'

I heard Jack take a long breath.

'OK,' he said. 'I'm sorry I bit your head off. We've got a major whale in the house today. He just checked in, and already he's got my goat. I hate the guy, but he drops a lot of money here.'

'Harry Bennett?'

'That's the scumbag.'

That much was true. Bennett was a scumbag, but he was a rich scumbag. And for some reason he looked down his nose at Jack.

'You have to deal with him, Eddie,' Jack said, 'or I'll kill him.'

'OK, Jack,' I said, 'I'll deal with him.'

'Thank you,' he said, and hung up.

'Trouble?' the bartender asked.

I handed him the phone and said, 'Yeah, but the best kind. The millionaire kind.'

'Wish I had that kind of trouble,' he said.

I just nodded, said, 'Thanks,' and left the lounge.

Harry Bennett answered his door and exclaimed, 'Hey, Jack Entratter's favorite pit boss.' He was holding a towel, wearing a white T-shirt and boxers, and his hair was wet.

5

'Not a pit boss anymore, Mr Bennett,' I said. 'I've got a new job now.'

'Oh yeah? What's that?'

'He's calling me a casino host,' I said. 'It's my job to get you and other guests playin' what they want.'

'Well, then, get your ass in here and we'll start workin' on that.'

I followed him, closing the door behind me. He had one of the big suites, like the ones Frank and Dean rated.

Bennett was in his fifties, thick around the middle – and in the head about most things, except his business. He was in real estate and knew his stuff. He lived in Boston, bought and sold up and down the East Coast. He came to Vegas several times a year to drop a couple of mil, most of it at the Sands.

'Make me a drink, will ya? Bourbon rocks. I'm gonna finish washin' up.'

'Comin' up.'

I got behind the bar and fixed him his drink. When he came back into the room, his hair was combed and he was wearing a button-down blue shirt and black slacks.

'Thanks,' he said, grabbing the drink from the bar. 'How about you?'

'Too early.'

'For Vegas?'

'I stay up late,' I said. 'I start drinkin' now, I'll be drunk by lunch.'

'Drunk by lunch sounds good to me.'

'Is there anythin' else I can get you?'

'Not right now, Eddie,' Bennett said. 'I'm

6

gonna drift a while, try my luck at some tables, but later I'll be lookin' for a big game – and a woman.'

'I can help you with both, Mr Bennett.'

'Good lad. I'll be in the Garden Room for dinner at seven. Check with me then. For now, I wanna be on my own.'

'You got it, sir.' I came around the bar and headed for the door.

'By the way,' Bennett said, 'will I be seein' Jack while I'm here?'

'I'm sure you will, Mr Bennett,' I said, and then thought, unless he sees you first.

Two

I had a dinner appointment with Dean at eight, so there was no trouble meeting Bennett in the Garden Room. He told me he was very satisfied with the action he had found that day, but he'd like a private game the next night. I told me I'd set it up. Then he said he also wanted a blonde, and I said I'd set that up, too.

I was in front of Dino's door at seven fifty-five, and knocked.

'Come on in, pally,' he said, 'I'm on the phone.'

I nodded and entered the room while he hurried back to his call. He picked up the receiver and pointed at the bar.

'Yes, Jeannie,' he said, 'I paid back the bet and was all set to come home tomorrow when Frank called. He wants me to hang around because he's coming to town . . . No, he's not performing . . . No, I don't know why . . . Yes, I'll let you know. Give the girls my love.'

By the time he hung up, I was behind the bar with a short bourbon – my first of the day.

'You ready for dinner?' he asked.

'I am,' I said. 'What about you?'

'A tie and a jacket and I'm all set.'

'What's this about Frank comin' to town?'

'He wanted me to tell you,' he said, heading for the bedroom. 'I'll do that at dinner!'

As usual, Dean had a car waiting out front. When we had dinner away from the Sands and off the strip, it was usually at the Bootlegger, an Italian place that Frank had introduced us to.

We were seated, got drinks and ordered before Dean brought up Frank again.

'Frank's comin' in tomorrow,' he said. 'He's got somethin' he wants to talk to you about.'

'Me?'

'That's right,' Dean said. 'And he asked me to stick around, said I might be interested, too.'

'Any idea what it is?'

'None,' Dean said. 'He was mum on the subject, said he'd tell us when he sees us.'

The waiter came over with the antipasto platter we'd ordered as an appetizer. I didn't like everything on it – the mushrooms and anchovies – but I attacked the meats, cheeses and olives. Dino, on the other hand, took a little bit of everything, including the artichoke hearts, something else I skipped.

8

We talked shop – his and mine. He talked about his last gig, his next one, and I mentioned Harry Bennett coming to town.

'He's an asshole, isn't he?' Dean asked. 'Doesn't Jack hate him?'

'He does. That's why I'm handling him.'

'Ah, as part of your new job.'

'Right.'

We finished off the antipasto in time for our main courses – lasagna for me, linguine with clams for Dino.

'So how do you like bein' a – what's Jack callin' you?'

'A casino host.'

'Doesn't have the same ring to it as pit boss, does it?'

'No, it doesn't,' I said.

'Well,' Dino suggested, 'do the job for a few weeks, then tell Jack you want back in the pit.'

'Yeah, maybe,' I said. 'We'll have to see how it goes. If I start feelin' like a pimp, that's just what I'll do.'

We finished off our meal with coffee and Italian pastries. After that we walked outside, where the car was waiting. It was parked across the street, with the driver, Andy, behind the wheel. Dean stopped to light a cigarette, so I started across the street. I heard rubber squeal and turned to see headlights bearing down on me. I thought I was a goner when something hit me in the lower back and I went flying. The car missed me, but not by much.

Andy got out of the car and rushed over to me. 'You guys all right?'

That's when I realized Dean had saved my bacon. He'd tackled me from behind, knocking me out of the path of the car.

'You OK, Dean?' I asked. He was lying on the ground next to me.

'I'm good,' he said, pushing himself up to a seated positon. 'You?'

'I think I'm OK,' I said, sitting up and taking stock. 'That was a great tackle. Somebody'd think you played football when you were younger, instead of boxing.'

'Let's get out of the street,' Dean suggested, 'before somebody tries to run you down again.'

'What do you mean, "tries"?' I asked as we got up.

'That was no accident,' Dean said.

'What?'

'That guy deliberately tried to run you down, Eddie. You seein' somebody's wife?'

'Not this week.'

We got into the back seat and Andy pulled the car away from the curb.

'Police?' he asked.

'No,' I said, leaning forward, 'back to the Sands.'

'But if Mr Martin is right—'

'I'm not sure that he is,' I said, cutting him off. 'Back to the Sands, Andy.'

'You're the boss, Eddie.'

I sat back.

'Eddie,' Dean said, 'I swear that guy was purposely headin' right for you.'

'But why?' I asked. 'I haven't pissed anybody off all month. It's more likely they were tryin' for you, Dino.'

10

'Not me,' Dean said. 'I was on the sidewalk lightin' a cigarette.'

'Maybe they got us mixed up.'

'Uh-uh,' he said. 'I'm taller, and a lot better lookin'.'

'I'm not gonna argue with you on that,' I said, 'but I can't see why anybody would want to run me down.'

'Come on, Eddie,' Dean said, 'you must've made some enemies in the past.'

'The only time I seem to get in trouble,' I said, 'is when I'm tryin' to help you guys out. The last time was earlier in the year when Eddie Robinson was here.'

'Maybe Bennett?' he asked.

'I haven't done anythin' to piss him off . . . yet.'

'Well,' he said, 'just to be on the safe side, you better watch your back.'

'I will.'

'And while I'm in town,' he said, slapping me on the back, 'so will I.'

Three

I drove home to my house in the Caddy, made a pot of coffee and sat in the living room, thinking about what had happened. I hadn't seen the car until I heard the tires squeal and saw the head-lights. So how could I say that Dean was wrong? He'd obviously seen more than I had, but if I admitted he was right, then I had to ask myself who wanted me dead, and why?

When I woke the next morning, I stopped at a local diner for breakfast before driving to the Sands. Frank was due after three. The Sands would send a car for him, so there was nothing for me to do until he got there.

I went to the Garden Room for a second cup of coffee. My job as a casino host required only that I be on the premises, and my hours exceeded the ones I worked as a pit boss. As far as I was concerned, seated in the Garden Room with a cup of coffee, I was at work.

Over a third cup I decided that the incident the night before had been an accident. I didn't have much choice. There was nobody I knew who was mad enough to try to kill me. And I'd given the matter enough of my time.

I asked the waitress to bring a phone over and I started making calls to get Harry Bennett his game, and his blonde.

I had just hung up the phone on the last player when Jack Entratter walked in. Resplendent as ever in one of his suits, tailored so his big shoulders wouldn't quite bust the seams, he spotted me, came over and slid into the booth across from me. A waitress appeared immediately with a cup of coffee for him, and another for me.

'I'm sorry I yelled at you yesterday,' he said, grudgingly. 'That guy gets my goat.'

'I know,' I said. 'He wanted to know if he was going to see you while he was here.'

'What did you tell him?'

'Not if you saw him first.'

'What? I never—'

'Relax,' I said, 'I only thought that. I told him I was sure he'd see you.'

'Oh, well, OK. So, what's he want so far?'

'Just a private game and an even more private blonde,' I said.

'Eddie,' he said, 'you're not a pimp—'

'It doesn't matter. The girl will make a pretty penny and won't kick any back to me.'

'Not much of a pimp, then, are you?'

'I don't have the flair.'

'Did you hear that Frank's comin' in today?'

'I heard from Dean,' I said. 'He's stayin' around to see him.'

'Any idea what it's about? Frank ain't playin' here for a while.'

'I've got no idea,' I said, 'but I'm sure he'll clue me in when he gets here.'

'I got a car pickin' him up at McCarran at three thirty,' Jack said. 'Anythin' else goin' on?'

I decided not to tell him about the car the night before. After all, if I was accepting it as an accident, what was there to tell? 'No, nothin',' I said. 'It's quiet.'

'Too quiet,' Jack said. 'But maybe with Bennett here, and Frank arrivin' today, that might change.'

'But not too much, I hope,' I said.

My Caddy was in the rear parking lot that day, because I didn't expect to have to use it until I went home. But it turned out one of the players I'd lined up for Harry Bennett backed out, and

13

I needed to find another one fast. I had a guy in mind, but he wasn't answering his phone.

I used a house phone in the lobby to call Jack's office. His new girl put me right through. She was the second one since his long-time secretary had been killed earlier in the year.

'Jack, I've got to go off the premises for a while,' I said. 'I need to hunt down my last player for Bennett's game.'

'Don't forget Frank's gettin' in at three thirty. He'll be in his room by four.'

'I'll be back by then,' I said, checking my watch. 'I've got an hour and a half.'

'OK, Eddie,' Jack said, 'but make it fast.'

'You got it.'

I hung up and went out the back way. I had the door open and was about to get in when somebody took a shot at me.

Not so quiet anymore.

Four

'One shot?'

'Do you need more?'

Jack rubbed his jaw. 'Why didn't you tell me about the car this mornin'?'

'I didn't think it was important,' I said. 'I thought it was just an accident.'

'Still could've been,' Jack said, 'but a shot – that's somethin' different. What've you been up to lately?'

'Nothin',' I said. 'My new job keeps me so busy I've been behavin' myself.'

'OK, next question. What about contacting the police?'

'Who do you suggest I call?' I asked. 'Hargrove?'

'There are other cops.'

'The story would get back to him,' I said, 'and he'd love it.'

'So what do you intend to do?' he asked.

'I don't know. For now, I've still got to find another player for Bennett's game.'

'Well,' Jack said, 'do it from the premises. I don't want you out and about, where somebody can try again.'

'I can't stay here forever,' I said. 'I've got to go home sometime.'

'Maybe we need to get you a bodyguard.'

'I don't want some gunsel followin' me around.'

'How about your buddy, Bardini?'

Now I rubbed my jaw. 'That's an idea.'

'Good,' Jack said, 'then call him.'

'I will,' I said, standing up, 'after I get Bennett's fifth for poker – and I'll do that after a good stiff drink.'

'You can have that here.'

'I'll have it downstairs, and use the phone at the bar.'

'Well, be careful, Eddie,' Jack said. 'Watch your back – and don't go outside.'

'I won't,' I said. 'Not today, anyway.'

I grabbed a stool at the Silver Queen Lounge, ordered a bourbon and asked the bartender for the phone. I still had an hour before Frank arrived.

15

I tried my poker player again and, thankfully, got him. With the game set, I called Danny Bardini's office.

'Bardini Investigations,' Danny said.

'Answerin' your own phone?'

'Penny's out shopping,' he said. 'You know, since this couple thing, she doesn't do what I tell her anymore – at least, not as much. It's your fault.' Like it was my idea for Danny to finally consummate a relationship with his secretary, Penny. Well, maybe it was . . . but it was for his own good.

'What's up, Eddie?' Danny asked. 'Rat Pack trouble?'

'No,' I said. Not yet, anyway. 'I've got some trouble of my own.'

'What kind?'

'There have been two attempts on my life since last night.'

'What? What kind of attempts?'

I told him about the car and the shot.

'Are you sure about the car?' Danny asked. 'Couldn't have been an accident?'

'I thought it was,' I said, 'but Dean thinks it was deliberate.'

'Dino was with you? What if he was the target?'

'That was a possibility, until somebody shot at me.'

'Any damage?'

'Driver's side mirror,' I said.

'You haven't called the police, have you?'

'No,' I said. 'I don't want Hargrove knowing about it. It would make him too damn happy.'

'What do you want me to be?' he asked. 'Bodyguard or detective?'

16

'Jack wants me to have a bodyguard,' I said, 'but I think I need a detective.'

'OK,' Danny said. 'I'll get right on it. I'll start with the car.'

'Talk to Dino,' I said. 'He'll be able to tell you more than I can. All I saw was some headlights.'

'He's still in town? At the Sands?'

'Yes,' I said. 'He's waiting for Frank, who gets in' – I checked my watch – 'just about now.'

'I'll be in touch,' Danny said. 'Meanwhile, watch your back.'

'I intend to.'

I hung up and gave the phone back to the bartender. I finished my drink. It was nearly four, time to go to Frank's suite and see what was on his mind. I was about to turn and get off my stool when something heavy fell on my shoulder.

'Mr G.!' Jerry Epstein said. 'Am I glad to see you!'

'Jerry,' I said, turning to face him, 'you scared the crap out of me.'

Five

'What are you doin' here?' I asked Jerry. The big guy usually didn't leave Brooklyn unless I asked him to. He was wearing a brown, lightweight sports coat and beige slacks, and a pair of loafers that would have looked like skis on me. His shirt, open at the collar, was an odd shade of purple.

'I came to protect you.'

'Protect me? How'd you know I'm in trouble?'

'You mean . . . it's already started?'

'What started?'

'The attempts.'

'What attempts? Come on, Jerry, make sense. Frank's waitin' for me.'

'Mr S. is here?'

'And Dino.'

'What's goin' on?'

'I don't know yet,' I said. 'Frank just arrived. But don't change the subject. How did you know I was in trouble?'

'I heard things,' he said, 'and as soon as I did, I got on a plane.'

'Heard what?'

'About the hit.'

I hesitated, then asked, 'What hit?'

'I thought that was what we were talkin' about, Mr G.,' Jerry said. 'Somebody put out a hit on you.'

I took Jerry with me up to see Frank. In the elevator I asked, 'What goddamned hit? Who put out a hit on me?'

'I don't know who,' Jerry said. 'I just heard that the word went out.'

'Who has the contract?'

'That's just it,' Jerry said. 'It's an open contract.'

'Open?'

'If I knew one guy had the contract, I'd take him out for you,' Jerry said. 'But this . . . anybody can pick this one up.'

'Jerry,' I said, 'what's the price tag?'

'Ten G's.'

18

'That's high, isn't it?'

'That's way high,' Jerry said. 'You musta really pissed somebody off, Mr G.'

The elevator stopped and I said, 'We'll talk about this later.'

'Hey,' he said, as we started down the hall, 'maybe Mr S. can help with this.'

'No,' I said, 'don't mention it to him. For now, I just want to see what's on Frank's mind.'

'Mr S. knows lots of people.'

'I get it, Jerry,' I said. 'Just do it my way, for now. OK?'

'Sure, Mr G.,' Jerry said. 'Whatever you say.'

For just a moment I wondered if Frank had heard about the hit, and *that's* what was on his mind. But as I knocked on the door, I doubted it.

Six

'Eddie!' Frank said, opening the door himself. 'And Big Jerry. How ya doin', boys?'

'Good, Frank,' I said. 'We're good.'

'Hello, Mr S.,' Jerry said.

'Come on in,' Frank said. 'Dino's here. Get yourselves some drinks.'

'I'll do it,' Jerry said, heading for the bar. 'Anything for you, Mr S.?'

'Jack Daniels, Jerry,' Frank said.

While Frank liked martinis, Jack Daniels had been a favorite of his ever since Jackie Gleason introduced him to it back in the forties.

'Same for me, Jerry.'

Dino was sitting on the sofa with a cup of coffee in front of him. He stood up and we shook hands. Both he and Frank were dressed casually, looking as if they were headed for the links any minute.

'I'm glad you're both here,' Frank said.

'Dean said it was important, Frank,' I said.

'It is,' Frank said. He accepted the drink Jerry brought him, and then the big guy handed me mine. 'Do you want a drink, Mr Martin?'

'No, Jerry, coffee's fine for me.'

He went back behind the bar and made himself one.

'So, OK,' Frank said, standing in the center of the room. Dino was still on the sofa, Jerry behind the bar, me in front of it. 'We're all here – more of us than I expected' – he gestured toward Jerry – 'but I'm glad you're here, Jerry.'

Jerry was smart enough to stay quiet.

'You all may or may not know about my . . . friendship with Judy Garland,' he said. 'Dean knows, of course. He and I did Judy's television show a couple of years ago.'

'Yeah, we did,' Dean said, sitting back. 'It was a big hit.'

'It was,' Frank said, 'but Judy . . . Judy's life hasn't been going the way she'd like it to.'

'How so?' I asked.

'Well, after that special they gave her a show of her own. It didn't last very long, for some reason. And her recent shows in Australia were . . . well, disastrous.'

'Why?' Dean asked.

'Judy still has certain problems with . . . booze,

20

drugs. She showed up for performances in less than perfect condition.'

'Didn't she just come back from London after doing a show with Liza?' Dean asked.

'Yes,' Frank said, 'and that went well – so well that they filmed it and are gonna show it on television next month.'

'Well, that's good,' I said.

'Yes, it is,' Frank said, 'but there's something else going on.'

'Like what?' I asked.

'Beats me. She can't talk to me about it.'

'But you're friends,' I said.

'Well,' Frank said, 'we had a relationship in the fifties, and since then I suppose you could say we've been friends, but not . . .'

'Close?' Dean asked.

'Intimates?' I said.

'Confidantes?' Jerry asked.

We all looked at him.

'Well,' Frank said, 'that's it, exactly. I'm not really in her confidence.'

'Who is?' I asked.

Frank looked at me.

'Ex-husband? Daughter? Any other friends?'

'Nobody that I know of,' Frank said. 'We're friends enough that she called me, told she was having trouble and asked me to . . .'

'To what?' Dean asked.

'To recommend somebody.'

'To do what?' Jerry asked.

'To help her.'

'So what'd you tell her?' Dean asked. 'Did you give her Fred Otash's number?'

Otash was the best-known private eye in Hollywood.

'No, Fred's too high profile,' Frank said.

'What about Eddie's friend?' Dean asked. 'Bardini. He's pretty good.

'No,' Frank said, 'she said she didn't really need a detective.'

'Then what does she need?' Dean asked.

'A fixer,' Frank said. 'Somebody who can see when something's wrong, and figure out how to fix it.'

'So,' Dean asked, 'did you recommend somebody?'

'I did.'

'Then why are we all here?' I asked.

'Because,' Frank said, looking at me, 'I recommended you, Eddie.'

Seven

'Why me?'

'That's what you do, Eddie,' Frank said, as if it was perfectly logical. 'You're a fixer.'

'I'm a pit boss turned casino host,' I argued.

'He's right, Mr G.,' Jerry said.

I gave him a look that said he wasn't helping.

'You do fix things,' the big guy said, with a shrug.

'Yeah,' I said, 'I fix it for a player to get into a poker game, for a high roller to get a girl, and I fix it for you to get pancakes when you want them – and you always want them.'

Jerry shrugged. 'I like pancakes.'

'Come on, Eddie,' Frank said. 'Look at all the times you've bailed us out of tight spots. Me, Dino, Sammy, over and over again.'

'That's because you're my friends.'

'Marilyn,' Frank said, 'and Ava?'

'That's because they were your friends.'

'And that's what Judy is,' Frank said. 'She's my friend, and Dean's.'

'And, by association,' Dean said, 'yours, pally.'

I glared at him, the same look I had given Jerry, times two. Dean shrugged and looked away.

'Frank, you don't even know what the problem is,' I argued. 'How could you tell her I can help her?'

He walked over to me and put his hand on my shoulder. 'Because, Eddie, it's been my experience – our experience,' he added, looking at Dean and then back to me, 'that you can fix anything.'

I frowned, but before I could say anything. Frank went on: 'Look, Eddie, all I'm askin' is that you go and talk to Judy. Hear her out, see what the problem is, and then decide if you can do anything to help.'

'Where does she live?'

'LA,' he said.

'I'd have to go to LA?'

'That might not be such a bad idea, Mr G.,' Jerry said.

I looked at him and he raised his eyebrows. I knew what he meant. With a hit out on me, it might be smart to get out of Las Vegas for a while.

'What do you mean?' Frank asked Jerry.

23

Jerry didn't even pause. 'Mr G. ain't had a vacation in a long time.'

I was impressed.

'Well, there you go,' Frank said. 'A free trip to LA.'

'Free?'

'On me,' Frank said.

'And me,' Dean added, raising his hand.

'All expenses paid,' Frank said.

'For both of you, if Big Jerry wants to go,' Dean said.

Frank and Dean exchanged a look, and then Frank said, 'That's right.'

'Sure, I'll go along,' Jerry said. 'Whatever Mr G. wants to do.'

Now they were all looking at me. I still had not recovered from Jerry telling me there was a hit out on me. An open contract. Somebody was really pissed and was putting up a lot of money.

Leaving town suddenly seemed very appealing.

'OK,' I said, 'I – *we'll* – go to LA and talk to Judy, see what the problem is.'

'Attaboy!' Frank said, grinning broadly. 'We'll all have dinner tonight – on me.'

'At the Bootlegger?' Jerry asked, hopefully.

Dino and I looked at each other, but kept quiet. Frank said, 'Sure, at the Bootlegger. Eight o'clock all right with everybody?'

'Good for me,' Dean said.

'Me, too,' Jerry said, happily.

'Yeah, sure,' I said, with a fatalistic shrug of my shoulders. 'Why not? Let's celebrate yet another new job for me. Eddie the Fixer.'

'I'll call Judy and tell her to expect you,' Frank said. 'Tomorrow too soon?'

'Tomorrow's fine, Frank. I'll have to clear it with Jack first—'

'I'll clear it with Jack.'

'No,' I said, 'that's OK, Frank. It's my job. I'll talk to him.'

'OK, Eddie,' Frank said, 'you call the shots.'

'Speaking of which,' I said, pushing away from the bar, 'I've got some work to do if I'm gonna be leavin' tomorrow.'

'OK, see you at eight,' Frank said.

'OK,' I said. 'Jerry?'

'Right with ya, Mr G.' He came around from behind the bar.

'I've got some things to do, too, Frank,' Dean said, standing. 'I'll see you later.'

'All my friends are deserting me,' Frank said, throwing his hands in the air. 'Ah, I'll just give Judy a call right now.'

I opened the door, let Jerry and Dean precede me into the hall, said, 'See you later, Frank,' and followed them.

Eight

Dino's room was two floors down. We rode there in silence, until the doors opened. He stepped out, then stopped the doors with his hand.

'I didn't know what it was about, Eddie,' he told me. 'Not until he just told the three of us.'

Frank and Dean were so close I wasn't sure that was true. Not that Dean would lie to me, but maybe he just thought I'd feel better hearing that.

'It's OK, Dean,' I said. 'Like Jerry said, I can use the time off.'

'OK, guys,' he said, releasing the door, 'see you at eight.'

Jerry and I rode down to the fourth floor, where Jack's office was.

'Jack's got a new girl, Jerry,' I said, as we walked down the hall. 'Don't scare her, OK?'

'Mr G.,' he said, reproachfully, 'why would I do that?'

'This one's kind of pretty.'

'I seen pretty girls before.'

I let that go.

We walked into Jack's office and the girl sitting at the desk there looked up at us. She had show-girl looks – the hair, the face, beautiful smile – but not the height, which was why she was working for Jack and not in the showroom.

'Hello, Diane,' I said. I'd made sure I learned her name early on – even though I didn't think she was going to last very long in the job. Jack wasn't an easy guy to work for day in, day out.

'Hello, Mr Gianelli.'

'This is my friend, Jerry Epstein. We'd like to see Jack. Is he in and available?'

'I have my orders, Mr Gianelli,' she said. 'You can go in any time.'

'Well,' I said, 'thanks.'

I started into Jack's office, but realized I'd lost Jerry. He was still standing in front of the desk, staring at the pretty girl.

26

'Come, Jerry,' I said. 'You've seen pretty girls before, remember?'

'Huh?' He looked at me, and it took an effort. 'Oh, sure, Mr G.'

I went into Jack's office with a reluctant Jerry right behind me.

'Eddie,' Jack said, 'and Big Jerry. What a . . . surprise.'

'For me, too,' I said. 'Jerry, why don't you close that door?'

'Somethin' you don't want my girl to hear?' Jack asked.

'Somethin' I don't want anybody to hear,' I said, sitting across from him. Jerry stood with his broad back to the door.

'And what could that be?'

'Jerry, tell Jack what you told me.'

'There's a hit out on Mr G.,' Jerry said. 'An open contract.'

'What the fuck – how much?'

'Ten G's.'

Jack looked as if he'd been punched between the eyes. He sat back in his chair and shook his head. Then he became pensive. 'Well, that explains the car and the shot,' he said. 'Could've been two different hitters tryin' for that jackpot.'

'That's what I thought.'

'What do you plan to do?'

'Well, for one thing,' I said, 'I'll leave town for a while, be hard to find.'

'What will that achieve?'

'It'll give Danny Bardini time to find out who put this hit out on me.'

27

'I can do that,' Jack said. 'I'll ask Momo.'

'What if Giancana doesn't know?'

'He's got to know,' Jack said. 'If he don't, he's gonna be pissed.'

'Well, I'm already pissed.'

Jack looked at Jerry. 'So you came to town to warn Eddie and . . . what?'

'Protect him.'

He looked at me again. 'Where you boys goin'?'

'We're doin' a job for Frank,' I said, 'so Frank and Dean will be the only ones who know where we are.'

Jack's eyes popped. 'You're not gonna tell me?'

'It's for your own good, Jack.'

He grumbled, but asked, 'How long you gonna be gone?'

'Until we finish our job, or until Danny – or you – finds the answer.'

Jack scowled.

'You can do without me for a while, Jack.'

'That ain't it,' he said. 'Of course I wanna do whatever's best for you, Eddie.'

'Then why the long face?'

'Ah,' he said, 'with you gone, I'm gonna have to look after that asshole Bennett myself.'

Nine

I made sure Harry Bennett got his poker game and his girl that night. After that, Jack was right; it was going to be up to him.

28

We met Frank and Dean at the Bootlegger at eight and talked about everything but Judy. The limo took us back to the Sands, and the subject finally came up again after Dean had already said goodnight and gone inside.

'This same car will take you guys to the airport in the morning,' Frank promised. 'Just let me know how things are progressing while you're there, and I'll keep Dino in the loop.'

'You got it, Frank.'

'And thanks again, both of you.' We shook hands and he went inside.

'Where we goin' now?' Jerry asked.

'I'm goin' home to pack.'

'Not without me, you ain't.'

'Come on, then.'

Outside, one of the valets brought my car around. Jerry almost cried when he saw the smashed mirror.

'That sonofabitch!' he swore. 'Whoever it was, I'm gonna kill him for this.'

'I'm glad to see you've got your priorities straight,' I said, tossing him the keys. 'You drive.'

'Yes, sir!'

We got in the car and he caressed the steering wheel before starting the engine.

'Can we get dessert along the way?' We'd all skipped dessert at the Bootlegger, which had made Jerry unhappy.

'Sure,' I said, 'I should see Danny before we leave, so let's get ahold of him and have him meet us at the Horseshoe.'

'Suits me!'

* * *

29

Danny was available, so we arranged to meet him at the Horseshoe coffee shop. He was waiting for us in a booth when we got there.

'Hey, Big Guy,' he said to Jerry.

'Hey, Shamus.'

I sat next to Danny, left the other side of the booth for Jerry.

It was late, so there were only a few diners who were taking a break from the tables and machines upstairs. We were intending to order pie, but Danny hadn't eaten so he ordered a burger.

'That sounds good,' Jerry said to the waitress. 'Me, too.'

'After what you ate at the Bootlegger?'

He stared at me.

'I know, what's my point?' I looked at the waitress and ordered apple pie and coffee.

'You want it heated?' she asked.

'Sure.'

Danny listened while I told him what Frank Sinatra wanted me to do.

'Judy Garland, this time,' Danny said, shaking his head. 'I had a real crush on her when she did those Andy Hardy movies. Whoo, boy!'

'Not my type,' Jerry said, with a shrug.

'Luckily, we're not tryin' to fix you up with her,' I said to him.

'So when are you leavin'?' Danny asked.

'Tomorrow.'

'You'll let me know where you land in case I find out anythin', right?'

'Right.'

'Jerry knows about the attempts on your life?'

'It was Jerry told me what's goin' on,' I said.

30

'Apparently, somebody put out an open contract on me.'

'Oh, man,' Danny said. 'How much?'

'Ten G's,' Jerry said, around a mouthful of burger.

'Jesus,' Danny said, 'an open contract like that will bring hitters out of the woodwork.'

'That's one of the reasons I'm leavin' town,' I said.

'Makes sense,' Danny said, 'although a good hitter will find you.'

'With an open contract like this,' Jerry said, 'they won't all be good.'

'He's got a point,' Danny said. 'But if somebody does make a try for you in LA, it'll be a pro.' He looked at Jerry. 'You better keep your eye on our buddy, Big Man.'

'That's what I intend to do, Shamus.'

I pointed at each of them in turn. 'You keep me alive,' I said to Jerry, then switched to Danny. 'And you find out who wants me dead. Then we'll all be happy.'

'You got it,' Danny said, and Jerry nodded with his mouth full.

I took my first bite of my now-cold pie.

Ten

Jerry slept on my couch.

We talked it over and decided that since one attempt had already taken place at the Sands, I should probably stay away from the place. We got up the next morning, I packed – Jerry's suitcase had never been unpacked – and then we had some coffee before going to the airport. We decided we'd probably have breakfast when we got to LAX.

We were sitting at the kitchen table, finishing our coffee, when there was a knock on the front door.

I stated to get up, but Jerry put out his hand and said, 'I'll get it, Mr G.' Suddenly, his .45 cannon was in his hand.

'Jerry,' I said, 'don't overreact.'

'Somebody took a shot at you, Mr G. I ain't overreacting.'

We both got up, and I followed him to the door. I looked out the front window, saw a car in my driveway that was easy to recognize.

'Cops,' I said.

'You sure?'

I leaned over so I could see who was on my front steps. It was two men in plain clothes. I only recognized one of them, but it was enough.

'Hargrove,' I said. 'Eighty-six the cannon.'

Jerry looked around, then opened the closet next to the front door and stowed the gun inside.

'OK,' he said.

I opened the door. Hargrove actually smiled at me, the sonofabitch.

'Eddie!'

'Detective Hargrove.'

'Mind if we come in a minute, Eddie?' he asked. 'I've got some questions for you.'

'About what?'

'I'd rather do it inside than on your doorstep.'

'Sure,' I said, 'come on in.'

I backed away. He entered, followed by a dour-looking man in his forties who had the saddest eyes I'd ever seen on a man. Maybe because he was Hargrove's new partner. The man went through partners like Jack Entratter was going through secretaries these days.

'This is my partner, Detective Holliday.'

Holliday nodded.

'And look who's here,' Hargrove said, his smile getting even wider. 'The Brooklyn Gunsel.'

Jerry didn't respond.

'He doesn't like me much, Doc,' Hargrove said to his partner.

Doc Holliday? Oh, brother.

'What's this about, Detective?'

'Can we sit down in the living room—'

'I think right here is good,' I said. 'We have to get to the airport. Make it quick.'

'Takin' a trip?'

I didn't answer. I just stared at him.

'We heard something about a shot bein' fired at the Sands,' Hargrove said. 'Would you know anything about that?'

'I wouldn't.'

'Really?' Hargrove turned and looked at his partner, who appeared bored. 'We also heard somethin' about a hit bein' put out on you. Did you know that?'

'Why do you care?' I asked.

'That's why this big freak is here, isn't it?' Hargrove went on. 'To protect you?'

33

'Again,' I said, 'why do you care?'

'Well,' he said, folding his arms, 'strictly speakin', I don't. I mean, on a personal level, I'd like nothin' better than to have you hit, successfully. But it's my job to see that doesn't happen.'

'It's not your job if I'm not here, in Vegas,' I pointed out.

'That's true,' he said. 'If you're goin' someplace else, you become their problem. So, where are you goin'?'

'You don't need to know that,' I said.

'No,' Hargrove said, 'I don't.' He looked at Jerry. 'You, put your arms out.'

Jerry stared at him.

'Do you want me to say "please"?'

Jerry raised his arms slowly. Hargrove started toward him and Jerry said, 'No, let him do it. I don't want you to touch me.'

Hargrove stepped back, looked at his partner and smiled.

'See? I told you, He doesn't like me.'

Holliday stepped forward and patted Jerry down.

'He's clean.'

Jerry lowered his arms.

'If we searched the house, we'd probably find that forty-five he likes so much.'

'Not without a warrant,' I said. 'You bring one with you? Or probable cause?'

'You takin' courses in the law now, Eddie?' Hargrove asked. 'No, I don't have either. But that's OK. I'll see you around.' He turned as his partner opened the door and went out. He stopped just in the doorway. 'Hey, do me a favor?'

'What?'

'If anybody manages to cash in on that contract,' he said, with a smile, 'have somebody let me know.'

He went out, closing the door behind him.

Eleven

The limo Frank sent to the airport to pick us up early that morning pulled to a stop in front of Judy Garland's home at 924 Bel Air Road in LA. According to Frank, she didn't spend much time there now, but during the tapings of her TV show in '63 and early '64 she had lived there. She still owned the house, however, and that's where we were to meet her.

Jerry kept turning in the back seat to look behind us.

'Could you stop doin' that?' I asked.

'What?'

'Lookin' over your shoulder,' I said. 'You've been doin' it since we left my house. You're makin' me nervous.'

'You should be nervous,' Jerry said. 'If I had an open contract out on me, I'd be nervous, too.'

'Why should I be lookin' over my shoulder?' I asked. 'I've got you for that.'

Jerry grinned and said, 'Fuckin' A.' And he looked out the back window again.

* * *

The car let us off in front of a black wrought-iron double gate. We rang the bell and the gates opened. The limo driver waved and indicated that he'd be waiting for us there. We walked up a winding path to a big white stuccoed house.

Jerry and I were both wearing sports coats and slacks, black shoes for me, brown for him. I felt kind of underdressed for the occasion. I wondered how he felt.

As we approached, the front door opened and Judy herself stood there. I'm one who always preferred Judy Garland's hair the way she wore it when she was younger, long rather than in a short, butch cut, but I had to admit she looked pretty regal standing there in a white silk blouse, black capri pants and flat slippers. She had dressed for comfort, not to impress, and suddenly I didn't feel so underdressed.

'Eddie Gianelli?' she asked.

'That's right, Miss Garland.'

She looked somewhat timid. 'Do you have some identification?' she asked.

'Would my driver's license do?' I asked.

'That would be fine.'

I took it out and showed it to her. She handed it back and looked up at Jerry.

'This is my colleague, Jerry Epstein,' I introduced.

'Miss Garland,' Jerry said, almost bashfully, 'I'm just the muscle.'

That comment seemed to perk her up, and she grinned.

'Well,' she said, 'you look perfectly cast for that role. Won't you both come in?'

36

We entered the house, and she led us to what appeared to be a playroom of sorts – furniture, yes, but also a bar, complete with bar stools.

'Can I get either of you a drink?' she asked.

'Ma'am,' Jerry asked, 'don't you have somebody who does that for ya?'

'Oh, it's just us here today. I didn't want anyone else around.'

'Then I'll get the drinks,' Jerry said, rushing behind the bar.

'You're so sweet,' she said. 'And please call me Judy – both of you.'

'Oh,' he said, 'I couldn't do that. What can I get ya?'

'Just a club soda, please,' she said, rubbing her upper arms as if she was cold. I'd seen the gesture before in drinkers who were trying to resist.

'Club soda for me, too, Jerry.'

He looked at me for a minute, then got it. 'I'll have the same.'

He put ice cubes into three highball glasses and filled them with club soda, came around the bar and handed them out, then went back there with his drink.

'Judy,' I said, 'I don't know what Frank might have told you about me—'

'He told me Eddie G. is the guy to go to when you need help,' she said. 'He said you've helped him, and Dino and Sammy . . . and so many others.'

'Well,' I said, 'I've gotten lucky a time—'

'You're being modest.'

'No, I'm not,' I said, 'but let's put that aside for a moment. Why don't you tell me what your

37

problem is, and I'll see if I think I can help you?'

'All right,' she said. 'Let's sit down.'

We went to the chairs, which were functional rather than comfortable. No cushions, just iron and leather. I guessed they were supposed to look futuristic.

Judy and I sat, while Jerry remained behind the bar, watching and listening.

Judy took a drink from her glass, as if she really needed it – only it wasn't what she really needed.

'I'm not at all sure where to start,' she said, putting one hand to her forehead.

'We can wait,' I said.

Twelve

'It's probably just a silly thing,' she said, 'but so much of my life is chaotic, I can't always tell the silly from the real.'

'That's OK,' I said. 'Just tell me what you're thinkin', and we'll go from there.'

But she had some things to talk out, and I decided to just let her.

'I've always had trouble with money.' She waved her hand, and her tone seemed to be on the verge of hysteria for a moment. Then she took a deep breath. 'But that's not your problem. And then there's my career . . . acting jobs have dried up, I've mostly just been singing for the past four or five years. When I did my TV show with Frank and Dean, it went so well, but then

38

they gave me a weekly show, and the viewers didn't show up.' She shrugged. I knew her show, though critically acclaimed, had recently been canceled. 'Everyone thinks I'm so successful . . . silly Oz thing . . . Andy Hardy movies notwithstanding . . .'

She trailed off, gulped the rest of her club soda, probably wishing there was something else mixed in with it. She looked nervous and fragile. This close, without the make-up afforded her by movie magic, she appeared older than her forty-two years. I thought I remembered that her drink of choice was vodka mixed with black tea.

'Let me get you some more club soda,' I offered, taking her glass to Jerry.

I wondered if I should have him spike it with just a touch of vodka. Maybe that would ease her somewhat and get her on track.

I decided to chance it. I located a bottle of vodka behind Jerry and pointed to it, then held my thumb and forefinger about half an inch apart, indicating that he should tip in just a touch. He did so and stirred it, and I returned the glass to Judy Garland. She tipped it to her mouth, sipped it, and her beautiful eyes widened for just a moment. She didn't say anything, however. She simply lowered the glass to her lap, where she clasped it in both hands and suddenly seemed a bit calmer.

I sat across from her. 'Go ahead, Judy. Get it finished.'

'With all of the ups and downs of my life,' she continued, 'I have never come up against any sort of . . . physical threat.'

'Until now?'

39

She sipped her drink again.

'It started in Australia,' she said. 'I was sure I was being followed. I couldn't concentrate. I was late for performances. People thought it was because I was . . . drunk . . . or high. I know what they say. I'm not deaf to the . . . gossip.' She finished her drink.

'More?' I asked.

'No!' she said firmly. 'No.' She took a deep breath, set the empty glass on a nearby table, then clasped her hands in her lap.

'England was much better,' she said. 'I had Liza with me, the shows went so well. But when we returned home, it started again.'

I looked at Jerry, who simply shrugged.

'Who have you seen?' I asked.

'Shadows.'

'But you've never actually seen anyone?' I asked. 'A man? A face?'

'Someone,' she said, raising one hand and wagging her finger as if admonishing me, 'has been in my house. I came home one day and found my things had been . . . gone through. Rifled.'

'Rifled?'

'A woman knows when someone has been through her underwear drawer.'

'Ah . . .'

'That's when I called Frank,' she said. 'I simply didn't know where else to turn.'

'What about the police?'

She shook her head.

'I can't afford the publicity,' she said. 'My reputation is already . . .' She waved a hand.

40

'I understand.'

'I just need to find out if I'm . . . imagining things, or if someone is really . . . following me, maybe even . . . stalking me, the way they'd stalk an animal before . . .'

Before striking, I thought. We had more in common, apparently, than I had initially thought when I first entered her house. I looked at Jerry again and he nodded.

'All right, Judy,' I said.

She looked at me, startled, as if I had just awakened her.

'You'll help me?'

'We'll see what we can find out,' I answered. 'Where are your children?'

'Somewhere safe.'

'And you?'

'I'm staying here at the moment.'

'Alone?'

'I have a staff. I gave them the day off. They'll be back this evening.'

'How many?'

'Two – a man and a woman.'

'It's better you stay inside,' Jerry said, speaking for the first time in a while. 'Stay behind these walls, until we come back. Can you do that?'

'I have some meetings,' she said, 'but things can be arranged. I can meet with people here.'

'People?' I asked.

'Studio people, people from my recording label, it's all business . . .'

'Don't let anyone in, unless they're with someone you do know.'

'A–All right,' she stammered.

I stood up and Jerry came from behind the bar. Judy stood and looked at us, wide-eyed, like Dorothy staring at the Wizard.

'You . . . you don't think I'm imagining things?'

'I might have,' I said, 'but then there's your underwear drawer, isn't there?'

Thirteen

We left Judy's house with the promise that we would return later.

'Will you . . . can you stay here?' she asked. 'I have rooms.'

'Frank has arranged for us to stay at the Beverly Hills Hotel,' I told her. 'That'll be our base of operations, for now.'

'A–All right.'

'Be sure the doors and gates are locked after we leave.'

'Eddie . . .' she said, and for the first time she looked frightened.

I touched her arm. 'We're going to have somebody watchin' the house while we're gone. I'll call you as soon as we have him in place. And we'll tell you who he is, in case he wants to come in. Actually, we'll bring him in and introduce him later this evening when we return.'

'Come back for dinner,' she said. 'I'll have Cook prepare something.'

'That's a deal.'

* * *

Back in the limo, Jerry asked, 'Who we gonna get to watch the house. The dick?'

'No,' I said, 'Danny's working the Vegas angle, tryin' to find out who's out to get me, remember?'

'Then who?'

'Danny was in LA last month and said he worked with a guy who was experienced and very good.'

'Who's that?'

'The Double-A Detective Agency,' I said. 'It's run by a fella named Nathan Hiller, who has offices in Chicago and LA. I thought I'd call Danny and make sure we've got a reference.'

'What about Otash?'

'Not this time,' I said. 'Otash is too concerned about headlines. When we get to the hotel, I'll try to arrange for Hiller, or somebody from his office.'

'You're the boss,' he said.

The last time we were at the Beverly Hills Hotel was a couple of years back when we were helping Ava Gardner – also at Frank's request. But I had gotten a lot closer to Ava than I'd ever get with Judy Garland.

The driver stopped in front of the hotel and we got out.

'What are you gonna do?' I asked the driver.

'I'll be around. Mr Sinatra said this car is yours for as long as you're in LA. That means you get me, too.'

He'd told me his name at the airport, and I didn't want to admit I'd forgotten it, so I took a moment to dredge it up.

'Greg, right?'

'That's right, sir.'

'OK, Greg,' I said. 'Stick around. We'll need you again today.'

'You got it, Mr Gianelli.'

'Just call me Eddie.'

'Yes, sir.'

We went inside, registered and discovered that Frank had booked us a two-bedroom bungalow. We took a peek into the Polo Lounge on the way, but didn't see anyone we knew at that time of day. A little later there'd be celebrities eating and drinking and making deals.

When we got to the bungalow, I got right on the phone to Danny in Vegas, but he didn't answer. Well, why would he? He was out trying to find out who was trying to kill me.

I hung up.

'What happened?' Jerry asked.

'He's not there.'

'So what do we do now?'

'Phone book,' I said.

Jerry found it and brought it over to me. Double-A was right at the beginning of the private investigator listings – no doubt why Hiller had chosen the name. I knew I could call and invoke Danny's name without getting him mad.

I dialed and, when it was answered, asked for Nathan Hiller.

'Who is calling, please?' she asked, politely.

'My name is Eddie Gianelli, from Las Vegas.'

'Does Mr Hiller know you?'

'No,' I said, 'but he knows a friend of mine, Danny Bardini.'

'I know Danny!' she said, excitedly. 'He was here last month.'

'That's right.'

'Are you the Eddie G. he told me about, from the Sands Casino?'

'I am,' I said. 'I hope he told you good things.'

'Hold on, please,' she said, without answering the question.

I waited a few minutes and then an authoritative voice came on the line.

'This is Nat Hiller.'

'Mr Hiller, my name is Eddie Gianelli,' I said. 'I'm a friend of Danny Bardini.'

'From Las Vegas, right?'

'That's right.'

'How's Danny doin'?'

'He's fine,' I said. Then decided to add, 'He's workin' a job for me right now, in Vegas.'

'And is that the reason you're calling me?' he asked. 'Danny's otherwise engaged.'

'That's it exactly.'

There was a moment's hesitation, and then he said, 'You mind if I ask what he's doing for you?'

'Not at all.' I'd already decided to be forth-coming with him. 'He's tryin' to keep me alive.'

'Come again?'

'There's an open contract out on me,' I said. 'Danny's tryin' to find out who's behind it.'

'You don't sound all that concerned,' Hiller said. 'Is this something that happens to you often?'

'Hardly ever,' I said, 'and it scares me shitless. But I'm here on another matter.'

'Staying out of Vegas for now, huh?'

45

'That's right.'

Suddenly – and maybe because I hadn't fed him any bullshit – his voice became warmer.

'All right, Eddie, what can I do for you?'

Fourteen

I explained to Nat – we had become 'Nat' and 'Eddie' – about the problem Judy Garland was having – without going into too much detail – and what we were planning to do to help her. I told him I needed somebody to keep an eye on her, and asked if he had an operative we could trust.

'I've got just the man,' he said. 'In fact, he was here working on a case, but he's from the Vegas office. Where are you staying?'

'The Beverly Hills Hotel.' I didn't know Double-A had a Vegas office, but didn't care where the man came from as long as he was good.

'Expense account?' he asked.

'Frank Sinatra's footing the bill.'

He whistled. 'You have important friends, Eddie.'

'As I understand it from Danny, Nat,' I said, 'so do you.'

'So where and when do you want my guy?'

'Outside of Judy's house,' I said, 'as soon as possible.'

'You got it.'

'I appreciate this.'

'You'll get my bill, Eddie.'

He told me the operative's name and said I could call him again if I needed any further help. Danny was right. He was a good guy.

Jerry was hungry, which was no great shock, so we walked down the street to a small diner, rather than eat in the hotel where I might run into somebody I knew. I'd been around enough celebrities over the past few years that it wasn't a stretch to think that one of them would come in to go to the Polo Lounge and recognize me.

'We coulda gone someplace better,' Jerry commented. 'Like maybe the Brown Derby?'

'Not right now, Jerry,' I said. 'The point is just to get something into our stomachs. This place is good enough.'

'I can go to a diner in Brooklyn,' he groused, but he sat down across from me in a booth.

A waitress came over, took drink orders and left us to read the menus. I looked out the window at the foot traffic on Sunset.

'Hey,' Jerry said, 'I wonder if we're anyplace near Seventy-Seven Sunset Strip? That's one of my favorite shows. I really get a kick out of Kookie.'

'We can't be.'

'Why not?'

'Because it's not a real address.'

'It ain't?' He seemed disappointed.

I shook my head. I didn't tell him I knew where the real address was.

* * *

'Well,' Jerry said, 'can we drive up and down the Strip and look for Dino's Lodge?' He leaned forward. 'That's real, ain't it?'

'Yeah, Dino's Lodge is real.'

'Mr Martin owns it, right?'

'No, not quite,' I said. 'See, after Dean and Jerry split, Jerry's first movie was a hit. Dean's, though, it was a flop. He fell on some hard times and needed money, so he sold his name to the owners of Dino's Lodge.'

'Mr Martin was broke?'

'It happens to everybody at one time or another, Jerry,' I said. 'What are you gonna have?' I hoped he'd forget the idea about driving up and down the Strip, looking for Dino's.

'The meat loaf looks good,' he said.

I cringed. When the waitress came, he ordered the meat loaf and asked for a double portion. She said she'd have to charge extra, and he said he didn't care. She shrugged, obviously feeling the same way. I ordered an open-faced roast beef sandwich with wet fries.

She frowned and asked, 'What the heck are wet fries?'

'It's a Brooklyn thing,' Jerry told her.

'Put the same brown gravy from the roast beef on the French fries, too,' I said. 'Wet fries.'

'Hmph,' she said, and wrote it down.

As she left, Jerry leaned forward and said, 'She's gonna ask if she can have one when she brings 'em.'

'No, she won't,' I said.

He sat back, a bemused smile on his face.

'So where are we gonna start?' he asked.

'I don't know,' I said, honestly. 'You know,

every time I get pulled into somethin' like this by the guys, I tell 'em I'm not a detective.'

'Mr G.,' Jerry said, 'you're a better detective than most detectives I know. Even your friend the Dick says that's so.'

'Yeah, maybe,' I said.

The waitress returned and set our platters down in front of us. When she didn't leave, I looked up at her. She had a tired look that aged her, making her appear fifty when she was probably forty. But at the moment there was a look of interest there, as well.

'You mind if I try one?' she asked.

I looked at Jerry, who smiled.

'Go ahead.'

She took an extra fork from among the straws in her apron and actually speared two of my wet fries. She stuck them in her mouth and chewed thoughtfully.

'Hey,' she said, nodding. 'Not bad. Wet fries, huh?'

'Wet fries,' I said.

'Well,' she said, 'both of you, enjoy.'

'Mr G. . . .' Jerry said, and I knew he was going to ask me again what our first move would be.

'Just eat, Jerry,' I said. 'We'll talk later.'

Fifteen

Jerry demolished his plate and ordered a second helping. He was almost done with that by the time I had finished mine.

49

'Dessert?' he asked, looking at me hopefully.

'Sure, why not?'

The food was really good, so I figured a piece of pie would be even better.

We both ordered apple, but Jerry ordered his with two scoops of ice cream, vanilla and chocolate. I took it plain.

'OK,' I said, over pie and coffee, 'this is what we're gonna do.'

Jerry stuck a heaped forkful of pie and ice cream into his mouth and gave me his full attention.

'I have some questions to ask Judy that I didn't think of before.'

'Like what?'

'Well, we need to talk to people who traveled with her, whoever made the travel arrangements. I guess that would be her manager.'

'So who's her manager?'

'That's the question,' I said.

'Do we have to go back?' he asked. 'Can't we just call her?'

'We could,' I said, 'but I'd like to check and see if Hiller has got his man in place yet.'

'He sounded like a man who gets his job done,' Jerry said.

'You're right about that,' I said. 'OK, we'll go back to the cottage and call her.' I started to slide out of the booth.

'Wait,' Jerry said.

'What for?'

'I want another piece of pie.'

I sat back down.

* * *

Finally back at the cottage, I dialed Judy Garland's phone number. She answered on the third ring.

'Is everything all right?' she asked after I identified myself.

'Fine,' I said. 'I just have some more questions.'

'So ask.'

'Who arranged your trips to Australia and England?'

'My managers, and my tour manager.'

'Who are they?'

'My managers are Freddie Fields and David Begelman,' she said.

'Offices?'

'Here in LA.' She gave me the address and I wrote it down.

'And the tour manager?'

'Why do you need to talk to him?'

'I'm going to talk to everyone connected with you, Judy.'

'Not my children.'

'No,' I said, 'not the kids. Don't worry. Now, what about the tour manager?'

'His name's Mark Herron,' she said, 'and he's a little more than my tour promoter.'

'What's that mean?'

She sighed into the phone. 'It's complicated. He produced the London show and was my tour promoter . . . and in a few days he'll be my fourth husband.'

'You're getting married?'

'Yes.'

That didn't make my job much easier.

'All right,' I said. 'Let me have Mark's address, too. Since he's family, I'll be . . . gentle.'

'Married?' Jerry asked. 'Again?'

I nodded. 'Fourth time.'

'Who's the guy?'

'Mark Herron,' I said. 'I'm not sure who he is, but we're gonna talk to him.'

'When?'

'Tomorrow,' I said. 'Today I want to see her managers, Fields and Begelman.'

'Where are they?' he asked.

'I've got the address here,' I said, waving the slip of paper I'd written it on. 'We'll give it to Greg and he'll take us there.'

'Why can't we get a car and drive ourselves?' he complained. 'Like a Caddy?'

'No,' I said, 'Frank gave us that limo; we might as well get some use out of it and its driver. Besides, we won't have to worry about directions.'

'I like directions,' Jerry said.

'Let's do it my way for now, Jerry.'

'Sure, Mr G.,' he said. 'You're still the boss.'

'Let's go out and see if Greg's waiting for us.'

Sixteen

We hadn't seen the driver or the limo when we went out to eat, but then we hadn't left the hotel by the front door. This time when we walked out

52

the front, there was Greg, leaning against the limo.

'Ain't you hungry?' Jerry asked.

'I had a hot dog.'

'You're a good-sized fella,' Jerry said. 'A hot dog ain't gonna hold you long.'

'You're probably right,' Greg said, laughing.

'Mr G., next time we eat we gotta take Greg with us.'

'Sure,' I said, 'but right now Greg's gonna take us for a ride.'

'Where to, boss?' Greg asked, straightening up to his full six feet.

I handed him the slip of paper with the address on it.

'Piece of cake,' he said. 'Hop in.'

Since Judy's TV show had been part of her deal with CBS, it was no surprise to find the offices of her managers in Studio City, down the street from CBS Studio Center, in the MGM Tower. Greg dropped us off in front, said he'd sit there as long as a cop didn't make him move.

Inside, we found Creative Management Associates on the lobby directory. Also listed separately were Fred Field and David Begelman. We took the elevator.

According to Judy, Fields and Begelman took over her management after her divorce from Sid Luft who, while her husband, had also acted as her manager. It was Fields and Begelman who got her the CBS television deal, and also arranged the Australia and London concerts.

When we stepped out of the elevator, we found

ourselves facing a perfect-looking blonde sitting at a large desk in front of letters on the wall that spelled out 'Creative Management Associates'.

'Gentlemen,' she said, giving Jerry a wary look, 'can I help you?'

'We're here to see Mr Fields and Mr Begelman.'

'Mr Fields is working from his home today,' she informed us. 'Do you have an appointment with Mr Begelman?'

'Why don't you ask him?' I suggested. Judy had said she'd call ahead to clear the way. At first I thought to tell her not to, choosing to surprise the two men, but in the end I opted for the easier way.

'One moment,' she said, picking up her phone. 'Mr Begelman, there are two gentlemen here to see you. Oh, yes, of course.' She covered the phone and asked, 'What are your names, please?'

'Eddie Gianelli and Jerry Epstein.'

'They are a Mr Gianelli and a Mr Epstein. Yes, sir, right away.' She hung up and said, 'He'll see you. Follow me, please.' She seemed neither surprised nor distressed by the news.

We followed her down the hall to large double doors with 'David Begelman' painted on them. We didn't pass any doors along the way that had Fields' name. She knocked, then opened Begelman's door. 'Gentlemen.'

A tall man in his early forties, wearing an expensive suit, stood up from behind a huge desk and came around, extending his hand. The smile on his face was practiced.

'Mr Gianelli?'

'That'd be me,' I said, giving him my hand. He pumped it as if he was trying to get water.

'And Mr Epstein?'

'Yes, sir,' Jerry said. Begelman's hand disappeared inside Jerry's big paw.

'Please, please,' he said, 'have a seat. Judy called and said you'd be here.' He went back around his desk. 'I'm sorry, Freddie isn't here. He's working from home today.'

'So your girl said,' I replied.

Jerry and I sat across the desk from him. It seemed a long way.

'So, what can I do for you gents?'

'Did Judy tell you anything?'

'Not a thing,' he said. 'In fact, she was very mysterious on the phone. Just said that two friends of hers were coming by and that I should give you some time.' He frowned. 'I must admit I've never heard her mention your names before.'

'We're friends of a friend of hers,' I said.

'Oh? Who would that be?'

'You've probably heard of him,' I answered. 'Frank Sinatra.' Frank had given me carte blanche to use his name while in LA if it would help to smooth the way.

'Ah,' he said, and no more. I couldn't tell what he was thinking. 'All right, then. What's it about?'

'It's about the tour Judy just came back from,' I said. 'Australia and England?'

'What about it?'

'Seems like there was some difficulty in Australia.'

'The shows didn't go well,' Begelman said.

'From what we heard, she was late a few times, not at her best—'

'Heard from who?' I asked. 'You fellas weren't there with her?'

'No,' Begelman said, 'neither Freddie nor I made the trip with her. She was in Mark's care.'

'Mark Herron?'

'That's right. He managed the tour and produced the shows.'

'Then I guess we should talk to him. Does he have an office here?'

'No,' Begelman said, 'Mark isn't part of our firm. But my girl can give you his addresses, both home and business.'

I didn't bother telling him we already had them. 'I'd also like to talk to Mr Fields.'

'Sure,' Begelman said. 'My girl can give you his home address, too.' He was being very helpful.

'I'd appreciate that.'

He sat back in his chair. 'Was that all you wanted?'

'Just a few more questions, if that's all right.'

'Of course.'

'Have you noticed anybody hangin' around Judy lately?' I asked. 'Any strangers, maybe?'

'Is that was this is about?' he said, as if pleased we had finally come to the point. 'She thinks she's being watched?'

'She also thinks somebody's been in her house,' I said. 'She's worried for the safety of her family.'

'Look,' Begelman said, 'the only threat to Judy's safety is Judy herself.'

'You wanna explain that?'

'You must know what I'm referring to,' he said. 'The drugs, the booze, the . . . sex.'

'How much of that is true?' I asked. 'And how much is just gossip?'

'Who knows?' Begelman said. 'She's probably the only one who knows the extent of her . . . addictions.'

'You're her manager,' I said. 'You're supposed to be her friend, aren't you?'

'Would you like a drink?' Begelman asked, standing. 'Or your friend?' He walked to a bar against the wall.

'No, not for me,' I said.

'Me, neither,' Jerry added.

He poured himself a drink from a decanter, then turned to face us.

'I appreciate you wanting to help Judy,' he said. 'Freddie and I both want to as well. That's why we got her the CBS deal, and the Australian and European engagements.'

'But what about helping her with her fears?' I asked.

'Mr Gianelli,' Begelman said, 'nobody is following Judy; nobody is breaking into her house. It's all in her head. To tell you the truth, nobody is really very interested in her these days.'

'I don't think that's so.'

'Well, excuse me,' he said, 'but I think I know her a little better than you do.' He drank from the tumbler he was holding.

'Longer maybe,' I said, standing, 'but not better. Thanks for your time.'

Jerry followed me out.

Seventeen

We gave Greg the address of Freddie Fields'
home in Beverly Hills and he drove us directly
there. He seemed to have a map of LA in his
head.

As homes of the stars went, this one might not
have been the biggest, but it was impressive. On
a third of an acre, it was a two-story Spanish
style home of more than six thousand square feet.
Enough room for almost anyone.

We were allowed through the gate, which
meant that Judy – and probably Begelman – had
called ahead. When we got to the front door, we
were greeted by a stunningly beautiful woman
wearing a filmy cover-all over a one-piece
bathing suit.

Fields' wife, actress Polly Bergen, answered
the door. She fixed us with her startling blue eyes.
I didn't know about Jerry, but I was almost struck
dumb. She was not what you'd call a huge star
in the business. She'd had a dramatic role opposite Gregory Peck and Robert Mitchum in *Cape
Fear* in '62, but was probably better known for
lighthearted films like *Move Over, Darling* and
Kisses for My President, or for her beautiful
singing voice. In fact, she'd had her own short-
lived TV variety show in '58. But in person she
was just, well, shockingly beautiful.

'Can I help you?' she asked.

'Uh,' I said. Jerry was no help, so I knew he was feeling the same effects. 'We're here to see Mr Fields.'

'Oh, yes,' she said, 'David called . . . are you Mr Gianelli?'

'That's right.'

'Then come this way, please.'

She led us through the step-down entryway, down a hall to an office in the rear of the house.

Fields was seated behind a more modest desk than his partner had been, but the view behind him – a swimming pool, fountain and koi pond – trumped Begelman's view of LA. In the near distance was a beautiful guest house.

'Thank you, darling,' Fields said to his wife, who withdrew. 'Gentlemen.'

He was a not overly tall, Hollywood-slick handsome man in his early forties, casually dressed in a polo shirt, shorts and sandals. To me, he demanded more attention than his nattily dressed partner had. We shook his hand and he waved us to chairs in front of his desk.

'Judy called ahead and asked me to speak to you,' Fields said. Behind him, Polly Bergen removed her filmy covering and reclined on a chaise-longue by the pool.

'I assume your partner called, as well?' I asked.

'Actually, he did,' Fields said. 'I'm going to guess that you didn't like David much.'

'You guess right, Mr Fields,' I said.

'Please, just call me Freddie,' Fields said. 'Everybody does.'

'Sure, Freddie,' I said. 'Whatever you say.' Having not liked David Begelman at all, I was also prepared to dislike his partner, but Fields was different. He drew you in rather than repelled you. 'I'm Eddie, and this is Jerry.'

'Welcome,' Fields said. 'David told me this is about Judy's fears.'

'It is,' I said. 'Your partner seems to think it's about her addictions, and her fears are just in her head.'

'And you disagree.'

'I do. I'd like to know how you feel about it.'

'I just want Judy to feel more at ease,' Fields said. 'That's all I care about. If having you in LA and in her corner does that, then I'm ready to give you whatever assistance I can.'

I could easily have felt that he was 'handling' us, but somehow I didn't.

'OK, then,' I said. 'The time you've spent with Judy, have you noticed anyone suspicious hanging around her?'

'I have, yes.'

'Well,' I said, 'that's something. Can you describe this person?'

'I can do better than that,' Fields said. 'I can give you his name.'

'Really?' I said, surprised. Was this job going to be so easy? And why hadn't David Begelman offered the information? 'Who is it?'

'His name is Mark Herron.'

Jerry and I exchanged a glance.

'Ain't that the guy she's supposed to marry?' the big guy asked.

'It is,' Fields said.

'Your partner didn't say a word about Herron,' I commented.

60

'David doesn't agree with my assessment of the man.'

'And what is that assessment?' I asked.

'Well, for one thing,' Fields said, 'he's an actor.' He said it as if that was enough to discredit the man.

'Aren't actors sort of your bread and butter?' I asked.

'Talented actors are,' Fields said. 'Herron's type are a dime a dozen.'

'And what type is that?'

'Wannabes,' he said. 'Actors with more ambition than talent.'

'So what does Judy see that you don't?' I asked.

'What do you think?' Fields asked. 'He's younger than she is, handsome, slick. He's pulled the wool completely over her eyes. And to top it off . . .' He stopped.

'What's that?'

'Look,' Fields said, 'I don't begrudge anybody their proclivities, but Judy has this bad habit . . .'

I waited for him to continue.

'Of choosing . . . gay men.'

'Herron's homosexual?'

'I'm sure of it.'

'But he's hasn't . . . said that he is.'

'No.'

'The director,' Jerry said, 'he was gay, right? What was his name?'

'Vincente Minnelli.'

'That's the guy.'

I looked at Jerry. The big guy sometimes surprised me with the things he knew.

'He's going to end up breaking her heart,' Fields

61

said. 'And he's after her money. Before Judy, he was sniffing around Tallulah Bankhead.'

'Judy mentioned something about money problems.'

'She doesn't handle money very well,' Fields said.

'So who manages her finances now?'

'We do,' Fields said. 'David and I.'

'And how does Herron figure he'll get his hands on it?'

'By marrying her, obviously.'

'Have you tried telling Judy your suspicions about her future husband?'

'She won't listen,' he said. 'Judy makes up her own mind about her men.'

'So there's nothing you can do?'

'Just wait,' Fields said. 'This marriage won't last. We'll be there to catch her when it falls apart.'

'So you haven't seen anyone else around her?'

'No.'

I wondered about her suspicions that someone had broken into her house. Maybe someone hadn't had to break in. Maybe he was already there.

Eighteen

Freddie Fields was more helpful than his partner, but that didn't mean I ended up liking him any better. In the end, I did decide he was trying to handle us. He was just too slick. His partner might have warned him to treat us in an entirely different way than he had.

As we approached the limo, Greg quickly opened the back door for us.

'Where to, boss?' he asked.

'Back to the hotel for now, Greg,' I said.

'I thought we were gonna eat at Miss Garland's house?' Jerry asked.

'We are,' I said, 'but we still have a few hours before that. Let's go back to the hotel and rehash what we've learned from these two managers.'

'I didn't like either one of 'em,' Jerry said, sitting back as Greg pulled away from the house.

'Can't say I cared for either of them, myself,' I agreed. 'That Begelman is slimy . . .'

'And this fella was too damn slick,' Jerry finished.

'Right.'

'Can we pick somethin' up on the way?' Jerry asked.

'Jerry—'

'That sounds good to me, guys,' Greg chimed in.

'I tell you what,' I said. 'You fellas drop me at the hotel and then go and get a snack. How's that sound?'

'Works for me,' Greg said.

'Me, too!'

While they went off to find some food, I got on the phone and tried to get Danny. He was at his desk, still answering his own phone.

63

'Your fault,' he said when I mentioned it. 'You're the one who suggested I make it official with Penny—'

'Yeah, yeah, OK,' I said. 'You gonna remind me of that every time we talk?'

'Probably. What's up?'

'I was gonna ask you that,' I said. 'Anything on my imminent demise?'

'Not a peep on the street,' Danny said. 'I'm startin' to dig a little deeper, though.'

'OK,' I said. 'Keep me in the loop, will you? Here's my number.' I gave it to him. 'The Beverly Hills Hotel.'

'Nice digs,' he said. 'Listen, Eddie, don't you wanna check in with Jack on this? Maybe some of his contacts—'

'I told Jack about it,' I said. 'If I know him, he's checking.'

'And Frank?'

'No,' I said, 'I haven't said a word to Frank. I want him to think all my attention is on Judy.'

'OK, I get it,' he said. 'I guess I was thinkin' about – well, you know – Momo.'

'If things get bad,' I said, 'I'll check in with Giancana. But I really don't want to be in Momo's debt.'

'Have you spotted anybody payin' you special attention since you've been in LA?'

'No . . . not yet, anyway.'

'Well, that's good. Maybe you've managed to hide yourself well enough.'

'Let's hope it stays that way.'

'How's the Judy Garland thing?'

64

'Not much happenin',' I said. 'Jerry wants to go look for Seventy-Seven Sunset Strip.'

'Did you tell him it doesn't exist?'

'I did. He was crushed.'

'Why don't you just take him to Dino's?'

'I might have to do that before we leave.'

'Oh, hey, Penny's here. I told her we'd go and have dinner.'

'Tell her I say hello.'

'I'll stay on this, Eddie,' he said, before hanging up. 'We'll find out who's behind it.'

'Thanks, Danny.' I hung up. The phone rang almost immediately. 'Hello?'

'Mr Gianelli, this is the front desk,' a man's voice said.

'Yes?'

'There's a man here asking for you, sir.'

'Is that so?' I asked. 'Did he give his name?'

'No,' the clerk said. 'He told me to tell you he'd be in the Polo Lounge.'

'How long has he been here?' I asked.

'Oh, he walked in about five minutes ago. Asked for you right off.'

'He wouldn't happen to be a policeman, would he?'

'He didn't say, sir,' the clerk said. 'He certainly didn't show me a badge.'

'What's he wearin'?' I asked.

'A blue suit,' the clerk said. 'Looks kinda nice.'

'OK. Thanks.'

I hung up, wondering how long it would be before Jerry got back.

Nineteen

I decided not to wait for Jerry. After all, even if the guy was a contract hitter, he wasn't about to kill me in the middle of the Polo Lounge.

I put my jacket back on and left the cottage. I'll admit to some butterflies in my stomach as I entered the hotel and walked to the lounge. I wasn't so jaded that having somebody out to kill me – more than one somebody – didn't make me nervous.

When I got to the entrance of the lounge, I stopped and looked in. There were still no big celebrities in view. Some of the people seated at tables could have been studio types taking meetings, or waiting for some big name to arrive, but at the moment there was nobody there I knew. I looked around, saw a tall fella in a blue suit sitting at the bar. There were some other blue suits, but this was the only man who was alone.

I went in and approached the bar, took the stool one to Blue Suit's left.

'Hello, sir?' the bartender said. 'Are you a guest?'

'I am,' I said.

'What can I get you?'

'Get me whatever this gentleman is having,' I said. 'After all, my drink is on him.'

The man in the suit stopped with his glass

66

halfway to his mouth, then turned his head to look at me. 'You Eddie Gianelli?' he asked.

'That's right.'

The bartender looked at the man.

'Get him his drink.'

'Yes, sir.'

The bartender put a glass with ice on the bar and poured some bourbon into it. Blue Suit watched. I could tell he was tall, even seated, in his late thirties, pretty fit. He could have been a cop or a hood. He was in shape for either one.

'Thanks.'

'Why don't you move over one?' Blue Suit invited.

'I like it here,' I said. 'At least until I know what you want.'

'Me?' he said. 'I'm just a guy who might know something of interest to you.'

'And what would that be?'

'Let's talk a while first,' he said. 'Maybe get acquainted.'

'A fella who wants to get acquainted with me,' I answered, 'usually starts with his name.'

'You can call me . . . Amico.'

'Amico,' I said. 'And there's no irony in that name, right?'

'Of course not.'

I picked up my drink and sipped it. I doubted he'd managed to coerce the bartender into drugging it, and he didn't look as if he was wearing a gun under that tailored suit jacket.

'What's on your mind, Mr Amico?'

'Not Mister,' he said, 'just Amico . . . Eddie.'

'Fine,' I said, 'we're Amico and Eddie. We're buddies now. What do you want?'

'I don't want you to get killed.'

'Why not?'

'Let's just say I have a vested interest in you staying alive.'

'But we don't know each other.'

'I know a lot of people,' he said. 'You know a lot of people. It only figures that some of them would know each other.'

'OK,' I said, 'this is a guessin' game.' I drank again. 'Somebody we both know sent you to warn me.'

He didn't answer or react. He just looked at the bartender and indicated two more drinks.

'OK,' I repeated, 'I'm warned. Where do we go from here?'

'I'd just like to be sure that you'll take the proper steps to stay alive.'

'I left Vegas, didn't I?'

'That was a good start,' he admitted, 'but it won't take long for somebody to find you here. After all . . . I did.'

'Point taken,' I said. 'I think I'm doin' what needs to be done, thanks.'

'Care to fill me in?'

'No,' I said, 'just on the off chance that you might be here to kill me, not help me.'

He smiled. It was a smile that should have been in the movies. I guess that was what kept me from seeing who and what he really was from the beginning.

He concentrated on his drink.

'Are we done?' I asked.

'I am,' he said. 'If you want another drink, you're going to have to pay for it yourself.'

'That's OK.' I put down my second drink, untouched. 'I've had enough, thanks.'

'I'll be seeing you,' he said.

'Will you?'

'Oh, yes.'

I left the Polo Lounge, unsure whether that was a promise or a threat.

Twenty

When Jerry returned, I filled him in on my meeting with Amico.

'Mr G.,' he said when I was done, 'you never shoulda went and met him.'

'It was in a public place, Jerry,' I said. 'If he was after me, I didn't think he'd try anything.'

'If somebody wants you bad enough' he said, 'they'll do it anyplace.'

'OK,' I said. 'I'll remember. But this . . . it was like he was sent here to warn me.'

'Sent by who?'

'I don't know,' I said. 'He was dressed too good to be a cop or a hood.'

'What'd he look like?'

I described him.

'I don't know him, neither,' he said, frowning.

'You think you know every hitter on the east and west coast?' I asked.

'Mr G.,' he said, reproachfully, 'such a question.'

'Is Greg outside?' I asked.

'Yeah. He's waitin' with the limo.'

'OK, we might as well go back to Judy's and talk to her some more.'

'And eat?'

'Yes,' I said, 'and eat.'

Greg drove us to Judy's house. In the car, Jerry spoke some more about Amico. He wanted to know exactly what he looked like, including any scars or marks, how he spoke, how he moved. He was looking for any kind of identifier that would help him figure out who the man was.

'You know,' I said, 'in the beginning, when I first started talkin' to him, I thought he was just a messenger, but now I'm not so sure. And the name.'

'Yeah,' Jerry said, 'what's that mean, "Amico"?'

'Friend,' I said. 'Jerry, it's Italian for "friend".'

As we pulled up in front of the house, I leaned forward and asked Greg, 'Do you want to come in? I'm sure Miss Garland won't mind.'

'I appreciate the offer, boss,' he said, turning to look at us, 'but the closest I want to get to these people is them in the back seat while I'm in the front. Or in the movies. But thanks for asking.'

'Suit yourself, then. Guess you can take off,' I said, 'do what you wanna do and come back for us in a couple of hours.'

'Thanks.'

As we walked to the door, Jerry said, 'He's a pretty OK fella.'

'I'm glad you guys got along.'

When we knocked this time the door was answered by a middle-aged man. He was clean-shaven – actually appeared to be newly shaved, shine and all – his hair slicked back, and he was dressed in a black suit.

'Gentlemen,' he said, executing just a slight bow, 'Miss Garland is waiting in the living room. Would you follow me this way, please?'

As we walked, I asked, 'How do you know who we are?' I was concerned that he had allowed us to enter without identification.

He pointed behind him, without looking, as he continued forward. 'That one,' he said, indicating Jerry, 'is hard to miss.'

Judy was, indeed, waiting for us in the living room. She was seated on the plush sofa – or maybe, in a house like that, it was called a divan. I really don't know the difference. Once again, she was dressed as casually as a movie star can dress, in a purple silk blouse and tight pedal pushers. On her feet were a simple pair of slippers.

'Eddie,' she said, breathlessly. 'I'm so glad to see you. You too, Jerry.'

'We told you we'd be back.'

'I had Cook whip up something I think you're going to like,' she said. 'We've just been waiting for you to get here. Harrington, will you tell Cook she can serve now?'

'Yes, Miss Garland.'

The man left the room and I walked over to join Judy on the sofa. Jerry remained standing, his hands clasped in front of him.

71

Judy reached out to take my hands. She was cold and clammy, and held on tightly.

'Have you found out anything?' she asked.

'Yes,' I said, 'I found out I don't like your managers.'

'I know,' she said, 'they're not very likeable, but they've been . . . well, they got me the CBS deal. It's not their fault the show was canceled.'

I had a feeling she was going to say something else and had changed midstream. I looked at her face and saw fear there. It made her look brittle and older. I hoped I was the person who was going to take that fear away from her, soften her look, take her back to the way she looked in *Meet Me in St. Louis*. The director of that film, Vincente Minnelli, had fallen in love with her and had lit her in such a way that even Judy thought she looked beautiful.

That was probably a little naïve on my part, since *St. Louis* was twenty years before, but I'd always felt Judy Garland had looked luminous in her movies. There was nothing of that in the Judy I was looking at now.

'Judy, your managers weren't very helpful,' I said, 'but they weren't on your tour with you, so tomorrow I'm going to talk to Mark Herron.'

'Oh, I'm sure Mark will be more helpful than they were,' she said. 'Mark understands what I'm going through.'

Harrington appeared at the doorway again. 'Miss Garland, dinner is ready.'

'Thank you, Harrington.' She stood up, squared her shoulders and spoke some of Jerry's favorite words: 'Come on, boys, let's eat!'

Jerry said, 'You don't gotta tell me twice,' but he was still gentleman enough to step aside and let Judy lead the way.

Twenty-One

I didn't know who Judy thought she was feeding. Even Jerry couldn't put much of a dent in the feast she had her cook lay out for us. From fried chicken to roast beef, with plenty of mashed potatoes and other vegetables. But as much as I dug in and Jerry plowed through, Judy herself ate very little of it. She seemed nervous to me, rubbing her hands together much more often then she used them to handle utensils.

When she spoke, she spoke quickly and with passion, but it seemed she might be trying to convince herself more than us. Mostly, she talked about Mark Herron.

'He's a wonderful young actor, handsome and charismatic, still to be discovered, but he put his career on hold to help me. Who does that in this town? Hollywood is a me, me, me place, Eddie. Always me first, but not Mark. He's putting my needs ahead of his own, and I love him for it.'

Well, her managers weren't so sure that Mark Herron was putting his own needs last. I was going to reserve my opinion until we spoke to him the next day.

'He sounds like a great guy.'

'He is,' she said. 'I've been around a lot of

73

great guys, Eddie. It may not be Frank's reputation, but he's a great guy. So is Dean, and so is Gene Kelly. I know a great one when I see him.' She pointed to me. 'You're a great guy. And you—' she started to say to Jerry, but he cut her off.

'That's OK, Miss Garland,' he said. 'Don't say it. I ain't no great guy. But you're right – Mr G. is.'

'You're too modest, Jerry,' she said. 'You're a great big teddy bear.' She looked at me. 'Does he always call you that? "Mr G."?'

'Lots of people call him that,' Jerry said. 'In Vegas, he's Mr G. He's the guy.'

'Well, Frank thinks he's the guy,' Judy said, 'and now that I've met you both, I'm putting my faith in you.'

The cook, a fifty-ish woman with a slight German accent, came out of the kitchen and asked, 'What can I bring you next, ma'am?'

'What do you say, Jerry?' Judy asked. 'Dessert?'

'Hell, yeah,' Jerry said. Then ducked his head and said, 'Uh, sorry.'

'Don't be sorry,' she said. She looked at the woman and said, 'You heard the man, Greta . . . hell, yeah!'

'Yes, ma'am.'

I had intended to skip dessert and just have coffee, but when I saw the chocolate layer cake, I had to go for a slice. Jerry had two. Judy had a sliver, and we all had coffee.

'Judy,' I said, 'do you mind if I ask you a few more questions?'

74

'Of course not,' she said. 'Ask all the questions you want.'

'Other than your house staff, your managers and Mark Herron, who else is part of your everyday life? I mean, other than your kids, of course.'

She thought a moment, then shrugged. 'No one – not really. I mean, I talk to some people on the phone, or I meet with studio or record execs, but no one else on a day-to-day basis.'

'Anyone else in this house besides Harrington and the cook?'

'No one.'

'So there's only Mark for us to talk to.'

'I suppose – but he'll probably be the most helpful.'

'I hope so.'

She frowned. 'What did David and Freddie tell you about Mark?'

'Well . . .'

'Nothing good, I'll bet. They think he's after me for his own benefit, don't they?'

Jerry and I exchanged a glance.

'They're wrong,' she said. 'He loves me. He does!'

I held my hands out in a back-up gesture. 'Take it easy, Judy,' I said. 'We're on your side, remember?'

She took a deep breath, let it out slowly. 'I'm sorry. I just get so tired of people . . .' She didn't finish the thought.

I washed down my last bite of cake with coffee. 'Jerry and I have to get going.'

'Oh, must you?'

'Yes,' I said, standing, 'but we have somebody outside watching the house.'

'Who is he?'

I hesitated. I didn't want to tell her that we hadn't met the man yet. All we had was the name Hiller had given me.

'He's a detective,' I said, 'a good man. He'll keep an eye on you while we keep looking.'

'Well, all right,' she said. 'If you say so, Eddie. I've pretty much put myself in your hands, haven't I?'

'Yes,' I said, not at all sure she had done so wisely, 'you have.'

Twenty-Two

Jerry and I left the house and stepped outside the gates. Greg wasn't back with the car yet.

'He'll be here in a minute or two,' Jerry said. 'I'm sure of it.'

I looked around.

'What are you lookin' for?' he asked.

'Hiller's man,' I said. 'He's supposed to be watching the house.'

'But he's not supposed to be seen, right?'

'Right.'

'Then you ain't gonna see 'im.'

'Then how do we know he's here?'

'Nat Hiller said he'd be here, and you said you trusted him.'

'Only because Danny does.'

Jerry shrugged. 'Same thing, right?'

'Well,' I said, 'I want to see him. I wanna meet 'im.'

'So,' Jerry said, 'all we gotta do is find 'im, or get 'im to come out.'

'If you wanted to watch this house and not be seen, where would you be?'

'Inside the walls,' Jerry said, 'not out here. Somebody comes over the wall, or forces the gate, they mean trouble.'

'OK, then,' I said, 'back inside.'

We hadn't closed the gate behind us yet, so we went back.

'You're the expert on the criminal mind, Jerry,' I said. 'Where would you look?'

'No place.'

'Then what do you suggest we do?'

'Just wait,' Jerry said. 'If he's any good, he'll come out to see what we want.'

'You think so?'

'That's what I'd do,' Jerry said. 'And ain't I the expert, like you said?'

'Yes, you are.'

'So that's what I say, Mr G. We just wait here.'

'It would help if we knew what the guy looked like. I should've asked Hiller—'

'I'd guess,' Jerry said, interrupting me, 'that he looks somethin' like that.'

I looked over to where Jerry was pointing and saw a man coming out from behind some trees. He was wearing a suit and a fedora, and as he approached he removed the fedora and started beating it on his suit.

'When I came here from Vegas,' he commented.

'I didn't realize I should have brought along some trail clothes.' He stopped and replaced the fedora on his head, then looked at us. 'You Eddie G.?' he asked me.

'That's right,' I said. 'I'm Eddie, and this is Jerry Epstein.'

'Nice to meet you.' He looked up at Jerry's six and half feet from his own five and a half. 'My name's Boyd – Kenny Boyd.'

I shook his hand, then watched as Jerry's hand engulfed his.

'You got some ID?' I asked.

'Oh, sure.' He took out his wallet and showed me his Las Vegas PI license. Boyd was the name Hiller had given me. I handed it back.

'I figured you guys were standing out here waitin' for me to show myself,' Boyd said. He looked to be about thirty, and his blue suit had seen better days but had once cost a few bucks.

'Have you seen anything in the short time you've been here?' I asked.

'Only you two, so far. Look, when do I get to go and have something to eat? Maybe clean up some?'

I stared at him for a moment, realizing that I should have asked Hiller for two men, one to relieve the other.

'I've got an idea, Kenny,' I said. 'How would you like to meet Judy Garland?'

'Would I?' Boyd asked. 'I thought I was just gonna get a chance to watch her house.'

'Come on,' I said. 'We'll get you something to eat at the same time.'

* * *

78

We left Kenny Boyd eating some of the fine dinner Judy's cook had prepared for us and went back out to the street, where we found Greg waiting with the limo.

'Sorry I was late, boss—'

'You're not late, Greg,' I said. 'You're just in time.'

Once we were in the back seat and the car was moving, Jerry said, 'That dick from Vegas was kinda small, wasn't he?'

'Hiller said he's a good man,' I said. 'We've got to take his word.'

'I didn't say he wasn't good,' Jerry argued. 'Just said he was small.'

Twenty-Three

When I got up the next morning, Jerry was in the bungalow's kitchen, making coffee.

'Where'd you get the coffee?' I asked.

'Paid a bellhop to bring it,' he said. 'Donuts, too.' He pointed to a bag on the counter.

'Coffee and donuts suits me fine.'

'Well,' Jerry said, 'it'll hold us until we can get to a diner.'

'Sure,' I said.

He poured me a cup of coffee, then carried his own and the donuts to the table. He pulled out a jelly and I grabbed a chocolate.

'What's first today?' he asked. 'We goin' to see that Mark Herron fella?'

'That's where we're goin', all right.'

79

'I wonder if he's so all-fired great as Miss Garland says he is.'

'Jerry,' I said, 'nobody's that great.'

He bit into his donut, then asked, 'But we're gonna go have breakfast first, right?'

Jerry agreed that the diner we'd gone to before would be fine for breakfast. Turns out the food there was pretty damn good. Once again, we sat at the window, watching the foot traffic on Sunset Boulevard. Greg and the limo were parked down the street.

'What are you lookin' so nervous about?' I asked Jerry after we'd given our orders.

'I was just wonderin' if somebody would have the balls to take a shot at you through this window,' Jerry said.

Now *I* was nervous.

'You might be right.'

We moved to another booth, this one away from a window. When the waitress came with our food, she looked around in confusion, then spotted us and came over.

'Switched tables on me,' she said.

'Too many people gettin' ready to watch us eat,' Jerry said.

'Well,' she said to him, putting plates of pancakes and eggs in front of him, 'if the last time you was here is any indication, watchin' you eat is somethin' else.'

'Not when you've done it as often as I have,' I told her.

She put my toast down in front of me and withdrew.

'That really all you're gonna have?' he asked, drowning his pancakes in syrup.

'I told you. The donuts were good enough for me.'

The bellhop had brought six donuts, and I managed to snag two of them. But the bacon on Jerry's plate looked good, so I stole a slice.

'Hey!'

'Sorry, Jerry,' I said. 'I lost my head. It won't happen again.'

'It better not.'

While we ate, I asked, 'What about Greg? He didn't wanna come in and eat?'

'He says you're the boss, and he should stay in the car,' Jerry said. 'I guess I know how he feels.'

I knew, too. He preferred to keep his business and pleasure separate. Eating with Jerry was OK, because he perceived Jerry as an employee. But I was the boss, so he preferred to keep things professional.

I eyed another slice of bacon on Jerry's plate, but he saw me and shook his head.

I ate my toast.

Twenty-Four

Mark Herron lived in an apartment complex in LA. It was two stories around a swimming pool, but the pool hadn't been very well cared for.

'I think I can see why he'd want to marry Miss

Garland,' Jerry said, looking around. 'He must not be doin' real well as an actor.'

'If he's livin' here,' I said, 'he's barely makin' a livin'.'

Once again, Greg stayed out by the car. I guessed that would be our pattern until we were finished in LA and he took us back to the airport.

'He's on the second floor,' I said. 'Come on.'

We walked along the pool to a stairway and up to the second floor. From up there the place looked even more deserted, the pool even dirtier. It hadn't been cleaned in so long that some of the dirt had settled on the bottom.

We reached Herron's door and knocked. When he didn't answer, I wondered if he was off somewhere, maybe working or maybe getting something to eat. I knocked a second time and the door opened.

'Can I help you?' he asked. Like Judy said, he was handsome and fit. Begelman had said he was younger than Judy. I put him in his mid- to late thirties.

'Mr Herron? My name's Eddie Gianelli. This is Jerry Epstein. We're—'

'Friends of Frank Sinatra,' Herron said. 'Judy called me. Come on in.'

He was wearing jeans, an open-neck polo shirt and a pair of slippers. The apartment was sparsely furnished with second-hand furniture. He was living the way most actors probably did while trying to hit it big. If he was marrying Judy Garland, then he was about to hit it real big.

'Sorry about the place,' he said. 'It's all I can afford right now.'

'But . . . you're marrying Miss Garland,' Jerry said.

Herron looked up at Jerry. He was about my height – six feet.

'She wanted to get me a better place,' Herron said, 'but I never wanted to be a kept man.'

'That's . . . admirable.'

'You fellas want a drink? I've got some beer in my fridge.'

'A little early for me,' I said.

'Me, too,' Jerry said.

'Coffee, then?'

'Sure,' I said, 'we'll have coffee.'

The apartment was an efficiency, so we watched as he went to the stove and heated some coffee. When we each had a cup, we sat on furniture that had no cush left in the cushions.

'Didn't you get paid for producing her tour?' I asked.

'I did,' Herron said. 'I used that money to get caught up on my bills.'

'Well,' Jerry said, 'you're gettin' married in a few days. You'll be better off then.'

'I'll be better off because I'll be with Judy,' Herron said, 'not because of her money.'

'I didn't mean nothin',' Jerry said.

'Sure,' Herron said, 'no problem. What can I do to help you fellas?'

'Tell us about Australia,' I said, 'and England.'

'What about it?'

'Judy said she had the feeling she was being watched. Did you ever see anyone?'

'No,' Herron said, 'I never did. I tried to keep her from being afraid, but it didn't help her that

83

I never saw anyone. It made her feel . . . well, that maybe I didn't believe her.'

'Did you believe her?' I asked. 'It doesn't seem that Fields and Begelman ever did.'

'They're a couple of crooks,' Herron said, 'especially Begelman. Once we're married, I'm going to try to convince Judy to fire them.'

'And then you'll take over as her manager?'

'I'm an actor, Mr Gianelli, not a manager.'

'You handled the tour.'

'I told Judy I'd do that as a favor,' he said. 'She insisted on paying me.'

'Then who do you think should manage her?'

'We'll have to find somebody,' he said, 'but I think Sid Luft should do it for a while, take over from Fields and Begelman.'

'Her ex-husband?' Jerry asked.

Herron nodded. 'He cares about her.'

'Won't that make you jealous?'

Herron grinned and said, 'No, I don't mind. If I was going to be jealous, I'd be jealous of Sinatra. After all, she called him for help and he sent you.'

I remembered what Begelman said about Herron being homosexual. Maybe that was why he had no feelings of jealousy. I didn't think he had any even toward Frank. He said he didn't want to be a kept man, but did he really love Judy?

'You really ain't jealous, are you?' Jerry asked.

'No.'

'You must think she loves you a lot.'

'She does.'

'I guess that makes you pretty lucky,' Jerry said.

'I guess it does.'

'What about Miss Garland?' I let Jerry continue to do the talking.

'What about her?'

'Does that make her lucky?'

'Well,' Herron said, 'I'd like to think so. Can I ask *you* something, now?'

'Go ahead.'

'What do you gents intend to do?'

I took it up from there.

'We intend to help Judy.'

'And what if – and I'm just saying *what if*, now – she's imagining things?'

'Well, if that's what I find out,' I said, 'then that's what I'll try to get her to understand. I just want to put her mind to rest.'

'I don't know if you know her well enough yet,' he said, 'but it'll take more than that to put her mind to rest.'

'I know the lady's got demons,' I said. 'We can't help her with that. But we can help her if we find some trouble that's more real.'

'Yes,' Herron said, 'yes, I suppose between the two of you, you can. You both look . . . quite capable.'

Jerry and I didn't talk until we got in the back seat of the limo.

'Where to, boss?' Greg asked.

'Back to the hotel for now.'

'Gotcha.'

'We didn't get much from him,' Jerry said, as we pulled away.

'No, we didn't.'

85

'You think Miss Garland's imaginin' things?'

'We don't have enough information yet to know that,' I said.

'Did you notice what I noticed back there?' he asked.

'I doubt it,' I said. 'What's that?'

'Two people live there.'

'How could you tell?'

'Plates and cups, silverware,' Jerry said, 'an' I could see into the bathroom. It was a mess.'

'So you think he's got a woman livin' with him?'

'Not the way that kitchen looked,' Jerry said, 'and the place needed cleanin'. Ain't no woman livin' there, Mr G.'

'So you're sayin' . . .'

'That he's livin' there with another man.'

'So,' I said, 'it could be a roommate . . .'

'Or that fella Begelman is right about him bein' . . . you know . . . what he is.'

Twenty-Five

When we got out of the car in front of the hotel, I told Greg to take off for a couple of hours. Then we went through the hotel lobby instead of heading straight for the bungalow.

'Any messages?' I asked at the desk.

'No, sir.'

'OK, thanks.'

'But there was someone asking about you.'

86

I studied the clerk for a moment. He was the young man who had told me the same thing before. 'Same man?' I asked.

'No, sir. A different man. Not as well dressed, or as well spoken.'

'He say what he wanted?'

'No, sir, but . . .'

'But what?'

'I'd hate to run up against him in a dark alley.'

I looked at Jerry, who just shrugged.

'If you see the man again,' I said to the clerk, 'or if anyone else asks about us, call the bungalow. OK?'

'Yes, sir.'

I handed him ten dollars.

'Yes, sir!'

'Nobody's been here,' Jerry said, after checking around for a few minutes.

'You sure?'

'Positive.'

'Well,' I said, 'somebody's found us.'

'Two somebodies,' Jerry said, 'but the second one sounds like a hitter.'

'Sure, boss.'

'There's some coffee left from this mornin',' Jerry said.

'Heat it up,' I said. 'I'm gonna call Judy and check in with her.'

'Right.'

I sat on the sofa and dialed Judy's phone number. Harrington answered. 'Harrington, it's Eddie G.'

'Yes, sir.'

'I'd like to talk to Judy.'

'I'll get her, sir.'

'Hold on. Is Boyd still in the house?'

'No, sir. He had something to eat and then went outside again.'

'OK, good,' I said. 'Put Judy on the line.'

Jerry came over while I was waiting and handed me a cup of coffee.

Twenty-Six

'Eddie?'

'You all right, Judy?'

'Why, yes,' she said. 'I had a wonderful talk with that young man you left here earlier. He's a big fan.'

'You have lots of fans, Judy,' I said. 'I need him there to protect you.'

'Well, he's outside, doing just that. He's kind of small, isn't he? But, then, Mickey was also short, and he's the biggest small man I ever met.'

I knew she was referring to Mickey Rooney.

'He'll do,' I said. 'Judy, we talked with Mark Herron. I'm afraid he wasn't very helpful.'

'I–I'm sure he tried his best,' she said. 'Maybe if I talked to him . . .'

'You go ahead and do that,' I said, 'and then Jerry and I will have another talk with him.'

'All right. I'll do that as soon as I hang up, Eddie.'

'Good.'

'What else are you doing?'

'We're going to keep lookin', Judy.'

'Come to the house for dinner again.'

'Yes,' I said. I'd already decided it would be a good idea to talk to her each night, until the matter was resolved . . . somehow.

'Can that young man come in and eat?' she asked, hopefully. 'He reminds me of Mickey.'

'Really?' I didn't see it, unless he had red hair beneath his fedora. 'Sure.'

'Wonderful,' she said. 'I'll see you and Jerry later. And I'll call Mark right now.'

'See you later,' I said, and hung up.

'What's up?' Jerry asked.

'She likes Kenny Boyd.'

'Really?' Jerry thought a moment. 'Probably because he reminds her of Mickey Rooney.'

'What? You, too?'

'Well, they're both little guys.'

'I don't see it,' I said.

'Maybe he's got red hair.'

'We'll find out tonight. She wants us all to come to dinner.'

'That's OK with me,' Jerry said. 'Her cook's pretty good.'

'Yeah, she is.'

'What's on your mind, Mr G.?'

'What?'

'You look like somethin's worryin' ya.'

'To tell you the truth,' I said, 'I'm just wonderin' if we're chasin' our tail on this, while there are men out there tryin' to figure out a way to kill me.'

'You got Danny workin' on it,' Jerry said. 'And maybe Mr Entratter.'

'I know,' I said, 'but the more we come up

empty on Judy, the more I think we should be out there lookin' for whoever put that contract out on me.'

'Who do you think it could be?'

'You know,' I said, 'for a few minutes I thought it might be Hargrove. Crazy, huh?'

'He pretty much hates your guts,' Jerry said, 'but he hates mine, too. I think he'd put out a hit on both of us.'

'You're probably right. So not him. Then who?'

'Who have you pissed off that much?'

'I've lain awake in bed a few nights tryin' to figure that one out,' I said. 'I'm not a cop, I haven't put criminals away.'

'You've helped Mr S. and Dino out over the past few years,' he said. 'Sammy Davis, too. Maybe somebody don't like your relationship with them.'

'You think this is jealousy?'

Jerry shrugged. 'If it's somebody's husband, it's because of jealousy,' he pointed out.

'A husband would come after me himself.'

'I've known jealous hubbies to hire hitmen.'

'Maybe – but to put out an open contract? For that much money? That would have to be a rich husband, and I haven't been with any rich women in the past – well, hardly ever! I think a husband is out.'

He sat down across from me. 'What about the Kennedys?' he asked, raising his eyebrows. 'They got the money.'

'I don't think I've pissed off Joe Kennedy that much.' Had I?

'I don't wanna say this but . . .'

90

'But what?'

'You got mob connections, Mr G.'

'You think Sam Giancana put out an open contract on me?' I asked.

Jerry shrugged. 'Why don't we ask him?'

I was wondering if Jack Entratter had already done that, decided to call him and find out.

'Have I what?'

'Asked Momo if he put out a contract on me?'

'You think I can just call Sam and ask him that?'

'I don't know, Jack,' I said. 'Can you?'

'I don't know what you think, Eddie, but Momo and I aren't asshole buddies. I've put the word out where I can, and I'm waitin' to hear, but nothin' yet.'

'OK, Jack.'

'Eddie!' he said, before I could hang up.

'Yeah?'

'If things get really bad,' he said, 'maybe you could get Frank to ask him.'

'I haven't told Frank a thing about this, Jack,' I said, 'but you're right. If things get real bad, I'll ask Frank.'

I hung up, thinking that somebody had put up a butt load of money for an open contract on my life. How much worse could things get?

We talked it over a bit more, and then I decided to call it quits. Jerry went into his bedroom for a nap; I turned on the TV and made some coffee. We'd talked to both of Judy's managers and her husband-to-be. Who was left?

When Jerry came back out a couple of hours later, rubbing his eyes, the TV was off and I was just staring at the wall.

'Sid Luft,' I said.

'Mr G., you think Sid Luft put a hit out on you?' he asked.

'No,' I said, 'I'm thinkin' about Judy's problem now. We have to talk to the ex-husband.'

'All of 'em?'

'Nope,' I said, 'just the last one. Sid Luft.'

'Where do we find him?'

'That's what we'll ask Judy tonight,' I replied. 'Also, we should probably talk to someone at the CBS studio, and her record label.'

'All good ideas, Mr G., but right now I'm kinda hungry.'

'For once,' I said, 'I'm with you, Jerry. Let's go.'

We went out to the front of the hotel and saw the limo sitting there, Greg behind the wheel. He must have been watching for us because he popped out immediately to open the door. Before coming around to our side, he slammed the driver's side door . . .

And the car went up in a ball of flames.

Twenty-Seven

We were approaching the car, and were close enough to be thrown off our feet by the explosion. As we were lying on the pavement, flaming pieces of metal and broken glass began to rain down on and around us. Before I knew it, Jerry had covered me with his big body.

'Jerry,' I yelled, 'get off me!'

He didn't respond immediately.

'Jerry?'

When he didn't move, I struggled out from beneath his weight. That's when I saw that a piece of metal had imbedded itself in his left shoulder. If he hadn't covered me, it would have been sticking out of my back.

People came streaming out of the hotel.

'Call an ambulance!' I shouted.

'For him,' somebody asked, 'or for you?'

I frowned, went to stand up and fell on to my back again, pain shooting through my leg. I looked down and saw a shard of glass sticking out of my thigh.

I passed out after that . . .

I woke in a hospital. It was easy to tell from the smells, even with my eyes closed. But I opened them anyway, just to make sure. All the people in white were the clincher.

'Hey?' I said.

A nurse stopped in mid-run and turned to look at me.

'You'll be all right, sir,' she said. 'Just don't move. There's an emergency right now.'

'What,' I called out, as she turned away, 'what emergency?'

'Don't worry,' a man said. 'It's not your friend.'

I turned my head in the other direction, saw a man in a cheap suit standing there.

'Cop?' I asked.

He nodded, arms folded.

'Where is my friend?'

'A few beds down,' he said. 'Resting comfortably, they tell me. They got that piece of metal out of his shoulder. It wasn't too bad.'

'But . . . he was out.'

'Yeah,' he said, 'another piece hit him on the head and knocked him out. He's got a nasty lump, maybe a concussion. But he'll be all right. And so will you. They bandaged your leg. The glass missed your femoral artery.'

'You know a lot,' I said.

'I got here fast,' he said. 'The name's Detective Lynn Franklin.'

'Don't you usually work in pairs?'

'My partner's still at the scene.'

'The scene . . .' I tried to sit up suddenly, which was a bad idea. Pain shot through my leg. I fell back on to my elbows. 'The driver?'

'He's not as lucky,' Franklin said.

'Is he dead?'

'No,' Franklin said, 'but he's unconscious. We assume he was outside the car—'

'He was.'

'And that probably saved him – that and the fact that the bomb was underneath the rear of the car, the passenger section.'

'That would put it near the gas tank, right?'

'Right,' he said. 'Somebody screwed up. If they meant to kill a person in the back seat, they forgot to allow for the gas tank, and . . . blooey.'

'Yeah,' I said, sourly, falling on to my back again, 'blooey.'

94

Franklin approached the emergency-room bed I was lying on. 'We got you and your buddy's names.' He took out a notebook. 'Eddie Gianelli from Las Vegas, and Jerry Epstein from Brooklyn.'

'And you're Detective Lynn Franklin from LA?'

'Beverly Hills, actually.'

'Wait a minute,' I said. 'I know that name. Franklin. You're the guy who pulled over Bobby Kennedy's car after Marilyn was . . . died.'

'Actually, Peter Lawford was drivin', but yeah, that's me.' He shrugged. 'I was still on patrol then. Lawford was drivin' erratically. I didn't know Kennedy was in it.'

'And that doctor – Greenberg – he was in it, too.'

'It was Dr Greenson, but that's right.' He frowned at me. 'How come you know so much?'

'I was friends with Marilyn.'

'Is that a fact?'

'It is.'

'And are you friends with Bobby Kennedy?'

'Bobby's no friend of mine,' I said.

'Well, then,' Franklin said, 'maybe we'll get along.'

'And do we have to get along?'

'I'm investigatin' this explosion, Mr Gianelli,' Franklin said. 'I'll need to speak with you, and your friend, as well as the driver . . . if and when he wakes up.'

'Of course.'

'I need to know,' Franklin went on, 'which of you this bomb might have been meant for.'

'Well . . .'

'Not the driver, I'm guessing. Besides, the bomb was under the passenger section. I guess that means it was meant for the passengers. Or . . . one of them in particular?'

I wasn't at all sure how to handle the situation and was about to plead a headache – or something – when a doctor appeared.

'Hey, Doc!' I said. I didn't remember the man, but was really glad to see him. He was bald, but young, with wire-rimmed glasses.

'Mr Gianelli,' he said. 'Am I . . . interrupting?'

'Huh? Oh, no,' I said. 'No, I, uh, I'm havin' a lot of pain. In my, uh, leg. Is there anythin' you can do for that? Like, now?'

The doctor looked at Franklin.

'Oh, OK,' the detective said. 'Mr Gianelli, we'll talk again. Soon.'

'Right,' I said, 'sure. I just need to, you know, clear my head.'

'Sure,' Franklin said, 'sure. Where are you stayin' while you're in Beverly Hills?'

'Actually, we're at the Beverly Hills Hotel. One of the bungalows.'

'Right,' Franklin said, 'right. Must be all that casino money, huh?'

'Yeah,' I said, 'that's right.'

'I'll need you to go now, Detective,' the doctor said.

'Yes, sir.'

As Franklin withdrew, the doctor looked at me and said, 'Now, about that pain.'

Twenty-Eight

'Never mind about the pain, Doc,' I said. 'How's my friend? Jerry Epstein?'

'I just came from him,' he said. 'I bandaged his shoulder. We'd like to keep him overnight, though, to be sure about the head injury.'

'That's OK.'

'Is it? He says he can't stay overnight.'

'Don't worry,' I said, 'he'll stay. Uh, what's your name?'

'Wyler, Dr Wyler.'

'Well, Doc, my friend can be very stubborn, but I'll make sure he stays put. Now, what about me?'

'I was going to say we could release you as long as you can walk, but you mentioned the pain—'

'Don't worry about that,' I said. 'That was for the cop's benefit.'

'Ah, I see. So there's no pain?'

'Well, there is,' I said, 'but I assume some aspirin will take care of that?'

'It should, yes,' he said. 'Unless it gets worse and you want something stronger.'

'No, no,' I said, 'somethin' stronger would knock me out, wouldn't it?'

He grinned. 'It would certainly take the starch out of you.'

'I kinda need all the starch I can get, so I'll make do with aspirin.'

'Very well, then,' Wyler said. 'I'll sign you out.'

'Can you tell me where Jerry is?'

'I'll take you to him.'

'Great.'

I moved to the edge of the bed, eased myself to the floor gingerly. When I put my weight on my leg, it wasn't too bad. Well, it was a little worse than I let on, what with the doctor watching me and all, but it wasn't unbearable.

'Lead the way,' I said.

Jerry looked up at me when the doctor pulled the curtain aside.

'Thanks, Doc.'

'I'll arrange for a room,' he said.

'A private room,' I said. 'Charge it to the Sands Casino in Las Vegas.'

'All right.'

'Hey, Mr G.,' Jerry asked, 'you OK?'

'Thanks to you, I am,' I said. 'Although you almost crushed me with your weight.'

'Sorry about that,' he said. 'I just meant to, you know . . .'

'Yeah, I know. How are you feelin'?'

'Just fine. Ready to get out of here?'

'I am,' I said. 'You're not.'

He was bare-chested, except for a swathe of bandage around his left shoulder.

'Whataya mean?'

'They're gonna keep you overnight to make sure your head injury isn't too bad.'

'My head's fine.'

'Got a headache?'

98

'A little one.'

'Yeah, well, we wanna make sure it ain't a big one.'

'Mr G.,' Jerry said, lowering his voice, 'I can't stay here while somebody's gunnin' for ya.'

'You won't do me any good if you can't even stand, Jerry.'

'I can stand.' As if to prove it, he moved to the edge of the bed, put his feet to the floor and then stood. Almost immediately he went white and I saw his eyes go out of focus. When he swayed, I moved fast, despite my leg, and eased him back on to the bed.

'Sure you can,' I said.

'I'll just have to do it slower.'

'Jerry,' I said, 'it's just gonna be overnight.'

'What about you?'

'I'll be fine. I can look after myself for one night.'

'Yeah, but' – he lowered his voice again – 'they tried to blow ya up.'

'They blew us up,' I said.

'Geez,' he said, 'how's Greg?'

'He's . . . not awake. They said the fact that he was out of the car may have saved him. The bomb was under the passenger section.'

'Meant for you,' he said.

'Or us.'

'So somebody tried to cash in.'

'But they were sloppy about it,' I said. 'The bomb was too close to the gas tank, and it probably shouldn't have gone off when Greg slammed his door.'

'Is that what happened?'

'That's sure what it looked like to me. Have the police talked to you?'

'Yeah, some dick named Franklin. I pretended I couldn't think. Ya know, the head wound?'

'Good.'

'But there's one other thing that might be a problem, Mr G.'

'What's that, Jerry?'

He dropped his voice to a new low. And looked around to make sure we were alone. 'Do you know what happened to my rod?'

'Your forty-five?' I said. 'You had it on you?'

'Well, yeah,' he said. 'How else was I gonna protect you?'

'The cops don't have it?' I asked.

'The detective didn't say nothin' about it.'

'What about the doctor? The nurse? Maybe they took it off you when they brought you in?'

'I don't know,' he said. 'They probably woulda turned it over to the cops.'

'Wait a minute,' I said.

'What?'

There was something – a memory, but fuzzy. As I concentrated harder, it sort of came into focus.

'Jerry,' I said, 'I think I may know what happened to your gun.'

Twenty-Nine

'Just before I passed out,' I told him, 'I saw the guy – what did he call himself? Amica?'

100

'Friend,' Jerry said.

'Yeah, right,' I said. 'Same blue suit.'

'Did he set the bomb?'

'No,' I said, 'he crouched over me, asked me if I had a gun. Then he asked if you had one. I said you probably did. He frisked you and came up with your forty-five. "You don't want the cops findin' this on him," Amico said. "I'll hold the piece for him until he's ready."'

'You didn't ask him why he was doin' that?' Jerry asked.

'I didn't get a chance to,' I said. 'That's when I passed out for real.'

'So where is this guy?' Jerry asked.

'I don't know,' I said, 'but he's got your gun. I'm sure of it.'

'He did us a favor, Mr G.,' Jerry said. 'I woulda had to explain that cannon.'

'I know,' I said, 'and now we only have to explain why somebody tried to kill us.'

'We could play dumb.'

'We could, but why?' I asked. 'What's the point? Somebody's tryin' to kill me – or us. We don't know who or why. And that's the truth. Where's the harm in tellin' it that way?'

'I see your point.'

'Besides,' I said, 'if they decided to check with the Vegas police, they'll find out for themselves. And then they'll wanna know why we didn't speak up.'

'So, OK,' Jerry said, 'we tell the truth.'

'I'll tell 'em,' I said, 'the next time Detective Franklin shows up. Meanwhile, you take it easy and relax. I'll come back and get you tomorrow.'

'An' you don't want me to tell it?'

'Only if they press you,' I said. 'It's probably better if I'm the one who talks to them. After all, it started with me.'

'OK, Mr G.,' he said, settling back. 'You're the boss.'

'You wait here and they'll take you to a room,' I said. 'It's all on the Sands, so you'll be in a private one. Meanwhile, I'll go and check on Greg.' I started away, then stopped. 'You guys had a meal together. Did he talk about any family?'

'Only to say he didn't have any.'

'Well, I'm sure the cops went through his pockets. If there's somebody to notify, they'll know.' I patted his foot. 'Do me a favor, Jerry. When they get you a room, stay put so I'll know where to find you.'

'OK, Mr G.'

Greg was hooked up to some beeping machines and was wrapped in bandages.

'How is he, Doc?' I asked.

'Mr Coleman is in pretty bad shape, Mr Gianelli,' Doc Wyler said. 'He's got a concussion, several broken ribs, several deep lacerations from flying glass and debris . . . but it's the head wound I'm worried about. If he doesn't wake up soon, he might never wake up.'

'Has anybody been notified about his injuries?'

'The police would know about that,' Wyler said, 'but I could check with billing.'

'If you don't find out anything from them, make

102

sure they send his bills to the Sands Casino in Vegas.'

'Him, too? Like your other friend?'

'Like my other friend,' I said.

'It sounds to me like you're a good man to know, Mr Gianelli.'

Considering both Jerry and Greg were in the hospital because they knew me, I said, 'Not necessarily, Doc.'

Thirty

I took a cab to Judy's, went through the gate and up the drive, keeping my eyes peeled for Kenny Boyd. When I knocked, it was Boyd who answered the door. He wasn't wearing his hat, and his hair was, indeed, ginger. So maybe I could see how he'd remind Judy of her friend Mickey Rooney. He was in shirt sleeves, with a .38 in a shoulder holster.

'You're late for dinner,' he started, then stopped. 'Say, what happened to you?'

'Somebody put a bomb in my limo,' I said.

'Anybody killed?'

'The driver's pretty bad. He might not pull through.'

'And the big guy?'

'He'll be in the hospital overnight,' I said. 'Can I come in and sit down? My leg's killin' me. I caught a piece of glass in my thigh and it took a few stitches to close it.'

103

'Sure, sure,' Boyd said, 'come on in. Judy's got the cook holdin' food for you.'

I followed Kenny to the living room, where Judy was sitting. She noticed my limp immediately.

'Oh, what happened?'

I sat down heavily in a chair and told her the same thing I'd told Boyd.

'Why would somebody do such a thing?' Judy asked.

'There's something I should have told you earlier, Judy.' I looked at Boyd. 'I should have told Hiller, too, Kenny. There were a couple of attempts on my life in Las Vegas. When Frank asked me to come and help you, Judy, I thought I was leaving that bad business behind.'

'So who's after you?' Boyd asked.

I looked at him, wishing he hadn't asked that. I didn't want to tell the whole truth in front of Judy. It would only serve to frighten her more than she already was. But it was probably unfair of me to keep it from her. If I was in danger, then so was she just by virtue of the fact she'd be close to me. The same went for Boyd, so I decided to tell him about it later.

'I don't know who it was,' I said, 'but I've got somebody workin' on findin' out.'

'Who?' Boyd asked.

'A friend of mine from Vegas,' I said. 'Danny Bardini.'

'I know Bardini's rep,' Boyd said. 'He's good.' He looked at Judy. 'He a PI.'

'And a friend of mine.'

'You must be starved,' Judy said to me. 'And in shock.'

'Starved for sure,' I said. 'I don't know about the shock.'

'Harrington,' Judy said. I turned and saw him standing in the doorway. It bothered me that I hadn't noticed him before that.

'Yes, Miss Garland?'

'Have Cook put out some food in the dining room for Eddie.'

'Yes, ma'am.'

'Come on, Eddie,' Judy said, standing. 'I'll sit with you while you eat. Kenny?'

'I better get back outside,' Kenny said to her. 'I think more than ever I should keep my eyes peeled out there.'

'All right,' she said, 'but come in if you need anything.'

'Yes, ma'am.' He looked at me. 'I'll see you on your way out.'

'Good idea,' I said. 'We'll talk.'

As Kenny grabbed his hat and jacket and headed for the door, Judy and I walked to the dining room. She was careful to walk at my pace.

Judy was right about one thing. My close call with death had somehow made me ravenous. While I consumed the feast her cook had laid out – one I wouldn't tell Jerry about, because he'd hate to hear what he missed – Judy and I talked about her problem, not mine.

'I spoke with Mark,' she said. 'He insists he told you all he could.'

'I don't know,' I said, 'I just had the feelin' he was holdin' somethin' back. Jerry felt the same way.'

'I don't know what that could be, Eddie,' she said. 'Mark loves me; he's willing to help all he can.'

'Is he willin' to talk to us again?'

'Absolutely.'

'All right,' I said. 'Tell me somethin' more about your managers.'

She bit her lip and stared across the table at me.

'What is it?' I asked.

'I – I don't quite trust them, Eddie.'

'Why not?'

'From the beginning, my ex-husband, Sid Luft, has had his doubts – about David specifically – so he had an independent audit done of David and Freddie and their handling of my business. Sid thinks David has been stealing, not passing on to me all the money I've been paid.'

'In the casino biz, we call that skimming.'

'Yes,' she said, pointing at me, 'that's the word Sid used. He said David was skimming.'

'Did you confront David?'

'I did.'

'And he's still representing you?'

'David and Freddie were very involved with the CBS deal,' she said. 'To split with them or sue them at that time would have been disastrous.'

I finished the chicken on my plate and cut into the steak. 'And?'

'And what?' Judy asked.

'I have the feeling there's somethin' else.'

I could see that there was, and it was something she didn't want to talk about.

'Judy,' I said, 'if I'm gonna help you, I need to know everything.'

She sat back in her chair, looked down at her hands, and then looked at me with an expression of abject misery. 'While we were negotiating with CBS, David came to me and said there was a photo of me . . .' She stopped.

'Judy? You can tell me anything.'

'There was a photo of me, partially nude, having my stomach pumped in a hospital.'

'A photo?' I said. 'Somebody was blackmailing you?'

'Yes,' she said. 'David said they wanted fifty thousand dollars.'

'And did you pay?'

'Yes.' she said. 'I could scarcely afford for a photo like that to come out.'

'Judy,' I asked, 'did you see the photo yourself?'

'No,' she said, 'David saw it.'

'He never showed it to you?'

She closed her eyes and held her hands out in front of her, as if warding something off.

'I didn't want to see it.'

'OK,' I said, 'but tell me somethin' else . . . did somethin' like that happen?'

She hesitated before answering, and I thought she was steeling herself to say 'yes', but instead she said, 'Eddie, I don't know.'

'You don't know?'

'I may have . . . blacked out,' she said. 'I may have been taken to a hospital and had my stomach pumped. I mean, it's happened before. Did it happen that time? Was my

107

stomach pumped and a photo taken? I don't remember.'

'But Begelman told you it did and there was a picture?'

'Yes.'

'Do you mind if I talk to him about this incident?'

'It's in the past,' she said. 'Why would you want to dredge it up?'

'Well, for one thing,' I said, 'I'd like to know if it actually happened. Wouldn't you?'

Thirty-One

As soon as I stepped out of Judy's house, Kenny Boyd appeared at my elbow.

'So, OK,' he said, 'what didn't you want to say in front of Judy?'

'Judy? You're on first-name terms?'

'She told me to call her that,' he said. 'She says I remind her of Mickey Rooney. I don't see it because, he's, ya know, short.'

'Yeah, he is,' I said. 'Look, a few days ago I found out there's an open contract out on me.'

'And you didn't think Nat Hiller should know that?'

'Actually, no, I didn't,' I said. 'I thought I was dealin' with two separate things. I thought the hitters would keep lookin' for me in Vegas.'

'It seems at least one found you here, huh?'

'Yeah,' I said, 'at least one, and he was an

amateur.' I told him about how sloppy the bomb was, going off too early and being placed too close to the gas tank.

'This ain't good news, you know?' he said.

'Believe me, I know.'

'No, I mean if amateurs are comin' out of the woodwork to cash in on this contract, it must be a lot of money.'

'It is.'

'I gotta tell Hiller about this, you know.'

'I do know,' I said. 'I hope he's not too mad.'

'Me, too,' he said. 'You wouldn't like him when he's mad.'

I limped through the hotel lobby, eager to get back to my bungalow and swallow a few aspirin.

'Mr Gianelli!'

I turned and looked at the front desk, where the young clerk was waving at me. With a sigh, I limped to the desk.

'Sir, are you all right?' he asked.

'I'll be fine,' I said. 'What have you got for me? Messages?'

'I have one, actually,' he said, handing me a message slip, 'and there's a gentleman waiting for you in the Polo Lounge.'

'A gentleman?' I asked. 'The same one as last time?'

'I believe so,' he said. 'He didn't give a name either time, but if it's him, then he's not wearing the same suit. I, uh, tend to remember how people dress.'

I assumed, in his job, he saw so many faces that he found it easier to remember clothes.

'Do you have any aspirin?' I asked.

'I don't,' he said, apologetically, 'but I'm sure the bartender will.'

When I entered the Polo Lounge it was almost midnight, but Hollywood – though not to the extent of Las Vegas – was an insomniac's heaven. There were still people in the room 'meeting' and 'concepting'.

I kept my eyes peeled for a familiar face, or anyone paying particular attention to me. A woman across the room waved and it took me a moment to realize it was Ruta Lee. Ruta was a beautiful blonde actress who was sort of an honorary member of the Rat Pack. I waved back. Luckily, she was seated with a man who was either her agent or a producer, so I didn't have to walk over.

A further study of the room revealed Henry Silva in another corner, sitting with two disreputable-looking men – probably producers. He gave me a nod, which for Henry was the equivalent of standing up and waving his arms.

When I turned my eyes to the bar, I saw Amico sitting there, this time in a more subtle, subdued-but-still-expensive suit. He waved at the bartender as I approached, and when I reached him there was a glass of bourbon on the bar.

'You got any aspirin?' I asked the bartender.

'Yessir, how many?'

'Three will do.'

'Yessir.'

I sat and took a sip of my drink while the bartender fetched my painkillers.

'I didn't expect you to be out of hospital so soon,' Amico said.

'Really?' I asked. 'Then why are you here?'

He laughed. 'You're right, of course,' he said. 'I figured you were not only tough but stubborn, too. But where's your big friend?'

'They're keepin' him overnight for observation.'

'Probably a good thing,' he commented. 'He took a nasty knock on the head.'

'You stood there and watched?' I asked.

'Well,' he said, 'I was watchin', and I did what I could do after the explosion. Speakin' of which, do you want the piece back?'

'Not here,' I said.

'No, of course not. Later.'

The bartender returned with the three aspirin and gave me a glass of water so I wouldn't have to take them with the alcohol.

'Thanks,' I said, and downed the little white pills. My leg was throbbing.

Amico was right about one thing: I had gotten out of that emergency room pretty quickly. I needed to be lying down somewhere as soon as possible.

'You got somethin' on your mind?' I asked, sipping the bourbon.

'I really just wanted to see if you were OK, and give you back the big guy's piece.' He moved his hand to his waist, as if he was going to produce it.

'Do you have it on you?'

'I do.'

'Then we better go outside so you can give it to me in private.'

111

'Why not in your cottage?'

'If you don't mind,' I said, 'I'm not in the mood for visitors, right now.'

'No, I don't suppose you are.' He tossed back the rest of his drink, stood up and buttoned his jacket. 'Shall we go?'

I took another sip, set my unfinished drink down on the bar and eased off my stool.

'By all means.'

Thirty-Two

I had decided that if Amico had intended to kill me, he could have done it already. So there was no danger going outside with him, alone.

We went out the exit that left us nearest to the path leading to the cottages. A match flared in the dark as Amico took the time to light a cigarette.

'The gun?' I said, hoping I was right about him.

'Of course.' He removed it from the back of his belt and handed it to me, butt first. I dropped it into my jacket pocket. A gun in my belt never felt comfortable to me.

'You got any more information for me?' I asked.

'Like what?'

'Like who sent you to be my guardian angel?'

'Sorry,' Amico said. 'Not at liberty to say, at the moment.'

'Well,' I said, 'you were at least helpful in

keepin' Jerry out of a prison hospital, which is probably where he'd be if the cops had found that gun on him. Thanks for that.'

'My pleasure.' He dropped the cigarette on to the path and ground it out with the toe of his shoe. 'I'll be seein' you around, Eddie.'

I watched him walk away, wondering if he'd been sent by Frank or Jack Entratter – or somebody else entirely – to help, or just watch. But then he was gone, and I had other problems, like not being able to stand for very much longer.

I went to the bungalow.

I woke up the next morning stiff and in pain. Sitting up and putting my feet on the floor was a chore. I probably should have stayed in the hospital myself over night, but Amico was right about one thing: I *was* stubborn.

I got up, tried stretching, walked into the kitchen. Moving around helped a bit, but I knew what would help more. I called room service.

'Coffee, toast and aspirin,' I told them. 'Lots of aspirin.'

'Yessir,' the room service voice said, 'right away.'

I could have made some coffee, since Jerry still had the makings in the kitchen, but I decided to spend my time showering and getting dressed. I tried my best not to get my bandage wet, but figured I could get it changed when I went to the hospital to pick up Jerry.

By the time I had struggled into a pair of trousers, there was a knock at the door. If it was a hitman, I knew I was dead. But it was room service.

'Here you go, sir,' he said, carrying a tray in.

'Just set it on the table.' I gave him a couple of bucks.

'Thanks,' he said. 'I'm Chris. Let me know if you need anything else.'

'Actually, I do need something,' I said. 'In half an hour. A cab, right out front.'

'Gotcha, boss.'

I gave him a five this time. Made him very happy.

After he left, I took four aspirin, then had my coffee and toast for breakfast. My first breakfast. I knew when I picked Jerry up he'd want food. He'd never be able to exist on hospital fare.

So I was only temporarily fortified when I left the bungalow, some of the stiffness gone, but not all. I got into the waiting cab and said, 'Cedars-Sinai.'

At the hospital I found Jerry's room and entered as he was getting dressed.

'It's about time,' he said. 'I'm starvin'. Do you know what they tried to feed me here?'

'I can imagine,' I said. 'How are you?'

'I jus' told ya.'

He was fine.

'Wait here, I'll find the doctor and get you signed out. Also, I need to get some bandages for my leg, so I can change them myself. And yours, for that matter.'

'OK, but hurry.'

Doctor Wyler wasn't on duty, but there was a young doctor named Owen who was able to sign Jerry out. He also arranged for a nurse to change my bandage, and then supply me with some extra. By the time I got back to Jerry he was almost manic, seated on the bed but ready to spring.

'Are we done?'

'*We're* done,' I said, 'but we need to check on Greg first.'

'I did that,' he said, standing.

'You did?'

He nodded. 'This mornin'. He's still unconscious. I left the phone number at the cottage so they can call us if he wakes up.'

'That was good thinkin', Jerry.'

'Well, I had to do somethin' to get my mind off my hunger,' he said. 'Mr G., they wanted me to eat lime jello. For breakfast!'

'Barbaric,' I said. 'Let's go.'

We grabbed a cab in front of the hospital and told him to take us to the nearest diner.

'There's one around the corner,' the driver said. 'You can walk.'

'We're a little beat up,' I said. 'I'll make it worth your while.'

'Suit yerself,' he said, with a shrug.

When we were seated in the diner and Jerry had a stack of pancakes in front of him, I said, 'Jerry, put your hand under the table.'

'Huh?'

'Under the table.'

'Sure, Mr G.'

He stuck his big hands under the table and I handed him his .45 cannon, which had been burning a huge hole in my jacket pocket.

'I wasn't sure, but I thought you'd want that.'

'You got that right, Mr G.' He tucked the gun into his belt.

'You sure you want to take the chance of carrying that around?' I asked. 'After all, the cops are gonna wanna talk to us again.'

'I'll take the chance,' he said. 'If somebody tries to blow us up again, they're gonna get a big hole blown in 'em.' He picked up his fork and asked, 'What are we gonna do for a car now?'

'We could call Frank,' I said, 'get another limo and driver, but we might just be puttin' him in a position to get blown up, too.'

'So we keep usin' cabs?'

'We keep usin' cabs. Did the police come by to talk to you again?'

He shook his head and swallowed.

'Not today.'

'No, me neither,' I said. 'They'll probably be lookin' for us today.'

Jerry seemed unconcerned about that. 'So, if they find us,' he said, 'we'll talk to 'em, right?'

'Yeah, right.'

He snagged a piece of bacon from my plate of bacon and eggs, moving faster than I'd ever seen him move before. I didn't complain.

I figured I had that one coming.

Thirty-Three

We decided to proceed as if somebody hadn't tried to kill us. It wasn't easy, but there was nothing we could do about that. The police were investigating on our end, and Danny was doing his best in Vegas. We had to go back to doing what we were supposed to be doing: trying to help Judy Garland.

We picked up another cab outside the diner. It was a conscious decision on our part to use a different one each time, and not keep the meter running on the same car all the way. It was safer for the driver and cheaper for us.

We went back to Mark Herron's apartment, this time without announcing ourselves ahead of time. When I knocked, the door was opened by a man who was not Mark Herron. He was handsome, in his early fifties. I was about to ask who he was when Jerry spoke first.

'Hey, Gator Joe!' he said.

'What?'

Jerry pointed and said, 'This guy played Gator Joe on an episode of *Bourbon Street Beat*.'

'You saw that, huh?' the man asked, with a smile.

'Sure did.'

'What can I do for you fellas?'

'Is Mark here?' I asked.

'Not right now,' he said. 'I'm Henry, Henry Brandon. Are you guys . . . producers?'

I had to admit, the guy did look familiar, like somebody I might have seen in a movie . . . maybe *Vera Cruz*?

'No,' I said.

'Well, he's working today.'

'Workin'?'

'On a commercial, actually. You know, making ends meet?'

He had a slight accent, maybe German.

'Can we come in?' I asked. 'Maybe you can help us.'

'What's it about?'

'Judy Garland.'

Suddenly, his face changed. 'Oh,' he said, 'her.'

'Yes, *her*.'

'You must be the fellas he talked to yesterday.'

'That's right,' I said. 'I'm Eddie Gianelli; this is Jerry Epstein.'

'All right,' he said, 'I suppose you should come in.'

He backed away, then turned and moved into the apartment. We followed and Jerry closed the door behind us.

'Do you live here?' I asked. 'With Mark?'

'We're roommates, yes,' he said. 'It's rather hard paying rent when you're not working steadily.'

'I'm sure it is.'

'I have some coffee on the stove,' Brandon said. 'Would either of you care for a cup?'

'No, thanks,' I said. Jerry just shook his head.

'What can I do for you, then?'

'To tell you the truth, I'm not sure,' I said. 'Did Mark talk to you about his recent trip with Judy?'

'Oh, yeah,' Brandon said, 'he talked about it a lot. "Judy this, and Judy that" . . . *ad nauseam*.'

He walked to the kitchen stove and poured himself a cup of coffee.

'Just what was the "this and that" he talked about, Mr Brandon?' I asked.

118

He looked as if he was about to answer, but then stopped himself.

'I don't think I should say,' he said, finally. 'I might paint an unkind picture of Mark's blushing bride.'

'Do you have a problem with Mark marrying Judy Garland?' Jerry asked.

Brandon looked at Jerry and said, 'You're quite something, aren't you?'

'Huh?'

'I'll bet you could have a career in Hollywood if you stuck around.'

'Me?' Jerry said. 'In the movies?'

'Or TV.'

'Like maybe *Sunset Strip*?'

'When it was on, yes,' Brandon said. 'It's too bad all those great Warner Brothers private eye shows have been canceled. You would have made a great hood.'

'Jerry – a hood?' I asked. 'Whatever makes you think that?'

'Well, look at him,' Brandon said. 'He's magnificent.'

'You better cut that out or you'll give him a swelled head,' I warned. 'And you haven't answered my question.'

'About Judy Garland?' Brandon said. 'I prefer not to say anything unkind.'

'So I'm assuming you won't be attending the wedding?' I asked.

'Hardly.'

'Well, then, just tell me if Mark mentioned anybody who may have been . . . stalking Judy on the trip.'

119

'That story?' Brandon asked. 'Is she still telling that one?'

'She is.'

'It's her imagination,' Brandon said. 'Even Mark thinks so.'

'Any idea when he'll be back?'

'Not till late this afternoon,' Brandon said. 'You can try again then.'

'Maybe we will,' I said. 'Thanks for your time.'

'Are you sure you wouldn't like to stay for a while?' Brandon asked. 'That leg looks painful. Some sort of . . . old wound?'

'Some sort of new one, I'm afraid,' I said. 'No, thanks. We have to be going.'

'How about you, Big Boy?' Brandon asked.

'Sorry,' Jerry said. 'I got to go with Mr G.'

'Pity.'

We headed for the door, and then I turned back.

'Did I see you in *Vera Cruz*?'

He brightened. 'Yes, I played a French Army Captain in that. I also did *The Searchers* with John Wayne. But of late I'm doing a lot of television. In addition to *Bourbon Street Beat*, I've done a couple of *Sunset Strips*, a couple of episodes of *Lawman*, one of *Maverick*—'

'Hey,' Jerry said, 'I saw you on *Wagon Train*.'

He didn't seem as happy about that. 'Yes, six times, all playing Indians.'

'Yeah, but usually a chief,' Jerry pointed out.

Brandon straightened his back and said, 'Well, yes, you have a point there.'

120

Thirty-Four

'Why didn't you ask for his autograph?' I asked Jerry when we got outside.

'Damn,' he said, 'I didn't think of it. He's a real star, you know.'

'Sounds more like a character actor,' I said. 'Maybe even a bit player.'

'Well, I've seen him on TV a lot. And he said he worked with John Wayne.'

'A lot of people worked with John Wayne.'

'So you weren't impressed?'

'Jerry,' I said, 'you and I have had dinner with Frank Sinatra, Dean Martin, Marilyn Monroe, Ava Gardner, and now Judy Garland. Why would I be impressed with Henry Brandon?'

He scowled. 'You got a point there.'

'He liked you, though.'

His scowl deepened. 'Whataya mean by that?'

'Just sayin' . . .'

'He asked you to stay a while, first.'

I looked up and down the street. 'Let's get a cab.'

In the cab Jerry fidgeted, trying to get comfortable.

'You OK?' I asked.

'This bandage itches,' he said, touching his shoulder.

'How's the head?'

'Throbbing.'

'I've got some aspirin.'

'I don't like pills.'

'You didn't need a bandage on your head?'

'It was mostly a bump,' he said, 'just a small cut that didn't even need stitches. What about your leg?'

'It itches,' I said, 'and throbs – and I do like aspirin.'

'That address you gave the driver,' Jerry said, 'it's that Bagel guy's office, ain't it?'

'Begelman,' I said, 'David Begelman.'

'That's what I said.'

'Yeah, well, I wanna talk to him about something Judy told me last night.'

'You saw her last night?'

'Yeah,' I said, 'I went to her house for . . . to tell her what happened. She was worried when she didn't hear from us.'

'What'd she tell you?'

I told him the story about the photo and the fifty thousand dollars.

'Fifty G's?' Jerry said. 'Did she see this picture herself?'

'Nope,' I said, 'she never did. That's what I want to talk to Begelman about. Also, I wanna know who he paid the money to.'

'Maybe that's the guy who's been followin' her,' Jerry said. 'And maybe he broke into her house lookin' for somethin' else he could sell back to her.'

'Yeah,' I said, 'if he even exists.'

'You think it was a scam?' Jerry asked. 'The Bagel guy kept the money?'

'That's what I'd like to find out, Jerry.'

We rode in silence again for a few minutes, and then he asked, 'You didn't eat nothin' with Miss Garland last night, didya?'

I was hoping he wouldn't go there. 'I just, uh, had a small snack, Jerry.'

He nodded, but after we drove in silence a few more miles he asked, 'What didya eat?'

Damn it, he went there.

Thirty-Five

When we arrived at Begelman's office, we were told he wasn't in. The pretty young woman at the reception desk wasn't forthcoming about where he was until we mentioned Judy Garland.

'Well,' she said, 'I guess if it's about Miss Garland, he'd want to talk to you.'

'You got that right, sister,' Jerry said. It also helped that she was obviously a little afraid of him.

'H–He's playing golf.' She leaned away from him and spoke to me.

'Where?' I asked.

'The Pine Ridge Country Club.'

'Thanks,' I said, feeling bad that she'd been frightened. 'You're a doll.'

She smiled at that and said, 'Why, thank you.' Then looked at Jerry and frowned.

'Come on, you big meanie,' I said to him.

On the way out he complained, 'Hey Mr G., I wasn't so mean . . .'

Another cab to Pine Ridge. Luckily, cabs were plentiful in Beverly Hills.

We had to invoke Begelman's name in order to be admitted to the club, claiming we were from his office and had some business to conduct that involved Judy Garland. Before long we were in a golf cart – Jerry behind the wheel – driving across the course looking for David Begelman, who was supposedly in a foursome playing somewhere on the back nine.

We found the front nine easily enough, but Jerry got turned around a couple of times before we finally found ourselves on the back.

'OK, so where is he?' Jerry asked, as we passed another foursome who hurled curses at us.

'Let's just keep goin' until we find him,' I said.

'Suits me,' he said. 'I like drivin' this thing. Hey, Mr G., you ever played golf?'

'A time or two,' I said. 'It's not my game.'

'I don't understand it,' Jerry said. 'Chasin' a little white ball around in the sun for hours. It ain't somethin' I'd do, and it sure as hell ain't somethin' I'd wanna watch. Gimme a good baseball game, any day.'

'OK, there's four guys,' I said. 'Let's check them.'

'Look at how silly they're dressed,' Jerry said. 'Get a load of those pants.'

I didn't know if he meant the stripes or the checks, but Begelman himself was wearing a pair of lime-green pants that should have been against the law. Made him easy to spot, though.

'There he is,' I said. 'Green pants.'

'Yikes,' Jerry said.

He drove the cart right up to the four men, who turned and stared in surprise, which turned to awe when they saw Jerry emerge from the cart. Begelman's shoulders slumped.

When I got out, Begelman turned to his friends – or clients, whatever – said something and then came walking over.

'Gents,' he said, 'this must be important for you to come out here and . . . interrupt me.'

'Nothin' important, I hope, Mr Begelman,' I said.

'Actually, I'm working on rather a big deal with these gentlemen—'

'Big?' I asked. 'You mean like fifty-thousand big?'

'Well,' he said, 'bigger than that . . . What made you come up with that figure?'

'That seems to be the amount you paid someone for a certain picture of Judy—'

'Shh, whoa,' he said, grabbing my elbow and pulling me further from the other three. 'Keep your voice down about that, will you?'

Jerry didn't move. He remained positioned between us and the other three men. He was staring at them, as if fascinated by their gaudy golf pants. For their part, the three men – of various sizes and ages – all seemed disconcerted by Jerry's attention.

'Why would you bring that up here?' Begelman asked me.

'I'm interested, Mr Begelman,' I said. 'That's the reason we drove out here.'

'To ask me about that picture?'

'That's right,' I said.

'I assume Judy told you about it?'

'Right again.'

'What do you want to know about it?'

'Why didn't you ever show the actual photo to Judy?'

'Why on earth would I want to do that?' he asked. 'It would have only upset her more.'

'It would have proved to her that the photo really existed,' I offered.

'As far as I know, she never doubted it,' Begelman said. 'Until now, that is, Mr Gianelli. You have to understand how delicate Judy is. She has to be . . . well, handled with care.'

'I don't understand,' I said. 'You manage her affairs – is that correct?'

'Freddie Fields and I, yes.'

'And that means her money, as well?'

'Yes, of course.'

'Then why wouldn't you have just paid the man and never let Judy know about the photo in the first place?' I asked. 'It seems to me *that* would have been handling her.'

'You expect me to just pay out fifty thousand dollars of Judy Garland's money without consulting her first? That's the kind of thing that can get a fella fired, you know. Or arrested, for that matter.'

'Then why not sugar-coat it – tell her the money was for something else?'

'By sugar-coat, you mean lie, of course. I don't

know what you think, Mr Gianelli, but I don't lie to my clients. Least of all to Judy.' He seemed genuinely insulted by the suggestion, but then again we were in a town where people lied for a living. Whether they were actors or not, they tended to become very good at it.

'OK,' I said, 'let me go at this a different way, then.'

'Is it going to take much longer?' he asked. 'I only have these gentlemen for a finite period of time.'

'It'll take as long as it takes, Begelman,' I said.

Dropping the 'Mister' from his name seemed to sober him some, as if he realized we were entering into deeper waters.

'Now look here—'

'Who was the man?' I asked.

'What?'

'I asked who the man was.'

'What man?'

'Don't be dense,' I said. 'The blackmailer you paid for the photo. What was his name?'

'I don't know!' he said, testily. 'Jesus Christ, how many blackmailers have you known who gave their names?'

'Then I assume you paid him in cash.'

'Of course I paid cash.'

'Who'd you give it to?'

He fell silent, shuffled his feet nervously.

'If the questions get harder, Begelman, I could have Jerry come over and ask them. He already doesn't like your green pants.'

Begelman took a quick, worried glance at Jerry, who at that moment happened to be looking at

127

us. He raised his eyebrows at the manager, which caused Begelman to look away.

'Now, look here, there's no need for threats. We're on the same side, aren't we?'

'I don't know – are we?'

Begelman seemed frustrated to me . . . or cornered.

'Are you gonna answer my question?' I asked. 'Who did you pay?'

'I don't know,' he said. 'I didn't make the payment—'

'What happened to the money, then?'

'No, you don't understand,' he said. 'The payment was made, but *I* didn't make it. I had someone else do it.'

'Who?' I asked. 'I need to speak to whoever handed the money over.'

'I really shouldn't say—'

He hadn't noticed Jerry moving closer, and now a big paw landed on his shoulder.

'Yeah,' Jerry said, 'I think you should.'

Thirty-Six

Jerry drove the cart back to the clubhouse.

'You buy it?' he asked. 'His story?'

'That he hired somebody to make the drop? It's possible, I guess.'

'We'll know when we find the guy.'

'If it's a phony story, he wouldn't give us the guy's name and address.'

'He would if he was gonna warn him.'

'Then I guess we better get there fast.'

We got back to the clubhouse, returned the cart and caught a cab out front. I gave the driver the address Begelman had given us.

'I think the address is legit,' Jerry said.

'Why?'

'He was too scared.'

'Of you?'

Jerry nodded. 'See, this time I was tryin' to be scary.'

'And a fine job you did of it, too.'

David Begelman told us he hired a PI to make the money drop, that his instructions came over the phone. The photo he received in the mail was supposedly a copy. When the PI made the payoff, he would get the other copies, the original and the negative . . .

'Did he?' I had asked.

'He gave me copies, what he said was an original, and some negatives.'

'And?'

'I burned them all.'

'So you have no way of knowing if there were any other copies? Or negatives?'

'No,' Begelman admitted, 'but I haven't heard from the blackmailer again.'

'How did you choose the PI who made the drop?'

'I didn't,' he admitted, 'the blackmailer did . . .'

'You know, Mr G. . . .' Jerry said.

'Yeah?'

'The PI who made the drop could also have been the blackmailer.'

I looked at him. 'Jerry, I was just having the same thought.'

The private dick's name was Jimmy Jacks, and he had an office in a seedy section of LA called the Nickel, on Fifth Street, right in the heart of Skid Row.

'Jeez, Mr G.,' Jerry said, as we drove down Fifth, 'you'd think somebody with the money that Bagel guy has would hire somebody better than this.'

'Remember,' I said, 'he said he didn't pick the guy.'

'Well, seein' where his office is – or maybe he even lives here – I don't guess he'd be the blackmailer himself.'

'Why's that?'

'If you had fifty grand, would you stay here?'

'If I didn't want people to know I was a blackmailer, I would – at least for a while.'

'I getcha, yeah. Maybe he's, whatayacallit, bidin' his time.'

The address we had was an office over a dive called Sammy's Bar.

'You guys sure this is where you wanna go?' the cab driver asked.

'We're sure,' I said, 'but maybe you could wait for us, with the meter runnin', of course.'

'No skin off my nose,' he said, with a shrug.

'Thanks.'

I had considered calling Nat Hiller to see if he knew anything about Jimmy Jacks, but his address seemed to say it all. Now that we saw his office, I knew I'd made the right decision. I may have been judging him too harshly, but that remained to be seen.

Jerry peered through the dirty front window at the interior of Sammy's Bar and said, 'Geez, even I wouldn't drink here, and I been in some pretty good Brooklyn dives.' Pretty good actually meaning pretty *bad*.

There was a door to the right of Sammy's which we found unlocked. There was a mailbox, but no indication if it was for a business or a residence. I figured it was for both. Who'd want to wake up in the morning at home and have to come here to work? Unless home was even worse.

We looked up at the long stairwell that barely had room for Jerry's shoulders. He almost had to turn sideways to go up. We came to a worn wooden door with worn gold lettering that stuttered: J–Ja–ks, In–est–ga–tio–s.

I knocked and there was no answer. A look at Jerry, who shrugged, told me we both had the same feeling. I tried the knob and it turned.

Inside, we found a cramped office with a scarred desk, chair and dented file cabinets. It looked as if Jacks had repatriated his furniture from a garbage dump. There were papers scattered on the desk and floor, and I would have thought the place had been tossed but for the fact that all the desk and cabinet drawers were still closed. Usually when rifling somebody's office, closing the drawers after you're done is not a priority.

'What a mess,' Jerry said.

'Yeah, but I get the feelin' it always looks this way.'

It was early, but as I peered out the dirty front window I could see that, after dark, Sammy's neon sign would be filling the room with a bright, perhaps even blinking light.

'Mr G.'

I looked over at Jerry, who was standing in an open doorway.

'In here.'

I walked over and followed him into an equally cramped room that became more so with both of us in it. There was a sagging bed with a poor excuse for a mattress, and a chest of drawers that looked as if it had come from the same dump as the office desk.

I walked over to the chest and checked the three drawers. The top two had clothing; the third was empty.

Jerry came and looked over my shoulder. 'No tellin' if there was anythin' in that bottom drawer,' he said.

'No.'

Jerry walked to another door, opened it to reveal a closet with one shirt and one pair of trousers hanging. On the floor was a worn pair of brown shoes. On the shelf was an old suitcase.

'Well,' I said, 'unless he had a set of suitcases, he didn't pack and leave.'

'With fifty grand, he could buy new clothes, a new suitcase, and move to a new neighborhood,' Jerry observed.

'You're right about that.'

132

'So if he is the blackmailer, he blew town with the money.'

'The blackmail took place months ago, before Judy's tour,' I said. 'Let's ask around, see if anyone has seen him recently.'

'Downstairs would be a good place to start,' Jerry said.

'Let's go.'

In the office I took the time to go through the desk drawers first, while Jerry checked the file cabinets.

'I got some pretty sloppy files,' Jerry said. 'Whatayou got?'

'Paper clips,' I said.

We both slammed our drawers and went downstairs.

Thirty-Seven

Sammy's clientele turned to look at us as we entered. All three were seated at the bar with drinks in front of them. From where I stood, I could see the dirt on the glasses.

Something crunched beneath our feet as we approached the bar. It wasn't peanut shells, so I decided not to look down to investigate.

As we got to the end, the bored barman came over and stared at us through bloodshot eyes. Surprisingly, he was about as tall as Jerry, but weighed about half as much. He looked as if a good breeze would knock him over. His grey pallor went with his bloodshot eyes. Add to that the broken blood vessels across his nose and cheeks, and it was obvious he sampled his own wares a little too much.

'What can I get ya?' he asked.

'Information.'

'Cops?' he asked. Then he looked at Jerry. 'You ain't no cop.'

'Neither is he,' Jerry said.

'So why should I talk to either of you?'

'Why not?' I asked.

'Well,' the bartender said, 'I guess it depends on what ya want.'

'Start with your name?'

'Leo.'

'Have you seen Jimmy Jacks lately?' I asked.

'Jacks?' he said. 'That's what you want? Why? He's a loser.'

'We know that,' I said. 'Have you seen him?'

'Well, not for . . . what? Coupla weeks?'

'A couple of weeks,' I said. 'Is that it? Or could it be a couple of months?'

'Months?' He scratched his head. The movement released a tuft of black hair and a foul odor from his armpit. It was stifling in the place, and that didn't help. I took a step back. 'I dunno.'

'What about these jokers?' I said, 'Are they regulars?'

'Them?' He looked over his shoulder. 'Oh, yeah. Their asses are bolted to them stools.'

'They have to go home some time,' Jerry said. 'Have any of them seen Jacks?'

'Ask 'em,' the bartender said, with a shrug. 'But you better buy 'em a round of drinks first.'

We looked over and realized they'd heard every word we'd said.

'Do it,' I said. 'A round of drinks for everybody!'

The jokers all grinned.

Once Leo the bartender had the three regulars set up with drinks, he allowed me to move in behind the bar.

'All right, guys,' I said, 'who wants to talk first?'

'What was the question again?' the first man asked.

'Have any of you seen Jimmy Jacks recently?'

'Ain't seen 'im,' the first man said.

'Not me,' the second man said.

The third man simply shrugged, shook his head and picked up his drink.

Jokers.

'Now, boys,' Jerry said. He had remained on the other side of the bar, and now he moved in behind the three men, who were sitting clustered on three consecutive stools in the center of the bar. They were dressed similarly, which is to say in clothes that had not been washed in – well, they never had been washed. They stank of dirt, sweat, whiskey, beer and urine, and in the cloying confines of that bar it was becoming unbearable. I decided just to let Jerry do what he did best.

He put a big hand on the shoulders of the men on the two outer stools and pushed them together so that the middle man was squashed between.

'The man was nice enough to buy you fellas a

135

drink,' he said, 'and all he wants is the answer to one question. And not just any answer, but the right answer.' He pressed them together so that they could hardly breathe. 'So don't make me have to pull your asses off these stools and pound 'em into the ground, huh?'

'OK, Jerry,' I said, 'they get the point.' I addressed the men again. 'Here's the deal. You each got a drink. I'll ask one more time. For the right answer you get a sawbuck, and Jerry doesn't kick your ass. Got it?'

They nodded. Jerry released them and stepped away, wrinkling his nose and wiping his palms on his thighs.

'OK,' I asked, 'who has seen Jimmy Jacks recently?'

Nobody moved or spoke, and then the man in the middle raised his hand tremulously.

'Yeah?' I said.

'Uh, whataya mean, exactly, um, by recently?'

'Let's say within the past month.'

The first man said, 'I seen him down the street last month. At least, I think it was last month.'

'Could it have been longer ago than that?' I asked.

'Nah,' he said, 'not longer. Maybe . . . sooner?'

'Now you,' I said, pointing to the second joker.

'I swear,' he said, 'I ain't seen him in . . . months, I think. Yeah, I, uh, I ain't.' He flinched, as if he thought Jerry was still behind him.

'And you?'

'I seen him,' joker number three said.

136

'When?'

'Coupla weeks ago?'

'Where?'

'Right out front, here.' He pointed over his shoulder.

'What was he doing?'

'He was in a hurry,' the man said. 'That's why I remember. I said, "Hey, Jimmy," and he just rushed past me and ran up the stairs to his place.'

'And then what?'

'And then . . . nothin'. I came in here and got a drink.'

'You didn't see him leave?'

'I didn't see him again,' he said, 'I swear.'

I stared at the three of them, then took out my wallet and put a sawbuck in front of each of them. 'Thanks,' I said, moving out from behind that bar. I wanted to get away from the stink.

When Jerry and I got to the front door and opened it, the fresh air must have jogged my brain. I thought of another question.

'Hey!' I said.

They jumped, startled, as if they thought we had already left.

'Yeah?' Leo asked.

'Would any of you put it past Jacks to blackmail somebody?' I asked.

They all kind of laughed, and then Leo said, 'Mister, I wouldn't put anything past Jimmy Jacks, if it meant money.'

'Yeah,' I said, 'right.'

Jerry and I stepped outside.

Thirty-Eight

The cab driver was still there, dozing behind the wheel. I didn't step immediately to the car.

'What's up, Mister G.?' Jerry asked, after taking several deep breaths.

'I wanted to find out more.'

'Well, one guy saw that Jacks guy when he was in a big hurry,' Jerry said. 'Maybe he packed another suitcase, took some of his clothes and blew town.'

'Yeah, maybe.'

'Or maybe somebody was up there waitin' for him.'

I thought a moment, then nodded.

'The place *is* a mess,' I observed, 'although it might just always look that way.'

'This guy still don't strike me as a blackmailer,' Jerry said. 'Just maybe a go-between.'

'So he did a job, got paid and then either left town . . .'

'Or *got* left someplace else.'

I took a deep breath and blew it out in frustration. 'Where to next?' I said out loud.

At that point the door opened and joker number three stuck his head out.

'Oh, hey, we wuz wonderin' if you wuz still here.'

'We are,' I said. 'So?'

'We wuz talkin', and we thought you might wanna know that Jimmy has a girlfriend.'

138

'He does?' This sounded promising. 'And would any of you happen to know who she is, and where we can find her?'

'Yeah,' he said, 'dat's why I'm out here. I know 'er.'

'That's great,' I said. 'So who is she?'

'Her name's Peggy,' he said, 'and she works at a club about two blocks down.'

'Stripper?' Jerry asked.

'Nope,' the guy said, 'she's a singer.'

'What's the name of the club?'

'The Starlight.'

'OK,' I said, 'thanks for the information. I guess it's a little early to find her there.'

The guy actually said something smart. 'Ya never know, she sometimes goes in early to rehearse.'

I passed him another sawbuck. 'Thanks.'

'Thank *you*,' he said, and slipped back inside with the money.

We got into the cab and I tapped the cabbie on the shoulder, rousing him.

'Hey, wha—'

'The Starlight club,' I said.

'Really? That's two blocks away.'

'I'll make it worth your while.'

'Hey,' he said, starting the engine, 'no skin off my nose.'

Once again we told the cabbie to wait. He was asleep behind the wheel before we hit the front door of the Starlight club. The door was unlocked, but as we entered it was clear the place was not yet open.

For a club on the Nickel it wasn't bad. At least the front windows were clean, even if they did have dingy curtains in front of them.

'We're closed!' a man yelled from behind the bar.

Some of the tables still had chairs piled on them, but up on stage a piano player was fiddling with the keys. A woman was leaning on the piano, a cigarette in one hand, reading some sheet music.

We walked over to the bar. The man who had shouted at us was in his mid-fifties, with steel-grey hair and a granite chin. He turned to face us with a bottle in each hand.

'Goddamn liquor prices keep goin' up,' he complained. 'Don't they know I own a fuckin' five on the Nickel, not an uptown club? I thought I told you we're closed.'

'We're lookin' for a girl named Peggy, supposed to sing here.'

'You ain't gonna take her away to the movies, are you?' the guy asked with heavy sarcasm.

'No.'

'Not cops?'

'Jesus, no,' Jerry said.

'Well, that's Peggy,' he said, gesturing to the stage with one bottle, 'and she sings, but she ain't no girl.'

'What's her last name?'

'Kendall.'

'Mind if we talk to her?'

'Why not? She's only rehearsing. Not that it'll help.' He turned back around, put the bottles on a shelf.

140

Jerry and I walked up to the stage, where the woman and the piano player were now conferring over the music.

'Peggy Kendall?' I said.

She turned, and I saw what the bartender meant. She was hardly a girl, probably on the wrong side of forty, and she'd had a hard life. Maybe at night, when she sang, make-up covered the bags beneath her eyes and lines at the corners of her mouth.

'I'm Peggy,' she said. 'Who are you?'

'My name's Eddie Gianelli,' I said. 'This is Jerry Epstein. We're from the Sands in Vegas.'

'The Sands?' Her eyes lit up. 'What are you doin' here?'

'Lookin' for talent,' I said. 'Can we talk somewhere?'

'My dressing room,' she said. She looked at the piano player. 'Be back in a jiff, Benny.'

Benny looked at me. 'Lemme know if you need somebody to tickle the ol' ivories, man.'

He was in his fifties, and this was probably his last stop.

'I'll keep you in mind,' I promised.

'Crazy,' the piano man said.

We followed Peggy to the back of the house, down a hall to a small dressing room.

'I know,' she said, 'it's barely the size of a closet. Your friend will have to stand in the hall.'

'No problem,' Jerry said.

She sat down on a rickety wooden chair in front of a scarred mirror. 'Where did you hear about me?' she asked.

'From Jimmy Jacks.'

'Jimmy!' Her eyes lit up. 'Where is he? Have you seen him?'

'Well,' I said, going with it, 'in Vegas, but we're supposed to see him here. He was going to introduce us to you.'

'That sweet man,' she said. 'B–but I haven't seen him in two weeks.'

'Two weeks?'

'That's right,' she said. 'When did you see him?'

'Well,' I said, 'actually, we haven't seen Jimmy at all, Miss Kendall.'

'What?' She looked confused.

'We're lookin' for Jimmy because he did a job for somebody,' I said.

'I don't understand,' she said. 'You're not from the Sands in Vegas?'

'Oh, I am. I just don't have anything to do with finding talent. But I do have something to do with finding Jimmy Jacks.'

'B–But . . . why? What job are you saying he did?'

'He made a drop,' I said, 'a blackmail drop.'

Her eyes got shifty as she said, 'W–what? I don't understand. Blackmail?'

'That's right,' I said. 'He was hired to make a payoff, and we want to know who hired him.'

'Or maybe,' Jerry said, 'he's the blackmailer himself.'

'A blackmailer? Not Jimmy!'

'No, not Jimmy,' I said, 'because he's a sweet man, right?'

'He'd never – he'd never blackmail anybody.'

'If you know where he is, Peggy,' I said, 'tell

142

him to contact Eddie G. at the Beverly Hills Hotel. It's the only way to prove he's innocent.'

'But – but—'

'If we don't hear from him,' I went on, 'we'll call the cops and tell them what we think. Then they'll be lookin' for him for blackmail.'

'B–But I told you, I haven't seen Jimmy—'

'I know,' I said, 'in a couple of weeks. Well, maybe he'll turn up. You never know.'

I looked at Jerry, who nodded and started down the hall. I left Peggy's dressing room and followed him.

Thirty-Nine

Outside the club, we didn't wake the cab driver until we actually decided where we wanted to go.

'Back to the hotel?' Jerry asked.

'No,' I said, 'I think the cops will be there. They're still wantin' to talk to us about the explosion.'

'Well, I need somethin' to eat,' Jerry said.

'We're not gonna eat anywhere down here,' I said. 'But I think we should wait a few minutes.'

'For what?'

'To see if she comes out.'

'You think she'll go straight to Jacks?'

'Maybe,' I said. 'I hope so.'

'What if she's tellin' the truth and she ain't seen him in two weeks?'

'Then we'll have to try somethin' else.'

We went to the cab and roused the driver.

'Now what?' he asked. 'Ya wanna go across the street?'

'Actually, we do,' I said, 'right in that alley.'

'What for?'

'You'll see.'

'What I ain't seen yet is any scratch, bub.'

I took some money out and shoved it into his hand. 'Now let's get into that alley.'

He tucked the money into his shirt pocket and said, 'Yer still the boss.'

It took ten minutes for her to come out.

'There she is,' Jerry said.

'We followin' her?' the cabbie asked.

'We're gonna try,' I said, 'if you're good enough.'

'Hah,' the driver said, 'you just happened to get the best driver in the city.'

'That a fact?' Jerry asked. 'What's your name?'

'Zack.'

'Well, Zack,' I said, 'if she has her own car—'

'She won't,' he said. 'Nobody brings their own cars down here. She'll look for a cab.'

The idea hit me like a bolt of lightning. 'Jerry, get out!'

He didn't hesitate. As he was climbing out, I said, 'Zack, go pick her up, then come back here and get us and take us to where you drop her. Got it?'

'I got it, boss.'

I hurried out and said, 'Go!'

144

As Zack pulled out into the street Jerry said, 'That was good thinkin', Mr G.'

'Let's hope so.'

A half-hour later we were still waiting in the alley.

'Either they went a long way,' Jerry said, 'or Zack forgot to come back.'

'The best driver in the city? I don't think so.' At least, I hoped not.

It was another half-hour before Zack pulled up in front of the alley.

'Bet ya thought I wasn't comin' back,' he said.

'Not me,' I said, as we piled into the back. 'Where'd she go?'

'To a house in the canyon.'

'She suspect anythin'?' Jerry asked.

'No,' Zack said, proudly.

'OK, then,' I said, 'let's go. Get us there as fast as you can, Zack.'

'You got it, boss.'

It wasn't fast enough.

Forty

The house he took Peggy Kendall to was in Laurel Canyon.

'Here?' I asked, when he pulled up in front.

'I swear.'

'Geez,' Jerry said, 'this is the opposite of the Nickel.'

'It sure is,' Zack said. 'The fella who owns this place has millions.'

'So why would Peggy Kendall come here?' I asked.

'Maybe he's her sugar daddy,' Zack said.

'Believe me,' I said, 'this dame doesn't have a sugar daddy. Those days are over for her.'

Zack shrugged. 'She looked pretty good to me.'

Jerry and I got out of the car.

'Am I waitin'?' Zack asked. 'Meter runnin'?'

'Meter runnin',' I said. 'Thanks, Zack.'

He nodded and closed his eyes.

Jerry and I walked up the path to the front door. It was the kind of house a rich-but-not-paranoid man would have, without iron gates and alarms.

'Pretty nice,' Jerry said. 'You think the Kendall babe owns it?'

'That'd be somethin', wouldn't it?' I asked. 'Why would she be singin' in a dive on the Nickel?'

'Maybe nobody else will hire her,' Jerry said. 'We ain't heard her sing. We don't know how good she is.'

'Well,' I said, 'that's not what we're here to find out.'

I rang the doorbell, then knocked. We went back to the cab.

'Zack?'

His eyes popped open. 'Done already?'

'No. Did you see the woman go in after you dropped her off?'

'I sure did,' he said. 'She rang the bell, and somebody opened the door.'

'OK,' I said, 'go back to sleep.'

Jerry and I returned to the front door. We tried the bell again, then knocked.

'Let's go around the back.' We started, and then I stopped. 'Maybe we should move Zack. Somebody might call the cops.'

'I don't think so, Mr G.,' he said. 'How many burglars do you know who take a cab to their job and have the driver wait out front?'

He was right. We were safer with Zack right where he was.

Around back we found a deck that overlooked a beautiful view of the canyons. At night you'd be able to make out city lights.

There were sliding glass doors on the deck that Jerry said he could open. It took him about twenty seconds to prove it.

'There ya go, Mr G., but lemme go in first, OK?'

'Be my guest.'

Jerry took the .45 from his belt and stepped inside. I went in behind him and was immediately hit by the air-conditioning. It was freezing inside.

Jerry held his arm out to keep me from moving past him until he was sure.

'I think it's clear, Mr G.'

'OK, let's have a look around.'

'But let's stay together.'

'OK, Mother.'

Actually, I was very happy to stay with Jerry. His presence and the gun in his fist were very comforting.

The house was quiet – too damn quiet. There was no movement and no voices.

'I don't like this,' I said.

'There ain't no cars outside,' Jerry said. 'Maybe the girl came and left.'

'Yeah, maybe.'

We moved around the first floor of the house and found it to be spotless.

'You know what this makes me think of, Mr G.?' Jerry asked.

'What?'

'One of them model houses,' he said. 'Like nobody lives here.'

'I agree,' I said. 'And I hope that's the case.'

We moved up to the second floor. All the bedroom doors were closed.

'I don't like this,' I said again.

'Me, neither.'

'OK,' I said, 'we'll open them together, one at a time.'

We moved down the hall. The first door opened on to a bedroom where the bed was made and the closet was empty. Jerry checked the dresser drawers, which were also empty.

'I don't get it,' I said, looking around.

'This could be a drop house,' Jerry said.

'Does that mean what it sounds like?'

'Yeah,' he said, 'just a place that's used for a ransom drop. Nobody lives here.'

'So why'd the woman come here?'

He shrugged. 'To meet somebody. And then they left.'

'I hope you're right.'

He wasn't.

Forty-One

We found Peggy Kendall in the third bedroom.

The second was the same as the first – pristine.

The third bedroom was as neat and tidy as the rest, except for the fact that Peggy Kendall was lying on her back on the bed.

'Crap,' I said.

Jerry moved to her. She'd been laid out right on top of the bedspread.

'She's dead, Mr G.,' he said. 'Strangled.'

'Shit,' I said, 'we should've stayed with her.'

'Not our fault, Mr G.,' Jerry said. 'Now we know why the air-conditioning is turned so high.'

'They were expectin' her to be here so long she might start to stink?' I asked.

'Or . . .' he said.

I knew what he meant.

We left the room to check the other bedrooms. In the last one we found a man, also lying on his back across a bed.

'Also strangled,' Jerry said, 'but I bet he's been dead for days, maybe longer.'

The air-conditioning again.

'Whataya wanna bet?' Jerry asked.

'Jimmy Jacks?'

'Who else?'

Jerry patted the corpse down, came up with a wallet. He opened it and pulled out a driver's license.

'James Jacks,' he read. 'Born 1918.'

That made Jacks forty-four years old, which matched what we were looking at. In fact, in death he looked even older.

'Brown hair, brown eyes,' Jerry said.

'Well, except for some of the grey in his hair, it matches,' I said.

'You want me to open his eyes?'

'No,' I said, 'just keep lookin' in his wallet until you come up with a PI license.'

'Right. Got it!' He held the ID up to show me.

'So it's him,' I said. 'Put it all back, Jerry, just in case we don't call the cops. We want everything to look untouched.'

He replaced the wallet inside the jacket of Jacks' cheap suit and smoothed down the lapels.

'Why would we call the cops, Mr G.?' he asked.

'Why, indeed?' I said.

'They'd have us stuck in interrogation for days,' Jerry said.

'It's the right thing for us to do, but . . .'

'It ain't the smart play,' Jerry finished.

'No, it's not,' I said. 'The smart play is for us to get out of here right now.'

We made sure the room was the way we found it, then wiped down all the doorknobs on our way back down the hall to the stairs.

On the first floor we did the same, using our handkerchiefs to wipe prints away, finally working our way back to the doors we used to get in.

'Better clean the glass,' I said. 'I don't remember if we touched it.'

We each worked on one of the doors, and then headed back to the cab.

'So,' Jerry said, 'what are these murders about – you or Miss Garland?'

'I don't see how this can be connected to the hit on me,' I said. 'It's got to be Judy.'

'I agree.'

'So what we have to figure out now is whether she's in any immediate danger?'

'What if somebody's tryin' to cover their tracks so they can make some more money off of her?'

'You might be right, but we can't take the chance.'

'So do we tell her managers so they can do somethin'?'

'You want to trust them with her safety?'

'Not a chance,' he said, 'and not that boyfriend of hers, neither.'

'It's up to us,' I said, 'or maybe I should say, Frank, to convince her.'

'Convince her of what?'

'To move.'

'Where do you wanna put 'er?'

'I don't know,' I said, as we got to the front of the house. 'We'll have to figure that out. For now, maybe we should just take her to the bungalow.'

'The cops'll be lookin' for us there.'

'We can talk to them about the car bomb,' I said. 'We've got nothin' to hide, there.'

'Except for the fact that there's a contract out on you.'

'Once they check me out and see who I work for and where, that won't surprise them. And if they talk to Hargrove in Vegas, they'll know all they need to know. He'll make sure of that.'

151

We got into the back seat of the cab, jarring Zack from his latest nap.

'Done already?' he asked. 'Where to?'

I gave him Judy Garland's address.

Forty-Two

When we reached her house, we immediately looked for Kenny Boyd.

'What's up?' he asked.

'You got a car?'

He nodded. 'Parked around the corner.'

I looked at Jerry. 'Pay Zack off and let him go. We'll use Kenny's car.'

'Right.'

'Use my car for what?' Boyd asked.

'Come inside,' I said. 'We'll tell you at the same time we tell Judy.'

He shrugged and followed. Harrington let us in, and I left the door ajar for Jerry, who joined us in the living room.

'Now what's this all about?' Judy asked.

'You have to pack,' I said.

'Why? Where am I going?'

I started to answer, then stopped and looked at Harrington.

'You can speak in front of him,' Judy said. 'He's been with me for years.'

I looked at Harrington, who sent an expressionless stare back at me.

'Judy, we found two dead bodies today.'

152

'That's awful!' She put her hands over her mouth. 'Who were they?'

'Well, one of them was a private detective who was involved in the blackmail payout earlier this year.'

'He made the drop?' Kenny Boyd asked.

'Right.'

'Who was he?'

'A guy named Jimmy Jacks.'

Boyd made a face. 'A bottom feeder. I wouldn't be surprised if he wasn't the blackmailer himself.'

'Maybe,' I said. 'We're talking about fifty grand. I think he would've blown town with that kind of money.'

'He might not have had time,' Jerry said.

'I can look into him, if you want.'

'I told Hiller I'd only be using you for surveillance.'

Boyd shrugged. 'I'd do it on my own time, off the clock.'

'That's so sweet of you, Kenny,' Judy said.

The tough little guy blushed.

'Kenny, for now I'd like you to stay with Judy.'

'Where?' he asked.

'At my hotel,' I said. 'We have a bungalow at the Beverly Hills.'

'I've never been there,' Kenny said.

'Oh, you'll love it, Kenny,' Judy said.

'We can take her in without going through the lobby,' I said.

'OK,' Boyd said, 'but I can do a lot just on the phone.'

'That's OK.' I looked at Judy. 'Can you travel light?'

153

'If I have to,' she said.

'Good,' I said. 'Pack a suitcase.'

'One?' she asked, shocked.

Apparently, Judy Garland's idea of travelling light was different from mine.

'OK,' I said, 'two.'

'I'll try. Harrington?'

'Yes, ma'am.'

She and her house man left the room, leaving Boyd, Jerry and me.

'Boyd, you carryin'?' Jerry asked.

'Always.'

'We may be running into cops when we get back to the hotel,' I warned.

'I got a carry permit.'

'OK, good, but Jerry doesn't. When we get there, can he leave his piece in your car until we determine whether or not the cops are there?'

'Sure, I got a panel in the trunk.'

'This is your own car?' I asked. 'Not a rental?'

'My own.'

'You drove from Vegas?' Jerry asked.

Boyd nodded. 'Fifty-six Chevy Corvette.'

Jerry's eyes lit up. 'With the second carburetor?'

Boyd nodded.

'Two hundred and twenty-five horses!' he told me, enthusiastically.

'Great.'

'Mr G.'s got a Caddy, but he really don't care much about cars.'

'Why would he have to,' Boyd asked, grinning, 'with a Caddy?'

Jerry's grin broadened.

154

'I'll bring my car around and keep an eye out up front,' Boyd said.

'Good.'

Boyd looked at Jerry.

'You wanna drive?'

'Hell, yes.'

'Well, come on.'

Jerry looked at me and I nodded.

Harrington came in first, carrying two suitcases, followed by Judy.

'Where are Jerry and Kenny?' she asked.

'Waiting outside,' I said. 'We don't want any surprises.'

'Like photographers?'

Like killers, I thought, but said, 'Sure.'

Forty-Three

When we got to the Beverly Hills, Jerry and I took Judy to the bungalow. Since Jerry wasn't armed, we figured it wouldn't hurt if we ran into the detectives. They'd probably be looking for us in the lobby, but might have a man watching the bungalow.

'Charming,' Judy said, as we entered.

'I'll get my stuff out of my room,' Jerry said. 'You can have that one.'

'Thank you, Jerry,' she said. 'You're very sweet.'

'Make the bed,' I suggested. We had told the

155

desk clerk we wouldn't need maid service, except for towels.

He gave me a reproachful look and said, 'I did that this morning, Mr G.'

'Of course,' I said. 'What was I thinking?'

There was a knock on the door and I let Kenny Boyd in.

'I parked in a lot down the street, came through the lobby,' he said. 'I think I spotted a cop there.'

'We figured that much,' I said. 'The detectives will probably be here soon.'

Boyd took out Jerry's .45. 'I figured the big guy would feel better with this inside.'

'Sure,' I said. 'Give it to him – let him hide it somewhere he can get to it quick.'

Boyd nodded.

'OK,' Jerry said, coming out of his room with his belongings, 'the room's ready for you, Miss Garland.'

'Thanks, Jerry.'

Judy went in and Boyd handed Jerry his .45, which he had retrieved from the car.

'Thanks.' Jerry looked at me. 'I'll find a safe place for it.'

'Good. Boyd spotted a cop in the lobby, so we probably don't have much time.'

At that moment there was a knock on the door.

'How do you want to play me?' Boyd asked.

'I don't,' I said. 'I wanna keep you a secret.'

'Closet, then?'

I had the feeling he was used to hiding in closets.

'You better go out the back,' I said.

'They might have a man out there.'

'They're only here to question us about the explosion.'

'Just in case, I'll go out a side window. Go ahead and get the door.'

'I'll get it,' Jerry said.

He walked to the door, waited until Boyd was out of the room, then opened it.

'Well,' Detective Franklin said, 'where have you two been?'

'Detective Franklin,' I called out. 'Come on in.'

Franklin entered with an older man after him. 'This is my partner, Detective Wilcox.'

'How are ya,' I said. 'That's Jerry.'

Jerry nodded and closed the door.

'We've been tryin' to find you two,' Franklin said. 'We need to talk about the car bomb.'

'Is this about Greg?' I asked. 'How is he?'

'Still alive,' Franklin said, 'still unconscious.'

Wilcox was looking around. I noticed he gave the air a sniff. Probably Judy's perfume.

'Anybody else here?' he asked.

'As a matter of fact, there is,' I said. 'Judy Garland.'

Wilcox gave me a hard look. 'Come on,' he said.

'She's in one of the bedrooms,' Jerry said.

Franklin and Wilcox exchanged a look.

'This could get interesting,' Wilcox said.

'You want some coffee?' Jerry asked. 'I can call room service; they're pretty quick.'

'Sure,' Franklin said, 'coffee's good.'

'And donuts,' Jerry said, heading for the phone. 'We need donuts.'

As he made the call, Franklin looked at me and asked, 'Is he joking?'

'He never jokes about donuts.'

Forty-Four

They still didn't believe us about Judy.

With a coffee pot in the center of the table, the four of us sat in the kitchen and talked. Franklin's partner, Wilcox, took notes.

First, they had me tell them why we were in Beverly Hills. I stayed as close to the truth as I could without mentioning Frank.

Wilcox shook his head as he wrote down the name 'Judy Garland'.

'Why would Judy Garland call you for help?' Wilcox asked.

'Maybe,' Franklin said, 'it's because Eddie, here, was also friends with Marilyn Monroe.'

'Get out!' Wilcox looked at his partner. 'Is he yankin' our dicks?'

'No, gentlemen,' Judy said, from the doorway, 'he's not yankin' your dicks.'

Both detectives looked at Judy, and Wilcox jumped to his feet.

'Holy crap!' he exclaimed. 'Judy Garland.'

'Eddie,' she said, 'why don't you introduce me to your friends?'

She was wearing cuffed jeans, a long-sleeved plaid shirt, and was barefoot. With carefully applied eye make-up and red lipstick, she looked

158

like she was due on set in twenty. She must have heard us talking and decided to put on a show.

'Judy,' I said, standing, 'this is Detective Franklin and Detective Wilcox. They're here about the car bomb yesterday.' Franklin got to his feet.

'Please,' she said, 'sit down and drink your coffee, gentlemen. That was a horrible thing with the car, horrible. Have you found out who tried to blow up Eddie and Jerry yet?'

'No, ma'am,' Wilcox said, 'not yet.'

'Well, get to it, will you?' she said. 'I don't want to lose these two. They're doing important work for me. Jerry, pour me a cup, will you?'

'You got it, Miss Garland.' Jerry poured and fixed it the way she liked it. I didn't know how he knew. 'I'll drink it in the bedroom and let you all finish talking.'

She turned and left the kitchen. The two detectives finally sat back down.

'Holy crap!' Wilcox said, looking at me. 'Did you really know Marilyn?'

'I really did.'

Forty-Five

'What are you doin' for Miss Garland?' Franklin asked.

'That's got nothin' to do with the car bomb,' I said.

'Are you sure?'

159

There was only one way to keep Judy's name out of their report and out of the press.

'Yeah.'

Franklin looked at his partner, who raised his eyebrows. Then he looked at me again.

'You mind tellin' us how you know that?'

'There's a contract out on me.'

'A what?'

'A hit,' Jerry said.

'Yes, we know what a contract is,' Wilcox said. 'Why didn't you tell me this before?'

'Do I have to answer that?'

Franklin looked at his partner and said, 'We didn't ask.'

'Well, we're askin' now,' Wilcox said. 'Who put out a hit on you?'

'I'd certainly tell you if I knew,' I said. 'All I know is it's an open contract, so I got out of Vegas for a while.'

'And how did you know Miss Garland needed a job done?'

'My boss at the Sands,' I said. 'He's got connections.'

'And who would that be?'

'Jack Entratter.'

'Can we check this story with him?'

'Be my guest.' My bet was they'd check Jack out before they called him. That gave me time to get to him first.

'What about Mr Epstein?' Franklin asked.

'Innocent bystander,' I said. 'He just happens to be helping me with Judy's problem.'

'Guess he was pretty pissed to find out you had a contract on you and didn't tell him,' Wilcox said.

'But I got over it.'

'And the driver?' Franklin asked.

'Just a driver,' I said. 'Wrong place, wrong time.'

'So that's why you're coverin' his expenses at the hospital,' Franklin said. 'Or, rather, the Sands is.'

'That's right,' I said. 'Do you have anything on the bomb?'

'Makeshift,' Franklin said. 'Dynamite and an alarm clock.'

'Amateur hour,' Wilcox said. 'This open contract must have them comin' out of the woodwork after you.'

'I guess so.'

'And you got no idea why?' Franklin asked.

'Not a one.'

'Anybody tryin' to find out for you?' Wilcox asked.

'I've got a couple of friends askin' questions,' I said.

'Will you let us know if they find out something?' Franklin asked.

'You guys'll be first on my list.'

Wilcox closed his notebook and the two cops stood up. I walked them to the door while Jerry washed the cups.

'I've got a question,' I said.

'What's that?' Franklin asked.

'You fellas haven't checked me out yet?'

Franklin smiled.

'We've got some friends workin' on it, Eddie,' he said. 'You and Jerry.'

'Well, let me know when you find out somethin', will you?' I asked.

'Sure, Eddie,' Wilcox said. 'You'll be first on our list.'

I watched them walk back towards the hotel. Apparently, they chose to go through the lobby. Maybe had some questions for the desk clerk.

When I got back to the kitchen, Jerry was eating another donut. The detectives had eaten one each and I'd had one. Judy came up behind me.

'Any donuts left?' she asked.

'Plenty,' Jerry said, pushing the box her way.

'Where's Kenny?' she asked, rooting around in it.

'He should be coming through an open window any minute now,' I said.

Jerry had washed the cups used by Franklin and Wilcox. His and mine were on the table, freshly filled. I snagged a jelly from the box.

'Any jelly left?' Boyd asked from the other room.

I looked and saw that I had taken the last one. I put it back, grabbed a Bavarian cream.

'One left,' Jerry said.

Boyd came in and said, 'Pour me a cup of joe, will ya, Jerry?'

Jerry did. We all sat down at the table, Judy and Boyd where the two detectives had been. Judy had brought her coffee back with her.

'What's this about a contract?' Judy asked.

I exchanged looks with Jerry and Boyd.

'Come on, come on,' she said. 'I'm not a little girl, you know. I watch gangster movies. A contract. Somebody's paying money to have you killed.' She looked at me.

'That's right.'

'Why?'

'I don't know.'

'And is that why you brought me here?' she asked. 'To keep me safe?'

'Seems ironic, don't it,' Jerry said, 'but yeah.'

'That's not all,' I said. 'The two people who were killed – the PI and his girlfriend – I don't think that had anything to do with me.'

'But it has something to do with me,' she said.

'That's what I think.'

'Seems logical,' Boyd said.

The room fell silent. Boyd grabbed another donut. 'I'll take this with me and have a look around outside.'

I waited till he was gone, then said to Judy, 'It looks like somebody hired this private detective, Jacks, to make the blackmail drop for your manager, Begelman.'

'And then killed him?'

I nodded.

'And his girlfriend? Why her?'

'She either knew somethin',' Jerry said, 'or just got in the way.'

'And what about David?' she asked. 'Will they try to kill him?'

I shook my head. 'Not if he's tellin' the truth. Everything was done by phone and he never saw anybody but Jacks.'

'I don't like David,' she said, 'but that doesn't mean I want to see him hurt.'

'Well,' I said, 'with Jacks dead and the girl the only link to him, we'll have to talk to him again.'

'That's fine,' she said. 'Listen, with the television show canceled, Sid wants me to sue both David and Freddie for back royalties. If you boys can find out anything that would help us with that, I'd be very grateful. Oh, I'd pay you!'

'No need for that, Judy,' I said. 'We'll do what we can.'

'You're both sweet,' she said. 'I'm so glad Frank suggested you, Eddie.'

'Judy, we have to go out, but Kenny will be here to look out for you.'

'All right,' she said. 'You know, I'm a little tired. I think I'm going to lie down. Let me know when you get back.'

'OK,' I said, 'and we'll bring some food.'

She stood up, then impulsively kissed me and Jerry both on the cheek before leaving the room.

Jerry touched his cheek and said, 'We goin' now?'

'We are.'

He stood up, opened the oven and took out his .45.

'That's where you hid it?'

He shrugged, tucked it into his belt and said, 'I thought that might be the last place they'd look.'

I stood up, slapped him on the shoulder and said, 'And you're probably right.'

Forty-Six

Outside, I snagged Kenny Boyd.

'You said you could do some phone work,' I reminded him.

'That's right.'

I handed him a slip of paper.

'See if you can find out who owns that house.'

It was the house where we had found Jimmy Jacks and Peggy Kendall.

'You got it, Eddie.'

'And you might as well stay inside with Judy,' I added. 'But keep your piece handy.'

He patted the iron under his arm and said, 'Always.'

We went out to the front of the hotel to find a cab. When we got to the street, there was Zack, leaning against his car.

'What are you doin' here?' I asked.

'I had a feelin' you guys would be needin' a cab again today,' he said.

'Well,' I said, 'you're right.'

'Keep the meter runnin'?' he asked.

'You got it,' I said.

'Let's make a detour,' I suggested to Jerry, after we got in the car.

'I thought we wanted to talk to the Bagel guy?'

'We do, but we also want to see Mark Herron again.'

'Yeah, that's right. His, uh, friend probably told him we was there.'

I gave the address to Zack and we sat back.

'I meant to ask Judy again when the wedding is set for,' I said.

'A coupla days, I think.'

'Maybe we can find somethin' that'll change her mind.'

'Let's hope so,' Jerry said. 'She's a nice lady and deserves better.'

I had to agree with him.

* * *

165

When we reached Herron's apartment complex, the pool was still filthy and empty. No one was on the grounds.

'This place is a ghost town,' I said. 'No wonder he wants to marry Judy. Whatever her money issue are, she's got to have more than he does.'

'The guy's a scumbag,' Jerry said.

We approached the door to Herron's apartment and knocked. I was hoping his friend Henry Brandon wouldn't answer again.

When Herron opened the door and saw us, he didn't look happy.

'You wouldn't happen to know where Judy is, would you?' he demanded.

'Maybe,' I said. 'Can we come in?'

We entered. He slammed the door and turned to face us.

'Brandon not around?' I asked.

'He's at the studio,' Herron said. 'Why can't I get Judy on the phone? We *are* getting married, you know.'

'I don't have anything to do with that, Mr Herron,' I said. 'If and when I see her, I'll tell her you're lookin' for her.'

'Which means you won't tell me where she is. Why? Is she in danger?'

He couldn't see our bandages, or he'd have known that we were the ones in danger.

I looked around. The place was cleaner than last time. Somebody had gone over it with a damp cloth or something.

'I can't offer you anything to drink,' Herron said. 'No, actually that's not true. I don't want to.'

'Do you know a man named Jimmy Jacks, Herron?' I asked.

'What? Jacks? No, never heard of him. Why?'

'He's dead,' Jerry said.

'What's that to me?'

'We don't know,' I said. 'What is it to you?'

'What is it to me? Nothing.'

People repeat when they lie. It's a pattern. It gives them time to think about their answer.

'Herron,' I said, 'if somebody's been following Judy, breaking into her house, and you haven't seen anyone suspicious, that means one of two things to us.'

'Which are?'

'Either you're very unaware of your surroundings, or . . .'

'It's you,' Jerry ended.

'It's me . . . what?'

'Tryin' to scare her.'

'W–why would I do that?'

'To get her to marry you,' I said. 'To make her think she needs you to be safe.'

'Th–That's . . . that's sick.'

'I agree,' I said. Jerry and I stared at him.

'Y–You can't think that I'd do that to Judy,' he said. 'Why would I?'

'You need her money,' I said.

'And her contacts,' Jerry added.

'You and your buddy, Brandon.'

'Henry?' he said. 'He works all the time.'

'In television, lately,' Jerry said. 'Lots of parts playin' Indians.'

'He didn't sound very happy about it when we

167

talked to him,' I said. 'Not happy at all with his career trajectory.'

'So you think . . . what? I'm going to marry Judy and use her money to support myself and Brandon?'

'You said it,' I replied.

'That's ridiculous,' Herron said. 'I love Judy. I demand to know where she is so I can speak with her. You're obviously trying to poison her against me.'

'Did you know about the blackmail?' I asked. 'Did she tell you?'

'What blackmail? What are you talking about?'

'Some time ago Begelman told Judy some-body had taken compromising photos of her,' I said. 'He wanted her OK to pay a fifty-thousand-dollar blackmail demand.'

'Did she let him?'

'She did.'

Herron shook his head. 'He probably kept the money for himself.'

'A private detective named Jimmy Jacks was chosen to make the drop.'

'The what?'

'The payoff,' Jerry said.

'And?'

'Now he's dead.'

'W–What?' Herron was aghast. 'What happened? Did the police kill him?'

'The police never knew about him,' I said. 'They know nothing about the blackmail. It looks like the blackmailer, whoever he was, killed Jacks and his girlfriend.'

'Christ!' Herron put his hands over his mouth. I had no idea how good an actor he was.

'Was it you?' Jerry asked.

'What?'

'Did you kill them?'

'You think . . . you think I tried to blackmail Judy?' he asked.

'You'd be in a position to take some revealing photos, wouldn't you?'

He launched a haymaker at me. If it had hit me, it might have done some damage, but Jerry hooked the arm with his, elbow to elbow, and stopped the blow.

'Hey,' I said, 'we were just askin'.'

Herron yanked his arm away from Jerry's and pointed his finger at me. 'I demand to talk to Judy.'

'I'll have her give you a call,' I said.

Jerry and I headed for the door.

'That's it?' Herron asked.

'For now,' I said. 'Unless we find out you had something to do with it, after all. The blackmail, the murder. All of it.'

'I'm innocent of everything.'

'Then you've got no worries,' I said, as Jerry opened the door. 'Have you?'

Forty-Seven

We stopped by the pool.

'Whataya think?' Jerry asked.

'I was surprised when he threw the punch.'

'Why? Because he's a homo?'

'No,' I said, 'that has nothing to do with it. I just didn't think he had that in him.'

'I guess anybody does, if they get mad enough.'

'You think he was acting?' I asked. 'You watch a lot of movies, a lot of TV.'

'If he was,' Jerry said, 'he was pretty convincing.'

'So if it wasn't him behind the blackmail,' I said, 'we have to concentrate on the managers.'

'The Bagel guy.'

'And Fields,' I said. 'We can't just forget about him. After all, they are partners.'

'So? Them next?'

I nodded. 'Let's do Begelman first.'

We walked away from the pool, heading for Zack's cab.

'Can we stop for a bagel on the way?' he asked.

'You know,' I said, 'that actually makes sense to me.'

It was getting late for business. I wondered if we'd still find Begelman at his office, or if we'd end up having to go to his house. As it turned out, his receptionist was still there, and said that he was, too. She showed us into his office.

'Thanks, Marie,' he said. 'You can go home now.'

'Goodnight, sir.'

'Goodnight.'

She gave me a look, then left the room.

'Pretty girl,' I said.

'Aspiring actress,' Begelman said. 'They all are – receptionists, secretaries, assistants – all trying to get discovered.'

'I haven't seen a secretary,' I said, 'either time we've been here.'

'I had one,' he said. 'She actually did get discovered by a producer who came up here for a meeting. Snatched her away from me. I haven't replaced her yet.'

'So she's an actress now?' Jerry asked.

'That all depends,' Begelman said, 'on how well she does in the audition. The guy probably has her on her knees, or her back, by now.' He sat back in his big desk chair. 'What can I do for you gentlemen now?'

'The PI you said delivered the money to the blackmailer has been found. He's dead.'

'Oh my God,' Begelman said. 'Will the police be questioning me?'

'We don't know.'

'You didn't tell them about me?'

'We haven't told them about the murder,' I said. 'Jimmy Jacks and his girlfriend were both killed. We haven't called it in, but we should.'

'No!' he said. 'Don't. That would involve Judy.'

'Mr Begelman,' I said, 'we need to know who else you spoke to, besides Jacks.'

'I . . . I only spoke to someone on the phone once. It was after I received the photo in the mail.'

'What did he say?'

'He told me how much he wanted, and that he'd be sending someone in to collect it and bring it to him.'

'And you agreed? Right away?'

'Yes,' Begelman said. 'I didn't want to take a chance on that photo getting out.'

'So you agreed even before you spoke to Judy.'

He hesitated, then said, 'Yes.'

171

'Did you make the payoff before you informed her?'

'I had to,' he insisted. 'I didn't have time.'

'OK, never mind that,' I said. 'How soon after you agreed did Jacks show up?'

'I don't know,' he said. 'Hours, I guess.'

'Give me a timeline, Begelman,' I said.

'I got the call around . . . three in the afternoon. Jacks showed up here after hours – around six.'

'And in those three hours you got fifty grand together?'

'Yes,' Begelman said. 'We had some on hand. I went to the bank and got the rest.'

'You did that yourself?'

'Yes. I didn't want anyone else to know about it.'

'What about Fields? Did you let him know?'

'Not till after.'

'You were able to lay your hands on fifty grand without talking to your partner or Judy first?'

'As it happens,' Begelman said, 'yes.'

'And then Jacks showed up to collect?'

'Yes.'

'And you just handed the money over,' Jerry said. 'How'd you know he was the right guy?'

'Well . . . he had the photos and the negatives.'

'And he gave them to you?' Jerry asked.

'When I paid him, yes.'

I looked at Jerry. He shook his head, which I assumed meant he had no more questions.

'All right, Mr Begelman,' I said. 'I think we're done, for now.'

'And you're not going to notify the police?' he asked.

'We probably will,' I said, 'but we'll do it anonymously. We don't want to connect Judy to this.'

'Thank you,' Begelman said.

'We're doin' it for her,' Jerry said, 'not for you.'

When we got down to the street, Jerry said, 'I don't like him.'

'That makes two of us.'

'And I don't believe him.'

'About what?'

'The way the payment was made,' Jerry said, 'and the way he got the negatives back.'

'If there were any negatives at all.'

Jerry nodded. 'He could've faked the whole thing to make fifty grand.'

'But why not more?' I asked. 'If he's gonna take the chance – steal not only from Judy Garland but from his partner – why only fifty grand?'

'Maybe,' Jerry said, 'he only needed fifty grand at the time.'

'Yeah,' I said, 'but for what?'

Forty-Eight

It was getting late and it had been a long day. We decided to leave Fields till morning and just pick up some food to take back to the bungalow. Naturally, that led to a discussion of what we should get. Aside from actually eating food, Jerry's favorite thing was talking about it.

'How about Chinks?' he asked, in the back of the cab.

'Fine.'

'Really?'

'Sure,' I said, 'it sounds fine. I'll bet Zack knows a good place.'

'You don't wanna maybe suggest somethin' else?' he asked.

'Nope,' I said. 'Chinese is fine.'

He fell silent, obviously disappointed that I wasn't going to argue.

'Hey, Zack,' I called, 'know a good place for Chinese food?'

'I know a great one!'

'OK,' I said, 'let's stop there.'

'You got it.'

We drove for a few minutes, and then Jerry asked, 'How about Mexican?'

We settled on Chinese, arrived at the bungalow with a couple of bags of it, along with some wine and a bag of donuts. As we entered, Boyd stuck the barrel of his gun in our faces.

'Oops,' he said, 'sorry.'

'Don't be,' Jerry said. 'Yer on yer toes.'

'Whataya got?' he asked.

'Chinks,' Jerry said.

'Chinese food,' I rephrased.

Boyd grinned. 'Don't worry,' he said, 'stuff like that don't insult me. I like Mex, Wop, Chinks, all kinds of food.' He followed us to the kitchen.

'You eat a lot?' Jerry asked, sounding surprised.

'Sure I do,' Boyd said. 'I eat like a horse. Why wouldn't I?'

174

'I dunno,' Jerry said. 'I just thought maybe, you know, because of your size.'

Boyd looked confused. 'Whataya mean?'

'I mean, ya know,' Jerry said, 'you're . . . kinda short.'

'I ain't short at all!' Boyd argued. 'I'm five seven.'

We both looked at him. If he was five three, it was a lot. Apparently, he felt that five seven was a lot better.

'What size are you?' Boyd asked Jerry.

'Six-six.'

That shut Boyd up. Apparently, he couldn't think of any reason to run Jerry down for being six and a half feet tall.

'I'll tell Judy we've got food,' Boyd said.

'You think he's on the level?' Jerry asked, removing cartons from the paper bags.

'About what?'

'He don't know he's short.'

'I think he knows it,' I said, 'and he doesn't like it. So don't keep remindin' him about it.'

'I don't know,' Jerry said. 'It might be fun, pokin' at him.'

'He's a tough little guy, Jerry.'

'Ya think?' Jerry asked. 'I wonder how tough a guy that small can be?'

'OK,' I said. 'I think I'm gonna stay out of this one. You guys can form your own little relationship.'

Jerry went to the cabinet and got some plates and glasses.

'That smells divine,' Judy said, coming into the kitchen, followed by Boyd.

'Have a seat,' Jerry said. 'We're gonna eat what the Chinks call family style. It helps to have a long reach.' He looked at Boyd. 'That gonna be a problem for you?'

Boyd grinned at him tightly and said, 'I'll manage, Godzilla.'

'Godzilla had tiny little arms and hands,' Jerry said. 'I think you mean King Kong.'

'Well,' Boyd said, 'since King Kong had a tiny little brain, I guess you're right.'

Jerry laughed and looked at me. 'See? I told you he'd be fun.'

I looked at Judy, but she just smiled a 'boys will be boys' smile.

Jerry opened all the boxes, set them in the center of the table, and then we all sat down and began passing them around.

Jerry and Boyd continued to fence while we ate. As it turned out, they liked each other, though they never would have admitted it. Boyd gave as good as he got, and the exchanges seemed to amuse Judy.

'Did you talk to David?' she asked, when there was a lapse in the banter.

A quick look passed between Jerry and me. We hadn't discussed how much we'd tell Judy.

'Judy, when are you getting married?'

'This month,' she said. 'In a few days.'

'Didn't you say that a couple of days ago?'

'Mark and I hadn't actually set a firm date,' she said. 'But it will be this month.'

I fell silent, concentrated on my moo goo gai pan.

'Did you talk to Mark?' she asked. 'And David?'

I hesitated, then said, 'Yes.'

'And?'

'Herron still claims he doesn't know anything,' I said, 'hasn't seen anyone around you. He also says he didn't know Jimmy Jacks.'

'The dead detective who made the payoff?'

'Yes.'

'See?' she said. 'I listen.'

'Yes, you do.'

'What about David?'

'He told us about the blackmail.' I explained to her how he had gone about making the payment, how he claimed to have spoken to the blackmailer only once, and then handed the money off to Jacks.

'Can I say somethin'?' Boyd asked.

'Go ahead,' I said. 'Make any contribution you can.'

'You was thinkin' maybe Jacks was the black-mailer himself?' Boyd asked.

'That was one idea,' Jerry said.

'Well, what about Begelman?'

'That's the other idea,' Jerry said.

'You think David faked the existence of the photo and stole the fifty thousand for himself?' Judy asked.

'It's a theory,' I said, 'but could he have done that without Fields being involved?'

'It's very possible,' she said. 'I told you Sid wants us to sue David and Freddie. He's sure David is stealing from me, and he doesn't think David could do it without Freddie knowing about it.'

'Maybe we should talk to Sid,' I said to Jerry. 'He sounds like he's got a lot on the ball.'

'He's a very smart man,' Judy said. 'And he still loves me.'

'Why'd you get divorced?' Jerry asked.

'Sid . . . he drank, gambled. We fought. Sometimes he got . . . abusive . . .' She waved her hand, not wanting to talk about it anymore. 'In any case, he's concerned about me and wants to help me get away from David and Freddie.'

'Can you?' I asked.

'We have a contract,' she said, 'but Sid thinks he can break it, and maybe even sue them.'

'But he needs some ammunition.'

'Yes.'

'All right,' I said, 'we still have to talk to Fields again tomorrow. Is Luft in town?'

'Yes.'

'Then we'll talk to him, too.'

'I'll call them both, let them know you're coming.'

'How are Freddie Fields and Begelman relating to each other?'

'They have different duties when it comes to the business,' she said. 'But if David is stealing and Freddie doesn't know about it, he'll help you.'

'Good. Now, let's get to something really important,' I said.

'What's that?' she asked.

'Stop hogging the fried rice.'

Forty-Nine

Jerry made some coffee to have with donuts, and this time I scored a jelly. We kept up the conversation about our situations, deciding to keep Boyd and Judy in the loop as far as the open contract went.

'So the car,' Boyd said, 'that was about the contract, and Jimmy Jacks and his girl – you figure that's gotta be connected to the blackmail.'

'It's gotta figure that way,' Jerry said.

'OK, then, I got a question.'

'Go ahead,' I told Boyd.

'If there was no blackmail, and this guy Begelman just kept the fifty grand, how does that involve Jacks? He'd only be involved if there actually had to be a drop. And that'd be the only reason to kill him.'

Jerry looked at me as if he expected me to have the answer.

'All I can figure,' I said, 'is that Begelman called Jacks, hired him to make the drop, then picked up the money himself, just so it'd look like a legit blackmail payoff.' The irony of using 'legit' and 'blackmail' in the same sentence did not escape me.

'So then Begelman killed Jacks and the girl?' Boyd asked.

'I can't believe that,' Judy said. 'I mean, stealing? Yes. Murder? No.'

'If she's right,' Boyd said, 'then who killed Jacks and why?'

'If there really was a blackmailer,' Jerry said, 'and he hired Jacks, then he killed him, too.'

'So now we're back to a real blackmailer?' Boyd asked.

'We were never off it,' I said. 'We've simply got two theories.'

'Maybe the Bagel guy got himself a partner he couldn't control,' Jerry said, 'and he killed Jacks and the girl.'

'Boyd,' I said, 'how you comin' findin' out who owns that house?'

'Still workin',' Boyd said. 'I'm waitin' for some callbacks.'

'The answer to that question might help us a lot,' I said, gesturing with the last bite of my donut before popping it into my mouth.

'As soon as I get it, I'll let you know. But I hadda give out the phone number here.'

'That's OK,' I said.

'Well, I'm stuffed,' Judy said.

'You're finished?' Jerry said.

'Yes, but you don't have to be,' she said. 'Keep eating. I'm going to watch some television.' She stood up to leave, then asked, 'Eddie, is it all right if I call Mark?'

'Sure,' I said, 'but how about tomorrow? Let's leave the phone open tonight so Kenny can get his callbacks.'

'OK,' she said. 'I guess I can do it when I call Sid and Freddie.'

'Right.'

She left the kitchen and the three of us continued

to eat. We had wine, but I'd noticed that Judy hadn't had any.

'You gonna let her talk to that Herron guy?' Jerry asked when we heard the TV go on.

'I don't know how long we can keep them from talkin',' I said.

'Ain't she gonna marry the guy?' Boyd asked.

'Yeah, but Jerry doesn't think it's such a good idea.'

Boyd looked at Jerry, who said, 'He ain't good enough for her,' and left it at that.

By the time we finished eating, there were still leftovers in the boxes, which made Jerry very happy. He had a snack all ready for later.

'You want me to stay around tonight?' Boyd asked. 'I can sack out on the couch.'

'Jerry's on the couch,' I said, 'but maybe we could get you a room.'

'Nah, I meant so's I'm around if there's trouble,' Boyd said. 'I could sleep in my car.'

'Kenny, why don't you go home and get a good night's rest,' I said. 'Come back in the morning, and you can stay with Judy while Jerry and I go out.'

'You got it, Eddie,' Boyd said. 'I'll have a look around outside before I go. I won't come back in unless I spot somethin'.'

'Good.'

He said goodnight, then went into the other room to say goodnight to Judy. We heard the front door open and close.

'I'm gonna clean up this mess,' Jerry said.

'I'm gonna go and sit with Judy for a while,' I said.

I started to leave the room and Jerry said, 'Hey, Mr G.'

When I turned, he nodded at the glass of wine in my hand. 'You think that's such a good idea?'

'You're right,' I said, and put the glass down. If Judy was trying to stay clean, there was no point in drinking in front of her. 'Good thinking.'

He gave me a nod and turned to the sink with an armful of dishes.

Fifty

Judy flashed me a big smile as I entered the room. She had her legs curled beneath her, and patted the cushion next to her.

'Come and sit with me.'

I sat down and stared at the TV. 'Red Skelton?' I said.

'I'm just staring. I actually turned the sound down.'

That was when I noticed it was just Skelton mugging for the camera, doing Gertrude and Heathcliffe.

'Who's he got tonight?' I asked.

'Vic Damone and Gale Garnett.'

I nodded.

'Do you want the sound on?' she asked.

'No, it's OK,' I said. 'I thought maybe we'd talk.'

'Of course. About what?'

'Everything,' I said, 'anything. Something you think might help?'

She shrugged. 'I don't know what I can tell you.'

'Have you been able to recall whether or not there actually was a photo taken like the one Begelman described?'

She sighed, put her hand to her forehead. 'No. Like I told you, there could have been, but I don't remember . . . I mean, I might not remember . . .'

She fell silent for a few moments. I felt she was working herself up to something, so I let her be.

'You know,' she said, 'when I was young – a little girl, really – and signed a studio contract, they were worried that I'd get fat. They supervised everything I ate, everything I put into my body, but in the end they figured out a way to keep me from gaining weight.'

'And that was?'

'Pills.'

'Jesus.'

'Oh, my mother got me started, really, first to keep me going, then to sleep. And then the studio ended up getting me hooked on pills,' she said. 'Once you're addicted to something, you have an addictive personality. Pills, booze, drugs . . . a little bit of everything. So, there have been times when I didn't know where I was or what I was doing. A photo could have been taken during one of my dark times.'

'I see.'

She was hugging herself, as if she was cold. On the screen Red was being Clem Kadiddlehopper, and Vic Damone played some other hick.

'Go ahead,' she said.

183

'What?'

'Ask what you want to ask,' she said, spreading her arms. 'I'm an open book to you, Eddie G. Otherwise, how can you help me?'

'Did you have any blackouts in Australia?' I asked. 'What was it, Sydney and . . .'

'Melbourne,' she said. 'Sydney went well, even though there was a problem accommodating all of the people who turned out. Melbourne . . . well, that was a disaster.'

'Why?'

'I was an hour late to the show. Everybody thought it was because I was drunk. After forty-five horrible minutes I ran off the stage.'

'But you weren't drunk.'

'No'

'Or high on anything?'

'No.'

'So what was it?'

'I was . . . scared. I felt I was being followed, watched – not just by an audience. I didn't know if someone was going to try to . . . hurt me while I was on stage.'

'What about London?'

'London was a dream,' she said. 'I had Mark with me, and Liza, of course. She was wonderful! I was so proud of her, I had no time to worry about anything else.'

'Wasn't Mark with you in Australia?'

'What?'

'You said London was a dream because you had Mark with you,' I repeated. 'But Mark was also with you in Australia – wasn't he?'

'Well, yes . . .'

'Why didn't you feel safe there but you did feel safe in London?'

She shrugged. 'Maybe because I had Liza with me in London. I trust her.'

There was a chink in the armor of the pending Judy/Mark Herron wedding.

'So . . . you don't trust Mark?'

She took a moment, as if composing her thoughts. 'I have a bad history when it comes to trusting people,' she said. 'My mother, Louis Mayer, my ex-husband Sid . . . I had someone I thought was a friend when I was twenty – Liz Asher. She was about five years older than me, and I thought . . . I thought we were like sisters, but I found out she was just a spy for Mayer, reporting back to him on everything I said and did. So, while I want to trust Mark, there's just too much in my history . . .' She trailed off, tears in her eyes.

'And Frank?'

'Frank is my friend,' she said. 'He proved that when he sent you to me.' She reached out and took my hand. 'I'd like to trust you, Eddie. So far, you haven't given me any reason not to.'

'I'll try hard never to do that, Judy. You can depend on me.'

'Thank you, Eddie. Hopefully, when all this is over, I'll be able to walk a new path in my life.'

'I noticed you didn't drink any wine with dinner,' I said.

'I'm trying to stay sober,' she said, releasing my hand. 'No booze, no pills. It's not easy, especially when I'm feeling stressed.'

'And this is about as stressful as it gets.'

'What about you?' she asked. 'Knowing that someone hates you enough to pay to have you killed? That must be stressful.'

'Very,' I said. 'I should probably apologize for putting you in the line of fire.'

'You didn't know they'd follow you here,' she said. 'Besides, they're after you, not me.'

'An innocent bystander has already been hurt,' I said.

'And somebody killed that private detective, Jacks, supposedly because of someone blackmailing me. See? We've each put the other in the line of fire. No apologies, OK, Mr Gianelli?'

I smiled. 'No apologies, Miss Garland.'

We turned the sound up in time to hear Gale Garnett sing 'We'll Sing in the Sunshine'.

'Nice song,' Judy said. 'Pretty voice.'

'Nice of you to say.'

'What, I can't compliment other female singers? I think a lot of them are wonderful. Peggy Lee, for instance.'

'What about Peggy Lee?' Jerry asked, entering the room.

'Good singer,' I said. 'At least, according to Judy.'

'Miss Garland should know,' Jerry said.

Judy unfurled herself from the sofa. 'I'm going to my room to read.'

'A new script?' Jerry asked.

'No,' she said, 'just a book. You fellas can turn the sound up more, if you like. It won't bother me.'

'Goodnight,' I said.

'Oh, I might come out later for a cup of tea.'

'I'll make it,' Jerry offered.

She blew him a kiss. He sat next to me on the sofa.

'What are ya gonna watch now?' he asked.

'I don't even know what's on next.'

'*Petticoat Junction.*'

I looked at the TV. It was a commercial.

'How do you know that?'

'I know my TV listings, Mr G.'

The opening of *Petticoat Junction* came on.

'I guess you do.'

'That's Jeannine Riley. She plays Billie Jo,' Jerry said. 'She's very sexy.'

'Which one is she?'

'The blonde.'

'Oh.'

'Ain't you ever watched this show?'

'No,' I said, 'I haven't.'

'See, all the girls are sisters, and they all got "Jo" in their names, like—'

'Jerry,' I said, 'that's OK. I don't need to know.'

He pointed to the TV and said, 'How you gonna know what's goin' on?'

'I'm sure you'll tell me, if I ask.'

'I get it,' Jerry said, folding his arms. 'You ain't interested.'

'Don't get sore,' I said. 'I just don't like sit-coms.'

'I ain't sore,' he said. 'I'd rather watch dramas, too. It's just . . . well, ya know . . . it's Billie Jo.'

'OK, then,' I said, 'let's watch Billie Jo.'

Fifty-One

We were halfway through *The Fugitive* when we heard a shot outside.

'What the hell—' Jerry said, getting to his feet.

'Easy,' I said. 'Don't go runnin' out there.'

Judy came hurrying out of her room. 'Was that a shot?' Her eyes were wide with fright.

'Sounded like it,' I said.

'It was,' Jerry said.

'Couldn't it have been a car backfiring?'

'No chance,' Jerry said. 'Mr G., you better stay inside with Miss Garland. I'll check it out.' He had his .45 in his fist.

'Eddie,' she said, 'you can't let him go out there by himself.'

'It's OK, Miss Garland,' Jerry said. 'This is what I do.'

He headed for the door. I hurried around and caught him before he went out.

'Somebody might be tryin' to draw us out, Jerry,' I said.

'I'll be careful.'

'OK, but let me get the lights first so you're not backlit.'

'Good thinkin', Mr G.'

I turned out all the lights in the room while instructing Judy to stay on the sofa. It was in the center of the room, away from the windows, and was probably the safest place – unless I stuck her under a bed.

'Eddie—' she said.

'Shhh. Just stay.'

She shut up.

I went to the front door, then took a quick step to one side, just in case, and waited . . .

Jerry told me later when he walked outside, gun in hand, he paused only long enough for his eyes to get used to the darkness. Then he moved forward in a crouch, which I didn't think would help him much. He moved to the end of the walk, where he could go either to the hotel lobby or to the street, and stopped to listen. He looked around, saw the hotel lights and heard low voices coming from there, but nothing else.

He moved toward the street, and the parking lot, where he assumed Boyd would have his car. The little PI had left some time ago, but he might have returned. Jerry would be able to spot his Corvette at a glance, if it was there.

It was.

'Shit,' he said under his breath. Why had Boyd come back? Or had he never left?

He moved into the parking lot, his head swiveling around, trying to look in every direction at one time. The parking lot seemed empty. Apparently, nobody else heard the shot, or they were simply not interested enough to come out and look.

Holding his .45 tightly, he moved toward the Corvette. All the doors were shut, but as he got closer he noticed a hole in the driver's side window. A bullet hole. The window had not shattered, but the glass was starred, cracks spreading out from the hole. He moved in closer, grabbed the handle and opened the door . . .

I jumped when Jerry knocked on the door. I opened it to let him in. His face looked grave. He was upset.

'Well?'

He looked over toward where Judy was seated.

'Can we turn on a light?' she asked.

'Sure,' I said.

She turned on a lamp near the sofa.

'Miss Garland, maybe you should—' Jerry started.

'Come on, Jerry,' she said. 'We're all in this together. What is it?'

He looked at me. 'Boyd's dead.'

There was a sharp intake of breath from Judy. When I looked at her, she had her hands over her mouth. Her eyes were wet.

'What happened?'

'I guess he must've come back,' Jerry said. 'Somebody must've been watchin' the parkin' lot. They fired one shot through his window. The bullet hit him square in the head.'

'Anybody else out there?'

'No.'

'No cops?'

'No,' Jerry said, 'not yet, anyways. Somebody might've called 'em, but nobody came out to take a look.'

'Christ,' I said.

'Is Kenny dead because of me?' Judy asked.

190

'No, no,' I said, 'of course not.' I looked at Jerry. 'This has to be because of me.'

Jerry looked me in the eye and held out a piece of paper. It was an envelope with Kenny's name on it.

'Turn it over.'

I did. Someone had written on the back: *You're just as dead as he is, you just don't know it yet.*

'They must have gotten this from his glove compartment,' Jerry said. 'Somebody was calm enough to take the time to look for some paper and then write this note.'

'A pro,' I said.

He nodded.

'I don't know what this all means,' Judy said.

'It means,' I said, 'that we're all going to Las Vegas.'

Jerry nodded his approval.

Fifty-Two

We had a lot of things to do before returning to Vegas.

'Do we call the cops?' Jerry asked.

I hesitated, then said, 'If we don't, we'll be in trouble. And if we do, they might keep us from leavin' town.'

Still shaken, Judy said, 'What if we left very early in the morning?'

'Then they'd wonder why,' I said. 'Sooner or later somebody's gonna find the body.'

191

'Nobody came out to see what happened, but somebody might have called,' Jerry said.

'Then we'd better call now, before they get here,' I said. 'Even if they've already been called, it'll look good if we phone, too.'

'Right,' Jerry said. 'You want me to do it?'

'I'll do it,' I said. 'In fact, I'll ask for Franklin personally. Might earn us some brownie points.'

'Right,' Jerry said. 'I'll go out and keep a lookout for the cops.'

As he left, I turned toward Judy, and she came and leaned her forehead against my chest.

'Poor Kenny.'

'Yeah,' I said. 'I got him killed. I feel like shit.'

She looked up at me. 'It's not your fault, Eddie.'

'I'll keep tellin' myself that while I make that call to the police.'

'I'll make some tea.'

'I'd prefer somethin' stronger.'

'So would I.'

She went to the kitchen. I felt like shit, again.

Jerry came in, said a patrol car had pulled up in the parking lot.

'Should we go out and talk to them?' he asked.

'Probably,' I said. 'After all, he was with us, and we heard the shot. You're the only one who went out to check on him. I talked to Franklin, and he's on his way.'

'Let's go, then.'

'What should I do?' Judy asked.

'Stay here,' I said. 'I don't want to involve you.'

'But I *am* involved.'

192

'No, you're not,' I said, 'and Jerry and I are gonna try to keep it that way.'

'All right.'

I pointed my finger at her. 'Stay inside. I mean it.'

She bit her lip and nodded.

When we got to the parking lot there was a second patrol car there. The cops looked over at us as we approached. One of them held his hand out. He was young, looked as if he hadn't started to shave yet.

'Don't come any closer, please. This is a crime scene.'

'We know,' I said. 'We called it in.'

Another cop came over, older, with some stripes on his arm. 'Do you know what happened?' he asked.

'We just heard the shot from our bungalow. We came out to see what happened.'

'Both of you?'

'Just me,' Jerry said.

'Why?'

'I know a shot when I hear one,' he said.

'And do you know the victim?'

'We do,' I said. 'He was a friend of ours. He was probably comin' to visit us. We were gonna buy him a drink.'

'Guess that ain't gonna happen now,' the young one said, with a smirk.

'Shut up, Benny,' the older cop said. 'Go and keep the people back.'

Guests who had not reacted to the shot had reacted to the presence of the police cars and were now beginning to crowd the parking lot.

'What did I sa—'

'Just go!'

Sullenly, the young cop turned and walked away.

'Sorry about that,' the older cop said. 'I'm Sergeant McDonough. Can I see some ID, please?'

We both took out our wallets. By the time he checked us out, Detective Franklin was there. I hadn't reached him at the station, but they'd promised to notify him. He looked as if he'd been dragged out of bed.

'What are you doin' here, Lynn?' the sergeant asked.

'I got a call, Andy,' Franklin said. 'I'm workin' on something that might be related.'

Sergeant McDonough looked from him to us and back to him. 'You know these fellas?'

'I do.'

He handed Franklin our wallets. 'It's all yours, then. Want us to canvas?'

'Sure, Andy,' Franklin said. 'That'd be fine.'

McDonough nodded to Franklin, looked at us and walked off.

Franklin handed us back our wallets. 'Who's the victim?' he asked.

'Kenny Boyd,' I said. 'He's a PI workin' for the Double-A agency.'

'Nat Hiller's outfit.'

'That's right.'

'Hiller involved?'

'No,' I said, 'Boyd was a loan.'

'What was he doin' for you?'

'Some legwork.'

194

'Is he from LA?'

'No, actually,' I said, 'he's from Hiller's Vegas office.'

'I didn't know Double-A was in Vegas,' Franklin said. 'What was Boyd doin' out here?'

'We don't know,' I said. 'We'd seen him earlier in the day, but thought he'd gone back to his hotel.'

'And where is that?'

Jerry and I looked at each other, and Jerry shook his head. 'We never asked.'

'When did you see him last?'

'Sometime after dinner.'

'When was that?'

This was a small lie, only because we'd already lied to the sergeant. We'd seen Boyd around eight, but I said, 'Six.' I felt it was a harmless lie, and saved us having to explain why we had lied to the sergeant before.

'Talk to him on the phone after that?'

'No.'

'So you have no idea why he was in this parking lot, or for how long.'

'No, we don't,' I said.

'What about Miss Garland?'

'What about her?'

'Could she have talked to him?'

'No.'

'How do you know?'

'Because since he left we've all been watchin' TV together.'

'TV? Really?'

'Why wouldn't she watch TV?'

He shrugged. 'No reason. What did you watch?'

'*Red Skelton*,' I said, and told him who was on the show, for good measure.

'And then?'

'*Petticoat Junction*,' Jerry said.

'Really?' Franklin said again.

I jerked my head toward Jerry. 'He likes Billie Jo.'

'Hmmm,' Franklin said, 'I'm kind of a Bobbie Jo man, myself.'

He turned to look as a white van pulled up. I assumed it was a lab truck.

'OK,' he said, 'that's it for now. We'll talk again.'

I told him which bungalow we were in.

'Stay there, please,' he said. 'I'll check in on you before I leave here.'

'Yes, sir,' I said.

'I'll bet Nat Hiller's not gonna be happy with you,' Franklin said.

'I'll bet you're right.'

Fifty-Three

We knew Boyd, and he was killed in the parking lot of our hotel. That's all the cops had on us.

Franklin came to our bungalow with Wilcox – who also looked as if he'd been dragged from bed – and they took our statements. They talked to Judy, who said she'd heard a sound, and that was all.

'Jerry and Eddie said it was a shot.' After that, they let her go to her room and agreed to keep her out of their report as much as possible.

'As far as I'm concerned,' Franklin said, at the door on his way out, 'I don't think either of you killed him, but I'd prefer you don't leave town. Or, at least, if you do, let me know.'

'Actually,' I said, 'we were going to head back to Vegas in the morning.'

'Where will you be?'

'You can find us at the Sands.'

'And Miss Garland?'

'She'll also be there,' I said. 'We're going to be discussin' the possibility of her performin' there.'

'I see.'

'If you need us, we're only a short plane ride away,' I said. 'We'll come back.'

'OK, as long as I have all your numbers.'

I gave him the number at the Sands, and my home phone. 'You'll find Jerry at those, too.'

They left and I looked at Jerry. 'Why do you think they're lettin' us go?'

'They're probably gonna have somebody in Vegas keep an eye on us.'

'I'll bet Hargrove would love to do that for him.'

'Probably.'

We all turned in after that – when everything had died down in the parking lot, and Boyd and his car had been taken away.

I had to call Hiller in the morning, tell him about his man.

'Does this have to do with the reason I loaned him to you?' he asked.

'Probably not.'

197

'Then was he killed instead of you because of the contract?'

'I think so,' I said. 'I'm sorry.'

There was a long pause and then he said, 'Well, you did tell me about it.'

I had that in my favor, at least.

'I'm still sorry. He was a good man.'

'Yeah, he was.'

'I would have called you sooner but I didn't have a home number.'

'Uh-huh.'

I had the feeling he wasn't happy with me and was trying to hold his temper.

'What's your next move?' he asked.

'We're headin' back to Vegas today,' I said. 'Obviously comin' here didn't throw anybody off my scent.'

'Well,' he said, 'watch your back, there.' He hung up without offering any more help, even though he had an office in Vegas.

I couldn't blame him.

'You didn't tell him about Judy comin' with us,' Jerry said.

'He didn't ask,' I replied. 'I think he's just glad we're leavin' town.'

'How are we gonna do that?' he asked. 'Fly?'

'I was thinkin' about drivin' in Boyd's car, but that's out now. I'll call Frank; he'll arrange for a plane.'

'I have a car,' Judy said, from behind us.

We turned, saw her standing there in her jeans and a sweater, the sleeves pulled up to her elbows.

'In fact,' she said, 'I have more than one.'

I looked at Jerry, who smiled.

198

Fifty-Four

As it turned out, Judy was afraid of flying. She was also afraid of guns, a fear she said materialized when she was making *Girl Crazy* with Mickey Rooney for Busby Berkeley. The constant gunfire all around so unnerved her that she had to take to her bed for five days.

So, because of her fear of airplanes, we agreed to drive to Las Vegas. Actually, by the time we could have contacted Frank, got a plane, driven to the airport, boarded and flown to Vegas, we would have been there by car. It was only 270 miles, after all.

Judy called Harrington in the morning and had him drive over in her car, which turned out to be a silver Rolls-Royce Phantom V MPW limo.

'Is this OK?' she asked hopefully as we stood in the parking lot.

Jerry was speechless.

'CBS insisted on this car,' she said. 'And they gave me a driver during the run of my show. Lately it hasn't been used much, though.'

'Well,' I said, 'Jerry's the driver. Is this OK, Big Guy?'

He was too busy running his hands over the finish to answer.

'It's OK,' I told Judy.

Harrington left to take a cab home. She told

him he could close up the house and take a few days off.

We went inside to get our bags, and Jerry stowed them in the trunk without ripping his stitches. Then Judy and I got in the back, while Jerry slid behind the wheel. The leather interior still smelled brand new. I hoped neither of us would bleed all over it.

Jerry didn't start the car right away, just sat there and ran his hands over the steering wheel.

'Jerry?'

'Yeah, Mr G.,' he said, 'I'm goin'. Just gimme a minute.'

I looked at Judy and said, 'He's just got to get his heartbeat down.'

She nodded, still unhappy that I hadn't let her call Mark Herron. I told her I thought it would be better to wait until we were in Vegas.

I hadn't even called Danny or Jack Entratter to tell them we were returning. I didn't want to give anyone a heads-up. We hadn't checked out of the hotel that morning; I'd let Entratter take care of the bill from Vegas.

However, before Harrington even arrived with the limo there was a knock on the door . . . and a bellhop handed me an envelope.

'Somebody left this at the front desk for you last night, sir.'

'Thanks.' I tipped him and sent him on his way. When I opened the envelope, I called out to Jerry, 'Well, now we know what Boyd was doin' back here last night.'

'What's that?' he called from the kitchen.

I joined him and waved the envelope.

200

'It's Boyd's report on the house where we found Jacks and Peggy.'

'Damn,' he said. 'He came back to drop that off and got killed for it? Wait till I get my hands on whoever pulled that trigger.'

We'd been in the middle of a simple breakfast of toast and coffee, so I sat back down across from him. Judy was in the bedroom, packing.

'What's it say?' Jerry asked.

'His note says there's a paper trail of companies that own the house, rent it out . . . a real estate rental office is involved . . . damn, he followed all this on the phone?' There were a few sheets of a typewritten report. I assumed he'd had a typewriter in his hotel room.

'Where does it lead?'

'Wait . . .' I went through the report, then put the pages down. 'He doesn't come to the end of it. He was still workin' on it. Damn.'

'Then why'd he bother bringin' it around?'

'I don't know,' I said. 'I wish I did. Maybe he just meant to give it to us, forgot and hurried back.'

'To die,' Jerry said. 'He was a good guy.'

'Yeah,' I said, 'he was.'

In the back seat, Judy was kind of quiet, pensive – or maybe just nervous about Jerry's driving. So far we'd only driven from her house to the hotel, but now we'd be on the highway.

'I hope he won't drive too fast,' she said. 'We're not in a hurry to get there, are we, Eddie?'

I took her hand and said, 'We're not in a hurry, at all, Judy. Don't worry.'

201

I leaned forward and banged on the open partition.

'Home, Jerry!'

Fifty-Five

As we pulled away from the Beverly Hills Hotel we spotted Zack and his cab out front.

'Mr G.?' Jerry said. 'Should we tell him we're leavin'?'

For a moment I thought we should, but then I said. 'Not if we're bein' watched. They've seen him drivin' for us. If they see him waitin' our front for us, it'll look like we're still inside.'

'Yeah, OK,' Jerry said. 'I just hate to leave the guy hangin'.'

'Better him than us,' I said.

We drove for an hour and Jerry couldn't take it anymore. That meant a proper breakfast in Riverside.

'This reminds me of when we did this with Miss Gardner,' Jerry said, putting the car in park.

'Ava Gardner?' Judy asked. 'Well, I'm in good company.'

'Yes, we drove with Ava from LA to Vegas a while back,' I said.

'Another favor for Frank, I suppose?'

'Yes.'

'Do you do favors for all Frank's women?'

I looked at her and said, 'Just the ones I like.

202

Do you have some dark glasses in your purse?'

'Always,' she said, 'and a scarf.'

'Good. Maybe we'll get away with this.'

'We will,' she said.

'Why do you say that?'

'Most people still expect me to look like Dorothy.'

We parked in the lot of a truck stop. Jerry got out and opened the back door for Judy, held his hand out to help her out. I was always amazed at how gentle the big man could be when he wanted to. I followed them to the diner.

Inside, we got a booth in the back, me and Judy on one side, Jerry by himself on the other.

'I love truck-stop breakfasts,' Jerry said, handing Judy a menu. 'Big ham steaks!'

'Ugh,' she said. 'I'll just have some coffee and a soft boiled egg.'

'Ugh!' Jerry said, and then smiled at her. She had no choice but to smile back.

Jerry and I both got scrambled eggs with a ham steak and home fries, while Judy stuck to her guns and had the soft boiled egg. I was surprised that a truck-stop cook got it so right for her. They brought her toast with it, so she ate two pieces.

We were still eating when she finished and lit up a Salem. I hadn't seen her smoke till then. I thought it was something else she was trying to give up. And I might have been right, judging by the way her hands were shaking.

'I'm sorry,' she said, 'do you mind?'

'Take more than that to stop me from eatin',' Jerry said.

'No problem,' I said.

She drew heavily on the cigarette, expelled the smoke shakily. 'I'm just a little on edge.'

'We understand,' I said.

'I thought I just had somebody following me, you know?' she said. 'To think that he might be a killer . . .'

'Blackmailers fall out,' Jerry told her. 'It could have nothin' to do with you, at all.'

'But I'm the one they were blackmailing.'

'Whether there were blackmailers,' I said, 'or whether Begelman pulled this and used Jacks to make it look like a payoff, them fallin' out doesn't put you in any danger. As far as Begelman's concerned, you're the goose.'

'The goose?' Jerry asked.

'That lays the golden eggs,' I said.

'Oh, yeah,' Jerry said. 'Jack and the Beanstalk. Abbott and Costello.'

'What?' Judy asked, puzzled.

'I mean, I know it's a fairy tale, but they did an Abbott and Costello movie about it.'

'Jerry,' she said, 'you're precious.'

I don't know if he was precious or not, but her hand had stopped shaking.

We finished breakfast, paid the tab and walked back to the car without anyone recognizing Judy. Jerry held the door for her. I walked to the other side and stopped him before getting in.

'Keep the speed down, Jerry,' I said. 'I get the feelin' she might lose it.'

'Sure thing, Mr G. I wouldn't do anythin' to hurt Miss Garland.'

'I know you wouldn't.'

204

We got in the car and Jerry pulled out on to the road.

'I haven't been to Vegas since I played the Frontier in fifty-eight,' she said.

'That was a triumph for you,' I said. I was in Vegas at the time, but didn't see her show and we never met. But I knew she was so good that they kept her over an extra fourth week.

'A triumph,' she said, then put her head back and closed her eyes.

Fifty-Six

It took longer than it should have because Jerry did keep his speed down. But Judy was right. We weren't in any hurry.

I told him to pull the limo around the back. I wanted to take Judy inside without anybody seeing her.

'What about the car?' Jerry asked. 'We can't just leave it. I mean . . . that's a car!'

'I'll have one of the valets look after it,' I promised.

Partially mollified, he followed us inside. I led the way directly to the elevators.

'Where we goin'?' Jerry asked.

'Right to Jack's office,' I said. I looked at Judy. 'He'll get you a suite with no fuss.'

'Whatever you say,' she said. She'd been very quiet the last couple of hours of the ride. I figured she had a lot on her mind. How much

205

she was willing to tell me, I hoped to find out later.

We took the elevator to Entratter's floor and entered his office. We passed two employees in the hall, and they both gaped at Judy. The same thing happened when we entered Jack's outer office. I didn't know anything about the girl sitting there, except that she was pretty and new. But she knew Judy when she saw her.

'Oh my God,' she said.

'Is Jack here?' I asked.

'Uh . . .' She pulled her eyes away from Judy. 'Who are you?'

'Eddie Gianelli.'

'Eddie G.!' she said. 'Yes, I was told about you. Yes, Mr Entratter is in his office.'

I looked at his closed door. That was unusual.

'Thanks,' I said and walked over to knock on the door.

'Come!' Jack yelled.

I held the door, allowed Judy to go in first. Jerry followed me in.

'What the—' Jack jumped up from behind his desk. 'Miss Garland. I didn't know . . . Eddie? What the—' He stopped himself again.

'Jack, I don't know if you've ever met Judy Garland before,' I said.

'Once or twice,' Judy said, before he could speak. 'How are you, Mr Entratter?'

'I'm fine, Miss Garland. Eddie, you wanna explain?'

'Judy needs a suite, Jack, and I don't want anyone to know. You'll have to tell your whole

206

staff, because a couple of them have seen her already, but I don't want them to talk.'

'The first one who talks gets fired,' he said. 'I'll see to it. But what's this about?'

'I'll have to tell you later,' I said, 'but it's important. Are Dean and Frank in town?'

'No, but Frank's in Tahoe. He can be here in a hurry if you need him.'

'I'll call him there,' I said. 'Meanwhile, Jerry and I have some other things to do.'

'Leave Miss Garland with me,' Jack said. 'I'll see that she's taken care of.'

I looked at Judy. She said, 'Go ahead. I'm sure I'll be fine with Jack.'

'All right,' I said. 'I'll check back in with you after you're settled.'

'Take me to dinner,' she said. 'Maybe Jack can join us?'

'Deal,' I said. 'Jack, I'll be back.'

'You better,' he said. 'You've got a lot of explainin' to do.'

'I can fill you in on some of it,' Judy said, then looked at me for approval.

'Sure,' I said, 'tell him as much as you know.'

She nodded and smiled.

'I'll take you to a suite personally,' he told Judy.

'Come on,' I said to Jerry.

We went out past the girl, who was still awed by Judy's presence.

'Where to?' Jerry asked in the elevator.

'Well, first we'll get that car you're so worried about taken care of, then we'll make some calls – get ahold of Danny and see what he's got.'

'And then?'

I looked at him. 'You're worried about eatin', aren't you?'

'Well . . .'

'Don't worry,' I said. 'We'll get somethin', and then we'll come back later to have dinner with Judy.'

'And Mr Entratter.'

'I doubt he'll be there,' I said, 'but Frank might. Once he knows Judy's here, he'll probably chopper in.'

'Where are we gonna make them from?'

'Jesus, Jerry,' I said, as the elevator doors opened on the main floor, 'all right, we'll make the calls from the Garden Café.'

Fifty-Seven

When we got a booth at the café, I had a phone brought over and plugged in. Jerry ordered for both of us. I called Danny's office, got lucky and found him there.

'I'm playin' some phone tag,' he said. 'You back?'

'Yeah, we're at the Garden Café. Come and join us.'

'On my way.'

I looked down when the waitress arrived with the food. Jerry had ordered exactly what I would have ordered for myself – a burger platter. I looked at him.

'I pay attention,' he said.

I took the top of the bun off to have a look and said, 'Yeah, you do.'

We started to eat and were only halfway through when Danny appeared.

'You started without me,' he said, sliding into the booth beside me.

'Order what you want,' I said. 'It's on the Sands.'

'I won't take advantage,' he promised, and ordered the same thing I had.

'Now what brings you back to Vegas?' he asked. 'I haven't found out who put that contract out on you yet.'

'Well, they found us in LA,' I said. 'They killed Kenny Boyd.'

'Boyd was OK,' Danny said. 'I'm sorry to hear he's dead. But why kill him?'

'I think they were sendin' me a message.'

'My guess is you received it loud and clear,' Danny said. 'What about Judy Garland?'

'She's here,' I said. 'We brought her back with us and put her in a suite.'

'Why?'

'Because we haven't solved her problem yet.'

'And what is her problem, specifically?'

Up to now we'd only told Danny about my troubles, so I filled him in on Judy's.

'And you don't think Jacks' death and the death of his girlfriend are a message to you?'

'No,' I said. 'For one thing, Jacks was probably killed even before we got to LA.'

'And you never did call the police and report it anonymously?'

Sheepishly, I said, 'We never got around to it.'

'Well, you might as well do it from here,' he said, meaning Vegas rather than the Sands, specifically. 'Let the cops get involved. Maybe they'll find out something.'

'Maybe they will,' I said. 'We did tell them that we were comin' back here.'

'I'll bet they call the Vegas cops to check up on you,' he said. 'You know what that means.'

'Hargrove will get involved.'

Danny nodded as the waitress set his platter down in front of him. 'A red flag goes up for him every time your name is mentioned.'

'Yeah,' I said, picking up a French fry, 'I'm sure he'll show his ugly face soon enough.' I popped the fry in my mouth, then reached into my pocket. I came out with the envelope Boyd had left for us. 'I have another favor to ask.'

'Shoot.'

I passed him the envelope.

'Boyd was workin' on findin' out who owned the house where Jacks was killed. This was what he had so far, until—'

'Somebody killed him,' Danny said, accepting the envelope. 'I'll see what I can do. I'll put Penny to work.'

'Remember what you just said,' I replied. 'Somebody killed him.'

'I'll put her to work on the contract,' he said, 'and I'll work on this. What about Entratter?'

I swallowed a mouthful of hamburger before answering. 'What about him?'

'Is he tryin' to help find out who put the contract out on you?'

210

'I haven't asked him.'

'Doesn't mean he's not tryin'.'

'I'll ask,' I said. 'It might be time to ask the hard questions.'

'Momo?' Jerry asked.

'Momo,' I said.

'I've got a question,' Danny said.

'What?'

'What if it turns out to be Momo Giancana who's responsible for all this shit? And if it is him, then it came from the top.'

'If Mr Giancana put the contract out,' Jerry said, 'then Mr G. is as good as dead.'

'Not if we have anythin' to say about it, right, Big Guy?' Danny asked.

'Right,' Jerry said, but he didn't seem all that sure about it.

Fifty-Eight

After we ate, Danny took off to put Penny to work on the contract while he followed up Boyd's work on the house in LA. Finding out who owned that place was going to go a long way toward telling us who was behind the whole mess. Judy's mess, anyway. My mess was still up in the air.

I made the call I should've made days ago, to the LA police, reporting a disturbance at the Laurel Canyon house.

'OK, that's done. I have to talk to Jack again,' I said, after hanging up.

211

'About Mr Giancana?' Jerry asked.

'Among other things,' I answered, 'like makin' sure you still have a room.'

'Thanks, Mr G. If I do have one, I think I'd like to go to it. I'll get our bags out of the car.'

'Good idea,' I said. 'Just put mine in your room for now. I'll take it home later.'

'You ain't goin' nowhere near your house, Mr G.,' he said. 'At least, not without me.'

'OK,' I said. 'We'll talk about it later. Let me get you situated.'

I picked up the phone and called the front desk, got Jerry a suite.

'They'll send somebody up with your key.'

'OK.'

'Then you might as well go up,' I said. 'I'll be OK as long as I stay inside. I don't think anybody's gonna try for me here.'

'Let's hope not.'

As Jerry left, I picked up the phone again and dialed the Cal-Neva in Tahoe.

'Mr Sinatra is not in his room,' the desk clerk said.

'Who is this?'

'Henry, sir.'

'Henry, this is Eddie G., from the Sands.'

'Oh, yes, sir.'

'Track Mr Sinatra down and get him on the phone to me as quick as you can,' I said. 'I'll be standin' by in the Garden Café.'

'I'll do what I can, sir.'

'Do more than that, Henry – much more.'

As I hung up, the waitress came by.

'Anything else, Mr Gianelli?'

'Coffee,' I said, 'although I need somethin' stronger.'

'I can get you something to spice it up,' she offered.

I looked at her, couldn't dredge up her name, so she must have been fairly new.

'Lexi,' she said, smiling prettily, 'my name is Lexi.'

'Well, Lexi, thanks for the offer, but for now coffee will have to do.'

'Yes, sir.'

I kept my hand on the phone, willing it to ring. If Frank would come back to Vegas and spend some time with Judy, it would free me and Jerry up for other things.

By the time Lexi brought me a fresh pot of coffee, the phone had still not rung. I was trying to decide who else to call – who needed to be called – when it finally rang. As ready as I was to pick it up, my first reaction was to pull my hand away as if it was hot. Feeling foolish, I answered it.

'Eddie?'

'Hey, Frank. I'm glad they found you.'

'Who?'

'The desk clerk at the Cal-Neva. I told him—'

'I'm not at the Cal-Neva, Eddie. I'm here, in the lobby. You still in the Garden Cafe?'

'I'm here.'

'Order me a cup.'

'You got it.'

Lexi had another pot on the table by the time Frank got there.

'Hoya, doll,' he said, and she giggled and went off. 'Eddie.'

213

'Frank. What are you doing here?'

'Jack called me, and I got a chopper. My feet are still vibrating.' He sipped his coffee. 'He said you had Judy with you. What's up?'

'Quite a bit, actually,' I said. 'It all started . . .'

Fifty-Nine

'First of all,' Frank said, when I'd finished, 'why didn't you tell me about this contract?'

'It was my problem, Frank. And I didn't want you to think I couldn't help Judy.'

'The point is,' Frank said, 'I could've helped you.'

'Well, I thought I'd have more time to find out who's behind it if I went to LA,' I said. 'Guess that was stupid. It didn't take them long to find me there.'

'I'm sorry about Greg,' Frank said. 'I'll check in on him, see how he's doing.'

'Is he a friend?'

He shrugged. 'Just a driver I use sometimes when I'm in LA. So, where's Judy?'

'Jack put her in a suite.'

'Is Jack trying to find out about this contract?'

'I didn't ask him to,' I said. 'I've got Danny workin' on it.'

'I can ask around.'

'I was thinkin' . . .' I said, and then stopped.

'About what?'

'Not what,' I said. '*Who*. Momo.'

214

Frank sat back. 'You think Momo would put a contract out on you? Why?'

'I don't know why,' I said, 'but does an open contract go out without him knowin' about it?'

'It shouldn't.'

'That's what I'm thinkin'.'

'You want me to ask him?'

'It might be better if I did,' I said.

'If you do it, you better do it in person.'

'That means goin' to Chicago.'

'I'll stay here and look after Judy, if that's what you want me to do,' he said. 'Take Jerry with you.'

'Definitely,' I said. 'I don't think he'd let me go to the corner without him.'

'I mean,' Frank said, 'Momo kind of likes him.'

'Oh.'

'I'll fill Dino in,' Frank said. 'He might have some thoughts.'

'OK,' I said, 'thanks.'

'You got any idea?' he asked. 'I mean, aside from Giancana?'

'Not really. Unless . . .

'Unless who?'

'Johnny Roselli?' I said.

'That thing with Elvis?'

I shrugged.

'I don't think Johnny would do it, but him I *can* ask straight out.'

'As long as you don't get jammed up.'

'By Johnny Roselli? Don't make me laugh. You piss anybody else off, lately?'

'No.'

'Husbands? Boyfriends?'

215

'Nope.'

He hesitated a moment, then asked, 'Cops?'

'The only cop who hates me that much is Hargrove,' I said, 'and he'd never do it that way. If he wanted me dead, he'd do it himself . . . and I don't think he hates me all that much – yet.'

'All right,' Frank said, 'then I'll go and see Judy. You go and see Momo. You want my plane?'

'Yeah,' I said, 'I'd rather do that than fly commercial. I'd be too big a target that way.'

'I'll have it waiting whenever you're ready for it.'

'I'll have to check with Jack, first.'

'Sure,' Frank said, 'he's your boss.'

We got up and left together, leaving a large tip for Lexi.

'Eddie,' Frank said, as we walked to the elevator, 'trouble.'

I looked across the lobby and saw Detective Hargrove, his partner and two uniformed policemen walking purposefully toward me.

'Oh, yeah,' I said.

'Want me to stay?' Frank asked.

'No,' I said, 'go to Judy's room. I'll deal with Hargrove. You might let Jack know, though, that I might need springin'.'

'I'll call him from Judy's suite.'

'Thanks.'

The elevator doors were closing on Frank when the cops reached me.

'Well, well,' Hargrove said, 'look who's still in one piece.'

'I guess you must've heard from the LA cops already, huh?'

216

'You should come with us for a little talk, Eddie,' he said. 'Whataya say?'

'Lead on.'

'Damn,' Hargrove said, 'and here I was hopin' you'd resist.'

Sixty

They let me cool my heels for an hour or so in an interrogation room. That was OK with me; it gave me time to collect my thoughts.

When the door opened, Hargrove entered without his new partner, Holliday.

'Thought you'd at least bring me some coffee,' I complained.

'Sorry,' Hargrove said, 'we're not in the habit of supplying creature comforts.' He sat across from me and folded his arms.

'That's OK,' I said, sitting back. 'I don't expect to be here very long.'

'That's not up to you.'

'Well,' I said, 'I assume I'm not under arrest.'

'What makes you say that?'

I spread my hands. 'No cuffs.'

'Well,' Hargrove said, 'actually, you're just here for a little talk. Shouldn't take long at all.'

'Talk about what?'

'Murder.'

'I haven't even been in town for the past few days, and you want to pin a murder on me?'

'I'm talking about murder in LA.'

'Isn't that the job of the LA police?'

He grinned. 'Well, they gave me a call and asked me some questions – about you.'

'That must have made you happy,' I replied. 'What terrible things did you tell them about me?'

'I told Detective Franklin that you were a troublemaker,' he said. 'I told him anythin' bad that might be happenin' in LA while you were there was probably your fault.'

'You give me a lot of credit.'

'But rather than you killing somebody,' he went on, 'he told me somebody was tryin' to kill you. Seems somebody's put out an open contract on you.'

'Now that,' I said, 'must've made you laugh.'

'Actually,' he said, 'I'm still laughin'. But I don't want any innocent people gettin' killed while they're tryin' to kill you – like with a bomb.'

'So . . . what? You want me to leave town?'

'I want you to give me some idea who you think hates you enough to put a contract out,' Hargrove said. 'Maybe I can find them.'

'You're kiddin', right?'

'Why would I be kiddin'?'

'You hate me,' I said. 'You'd love it if somebody blew me up. Why would you go to any trouble to find out who's got it in for me?'

'I'd blow you up myself if I could figure out a way to get away with it,' he said, 'but I'd make sure no innocents got killed in the process. Now,' he leaned forward, 'who's on your list?'

'Well,' I said, 'you were at the top.'

'Who else?'

I thought a moment. 'Nope, that's it. Only you. And you're sayin' you didn't do it?'

'Not a chance.'

I shrugged. 'Then I'm stumped.'

'Come on, Eddie,' he said, 'you work for the mob. You've got to have some idea who'd put this kind of contract out on you.'

'I'm still tryin' to figure it out.'

'You and that big idiot from Brooklyn?'

I nodded. 'Me and Jerry.'

'And I'm sure your trained private dick friend is involved.'

'I'm usin' whatever resources I've got at my disposal, Hargrove,' I explained. 'I don't want any innocents to die, either.'

He nodded.

'Anythin' else?'

He pointed his finger at me. 'If you and your mob buddies make Las Vegas into a shooting gallery, I'll make you pay. Understand?'

I leaned forward in an attempt to give my words more gravity. 'I don't have any mob buddies.'

'Uh-huh.' He stood up.

'Can I go now?'

'Not just yet,' he said. 'I'll let you know.'

'Well, if you're gonna keep me here any longer, you might consider sendin' in some of those creature comforts you mentioned before.'

He went out the door without replying.

'Just a cup of coffee would be nice,' I called after him. 'Black, no sugar!'

He left, and I sat back, prepared to cool my heels a little longer.

Sixty-One

When I stepped outside I started to look for a cab, but instead my own car pulled up in front of the station with Jerry behind the wheel.

'How'd you know I was here?' I asked, getting in.

'Mr S. filled me in.'

'And how'd you know when I'd be comin' out?'

'From experience I figured that scumbag Hargrove would sweat you at least two hours.'

'So you figured it perfectly?' I said. 'I'm impressed.'

'Well, don't be,' he said, putting the car in drive, 'I was parked down the street for about half an hour.'

He pulled away from the curb, leaving some rubber in his haste to put some space between us and the police station.

'Somebody's on our tail,' Jerry said, a few minutes later.

'You sure?' I asked, twisting in my seat.

'I'm sure.'

I turned back around.

'Whataya wanna do?' he asked.

'I want to find out who it is and what he wants,' I said.

'And if he's got a gun?'

220

'Then he's your business.'

'All right! Where should we take him?'

'Where else?' I asked. 'Industrial Road.'

Industrial was off the main drag – lots of strip clubs, liquor stores and empty lots.

'Think he's gonna get wise?' Jerry asked. 'I mean, us leadin' him out here like this?'

'Maybe,' I said, 'or maybe he's got enough dollar signs dancin' in his head it makes no difference.'

'OK,' Jerry said, looking in the rear-view mirror, 'here he comes.'

I took a look. The guy was driving a Mercury Marauder, a big muscle car, and was speeding up.

'He's comin' up on your side, Mr G.,' Jerry said. 'You want my piece?'

'No,' I said, 'I'll shoot myself in the foot. I'm gonna depend on your drivin' ability.'

'Well, OK,' he said, 'but if he scratches this car, he's gonna be one sorry-ass hitman.'

'That's what I'm countin' on.'

We didn't know what he was waiting for.

He had increased his speed until he was practically right on us, and then he maintained. It was as if all he wanted was us to know he was there.

'This guy's gettin' on my nerves,' Jerry said. 'It's like he don't wanna catch us.'

'Let's see,' I said. 'Turn right on Grove.'

He did it. Grove was a stretch of empty lots, with the exception of a nursery school.

'Pull over.'

'Where?'

'Pass the nursery school . . . keep goin' . . . OK, right here.'

'It's an empty lot.'

'Right. Pull over. Let's see what he does.'

We braked immediately, pulling over to the curb in front of a vacant lot that was just dirt – no grass, gravel or even a fence.

We both turned to look at the car which also pulled over right behind us. Nobody got out.

'What's he doin'?' Jerry asked.

'He's doin' the same thing we are,' I said. 'He's waitin'.'

'For what? He's got a clear shot.'

'If that's what he wants,' I said.

Jerry filled his right fist with his .45 and reached for the door.

'Hold it!' I put my hand on his arm. 'Somebody's gettin' out of the car.'

'One guy or two?' he asked.

'One,' I said. 'Driver's side.'

'I'll get 'im when he comes closer—'

'Jerry,' I said, 'put the gun away.'

'What?'

'Stash it. Now!'

Jerry reached down and stuck the gun underneath his seat. As the man came closer, I noticed he had something in his hand, but it wasn't a gun.

'Eddie Gianelli?' he asked. He was medium height, in his late thirties, wearing a brown suit with a beige tie. Very plain.

'That's right.'

He showed me what he had in his hand. It was a wallet with an ID. I leaned into Jerry to take a look.

222

'FBI?'

'That's right,' the man said. 'Agent Seagrave. Can we talk?'

'Get back in your car and follow us, Agent Seagrave,' I said, 'and we'll talk.'

Sixty-Two

I wanted neutral ground, so we didn't take him to the Sands or to my house.

'Where to, Mr G.?' Jerry asked.

'The Golden Nugget.'

'Why there?'

'One of the best-known and busiest casinos in town,' I said. 'And pretty far from the Sands, where Judy is.'

'Neutral ground?'

'Exactly.'

'You think this guy is on the level?'

'Well,' I said, 'he could've shot us. And his ID looked real.'

'You ever seen a real FBI ID?' Jerry asked.

'No.'

'I have,' Jerry said. 'When we get there, I'll take a good look.'

We pulled in behind the Nugget.

'Leave the gun,' I said, as he reached under the seat.

'Why?'

'If he's legit and he catches you carrying—'

223

'I'll take the chance, Mr G.,' he said, tucking the gun into his belt, behind his back where his sports jacket would cover it.

'OK,' I said. 'Have it your way.'

We got out of the car, met up with Agent Seagrave behind it.

'Can I see that ID?' Jerry asked.

'Of course,' Seagrave said. He took it out and handed it to Jerry. The big man studied it, then flipped to the man's driver's license, studied that, too. He handed it back.

'OK?'

'So far,' Jerry said. 'Don't you jokers usually travel in pairs?'

Seagrave smiled.

'The other joker is otherwise engaged,' Seagrave said. 'Besides, I didn't think I'd have any trouble with you fellas. I only want to talk. Is here good?'

'Inside,' I said.

'Lead the way.'

I did, but Jerry took up the rear, keeping Seagrave between us.

Inside, I paused, but Jerry said, 'It's dinner time.'

'Yeah,' I said, 'it is.'

'I could eat,' Seagrave said.

I didn't want to hit any of the major restaurants in the Nugget, so I led the way to the lounge.

'We're eatin' here?' Jerry asked.

'They have a good menu,' I said.

'As long as they have something,' Agent Seagrave said.

I waved over a waitress who happened to recognize me.

'Hey, Eddie G. in the Nugget. What brings you here, handsome? Recruitin' for the Sands?'

'If I was, I'd snatch you up, Molly,' I said. 'We just need drinks and somethin' to eat.'

Molly gave Jerry an appraising look and said, 'I'm glad we don't have a buffet up. You look like you could do some damage.'

'You got that right, lady,' Jerry said.

'Whataya need, Eddie?'

'Three beers and some appetizers would be OK.'

'Comin' up.' She flounced away.

'Waitresses at the other casinos know you?' Seagrave asked.

'Mr G. gets around,' Jerry said.

'Speakin' of gettin' around,' I said, 'you might wanna tell us why you were tailin' us.'

Seagrave grinned. 'Who'd you think I was?' he asked. 'Another hitter trying to cash in?'

'What were we supposed to think?' I asked.

'So that's why you were leading me to the middle of nowhere? You were going to take me out?'

'If we had to,' Jerry said.

Seagrave pointed his finger at Jerry. He was about my height, maybe even a little less than six feet, and slender. It wasn't a very threatening move. 'You wouldn't even want to bruise an FBI agent, Jack.'

'The name's Jerry,' the big man said, 'and try me. I'd do a lot more than bruise ya.'

'You wouldn't be carrying, would you, Tough Guy?'

'Trying searchin' me,' Jerry invited.

225

They glared at each other.

'OK, OK,' I said, 'let's cut the crap. What do you want, Seagrave?'

Molly came with the three mugs of beer, and we waited while she set them down, giving us a good look at some generous cleavage. Seagrave took full advantage.

When she was gone, Seagrave took a moment to down some beer.

'OK,' I said, 'what's the big idea?'

'You and your friend here walked in on something in LA, Eddie,' Seagrave said, 'and all of a sudden, people started to die. That sort of got us pissed initially, but then we got curious.'

'And?'

'We're the FBI,' he said. 'We poked around a bit and found out about the open contract.'

'So you weren't watchin' us in LA because of the contract?'

'Hell, no,' Seagrave said. 'We were working on something else.'

'That we walked into?' I asked. 'The only thing we went to LA to do was help Judy Garland out with something.' I leaned forward. 'FBI not investigating Judy, are they?'

Before he could answer, Molly returned with a couple of platters of finger food. Both Seagrave and Jerry reached for them immediately. Luckily, they each went for a different platter.

'No,' he said, around a pig-in-a-blanket, 'not Judy Garland.'

'Who, then?'

He sat back and licked his fingers. 'OK, you didn't hear this from me.'

226

'We ain't heard nothin' from you, so far,' Jerry said.

'Yeah, OK,' Seagrave said, 'settle down, Godzilla.'

'That the best insult you got?' Jerry asked. 'I heard 'em all.'

'Jesus,' I said, 'don't make me send you both to a damn neutral corner.'

'Sorry, Mr G.,' Jerry said. 'I don't like this guy.'

'I'll try to cope,' Seagrave said, grabbing what looked like some kind of potato puff.

'Let's have the whole story, Seagrave,' I said, 'before I walk away and let you deal with Jerry one-on-one.'

Jerry looked real happy at that prospect.

'We've had some reports about the business practices of Miss Garland's management team, Freddie Fields and Dave Begelman,' he said. 'We're looking into it.'

'Why's the FBI interested in some actress being cheated by her manager?'

'Could be these boys are breaking some banking laws,' Seagrave said. 'Also, if they're doing some skimming, that's embezzlement, and that interests us.'

'How long has this investigation been goin' on?'

'Months.'

'Then it must have been in place when Begelman told Judy somebody was blackmailin' her.'

'It was.'

'So you knew about that photo?'

'We knew there was something going on

227

between Begelman and the PI, Jacks,' Seagrave said. 'We didn't know if a photo really existed. We were going to go after Jacks and see if we could get him to flip on Begelman, but then he disappeared – until he turned up dead the other day in a house in the canyon, along with his girl.' He leaned forward. 'You fellas wouldn't know anything about that, would you?'

'Not a thing,' I said, reaching for a chip and stuffing it into my mouth.

Sixty-Three

'We know you snatched Judy Garland away to Vegas,' Seagrave said. 'Is she at the Sands?'

'Do you have any reason to bother her?'

'We've been talking with Sid Luft, who apparently is going to represent her when she sues her management team.'

'Does she know you've been talkin' to Luft?' I asked.

'I don't know,' he said. 'That's between them.'

'So you were tailin' us to find her?' I asked.

'Not exactly,' Seagrave said. 'More like we wanted to see what you were up to.'

'Why didn't you just ask?' I said.

'That ain't the way the FBI works, Mr G.,' Jerry said.

'And what would you know about the way we work?' Seagrave asked.

Jerry just glared at him.

'Jerry?' I prodded.

'They never do anythin' the easy way, Mr G.,' Jerry said. 'And if they can mess things up, they will.'

'Now wait just a minute—'

'Are you gonna say you've never messed anythin' up?' I asked him.

'Well . . . everybody makes mistakes . . . but what he's saying isn't—'

'Just come out and tell us what you want to know, Agent Seagrave,' I suggested. 'We have to get on with our day.'

'What specifically are you doing for Miss Garland?'

'That's between us and her.'

'Does it have anything to do with possible embezzlement?'

I didn't answer.

'OK, then, where is she?'

I kept silent.

'At the Sands? In the hotel?'

'Look,' I said, 'if you're talkin' to Sid Luft and he's representin' her, then why do you need to see Judy?'

'We just want to . . . ask her a few questions.'

'Ask Sid Luft,' I said. 'I'm not gonna let you bother Judy Garland. I'm not gonna let you . . . drag her through the press, cause her unnecessary publicity – bad publicity.'

'What makes you think—'

'How else would it look if it got out that she was being investigated by the FBI,' I asked, 'but bad?'

229

'OK,' Seagrave said. 'How about this? You ask Miss Garland if she wants to talk to us. Let her make the decision. Whataya say?'

I hesitated, then said, 'I'll mention it, if I happen to see her.'

'That'll do for now.' He stood up. 'Oh, just to cover all the bases . . . neither of you has killed anybody in the last . . . say . . . week?'

'No,' I said, 'I don't kill people.'

He looked at Jerry.

'Not this week,' the big man said.

Seagrave snorted, looked at me, pointed at Jerry and said, 'He's a riot.' He started away, then turned back. 'You'll hear from me, again.'

'Next time, just call,' I said to his retreating back.

'Next time he follows us like that, I'll put a bullet in him,' Jerry said.

'What would that accomplish?'

'I don't like him,' he said. 'It would just make me feel good.'

'I getcha.'

'Are you gonna tell Miss Garland it's the FBI that's been watchin' her?'

'I don't think they broke into her house and looked in her underwear drawer,' I replied.

'So . . . maybe that didn't really happen?'

I looked at him. He was probably right. If she noticed she was being watched, her imagination could have conjured up the rest of it. Could I tell her about the FBI and then convince her that no one had entered her house? And between me and Sid Luft – and the FBI – could we convince her there had never been any blackmail? And that she should probably go ahead and sever her relationship with Fields and Begelman, then sue them.

But it would probably be best to do all that a little at a time . . .

'You gonna eat any more of this food?' I asked.

Jerry looked down at it and said, 'Finger food,' as if it was a dirty phrase. Then he looked at me. 'Ain't the Horseshoe down the block?'

'Yep, it is,' I said. 'But let's go back to the Sands and take Judy to dinner – that is, if Frank hasn't beaten us to it.'

'OK, Mr G.,' he said. 'Sounds good.'

Frank answered Judy's door. 'Hey, guys.'

'Thought you might have gone to dinner already,' I said.

'I suggested it,' he said. 'She said she wanted to wait for you. Seems you've made a pretty good impression on her.' He looked past me at Jerry. 'Both of you.'

'Good to hear,' I said.

'Come on in,' Frank said. 'Now that you're here, I've gotta get going. I just didn't want to leave her alone.'

'Is she OK?' I asked.

'She's fine,' he said. 'A little jumpy. She wanted to call that fella Herron, said you didn't want her to. I suggested she wait until you got back.'

'Where is she?'

'In the bathroom.' Judy had often said the bathroom was the only room she felt safe in.

'How do you know she's not on the phone right now?'

231

'I don't,' he said, picking his sports jacket up off the sofa. 'But I couldn't sit on her shoulder.'

'No,' I said, 'that's my job.'

'Favor,' he reminded me. 'That's your favor, pally. Remember?'

'I remember.'

I walked to the door with him.

'So you're still planning on talking to Momo about the contract?'

I nodded.

'I'll set it up, but I doubt Momo had anything to do with it, Eddie.'

'Guess I won't feel sure until I ask. If not him, maybe he knows who did.'

'If it's a good contract, it'd have to go through him,' Frank said. 'If it didn't, he's gonna be pissed. Once you tell him, Eddie, and he tells you it didn't go through him, he'll find out who did.'

'Then I guess I should've asked him from the start,' I said.

'There aren't too many people who'd have the nerve to ask Momo somethin' like that,' Frank said. 'I got a lot of respect for you, but it's gonna double if you do that.'

'I'll try to suck it up.'

He reached out, patted me on the arm, then left the room. I turned and looked at Jerry.

'You got balls, Mr G.,' he said, 'if you're gonna ask Mr Giancana about the contract.'

'I don't know, Jerry,' I said, 'but maybe we're gonna find out, huh?'

Sixty-Four

On the one hand, it wouldn't be unusual for someone like Judy Garland to be spotted in Las Vegas. On the other hand, how safe was she with me?

'Jerry,' I said, while we waited for Judy to come out of the bathroom, 'why don't you take Judy to dinner?'

'Without you?'

'She'll probably be safer that way.'

'Mr G.,' he said, 'I gotta stay with you.'

'I'll be OK,' I promised. 'I'll stay inside—'

'A pro ain't gonna let somethin' like that stop him,' Jerry said.

'Maybe not.'

'I gotta watch your back, Mr G.,' he said in a no-nonsense tone.

'Yeah,' I said, 'well . . . my other idea is we have dinner right here.'

'Room service?' he said.

'Right.'

'I like room service.'

'Did somebody say room service?' Judy asked, entering the room. 'I'm hungry.'

We turned and looked at her. She appeared neat in a white shirt, black capri pants and a pair of black slippers. Her hair looked wet, as if she'd washed her hands and run them through it. Her eye make-up and red lipstick had been meticulously applied.

'Were you on the phone?' I asked.

'I – uh, no.'

Who would have thought that an actress of Judy Garland's caliber would be such a bad liar.

'You called Herron?'

'I just had to talk to him, Eddie,' she said. 'I just had to.'

'Did you tell him where you are?'

'No. He asked, but I didn't tell him, honest I didn't.' Her wide-eyed innocence convinced me.

'All right,' I said. 'Jerry and I figured to have a room service dinner.'

'We can't go out?'

'I think we're all safer inside, Judy,' I said, 'for now. Believe me, I can get a helluva spread brought up here.'

She smiled and said, 'Prove it!'

'Ah,' I said, 'A challenge. OK, wait and see.'

I went to the phone. When room service picked up, I said, 'This is Eddie G. in Judy Garland's suite. I want the works.'

The works was shrimp cocktail, soups, salads, steak-and-lobster, all kinds of vegetables – and champagne. It took three bellhops and three carts.

I had called Jack, but he said he couldn't join us for dinner. I told him we would get over it. I also asked him to have the house doctor come up and change our bandages. He said he'd get him right there.

Dr Abe Sandborn came up and got us cleaned and rebandaged before the food got there. In fact, he passed the bellhops on the way out and looked longingly at the trays.

'I'm impressed,' Judy said as we sat down to eat.

Jerry made a bigger dent in the fare than Judy and I did, but that was to be expected. I ate my share, but Judy just picked and stared into her plate, despite professing her hunger earlier.

'How's Herron?' I asked.

Her head jerked up. 'Hm? Oh, Mark? He's . . . confused. He thought we'd be married by now.'

'He's in a hurry,' Jerry said.

'Actually,' she said, 'we got married once already, on a ship. Only I was foolish – I hadn't realized that my marriage to Sid hadn't been dissolved.'

Jerry and I exchanged a glance. How could she have not known that? Maybe it was just wishful thinking.

She shrugged, as if it was of no importance. 'I told him not to worry,' she said. 'We'll be getting married – for real.'

Jerry and I didn't look at her.

'You boys don't approve of Mark, do you?' she asked.

'Honest?' Jerry asked.

She nodded. 'Honest.'

'I don't like him.'

'Why not, Jerry?'

'He ain't good enough for you,'

'That's sweet,' she said, 'but you must have a reason.'

We had a reason, but it wasn't one we wanted to reveal. I also believed it was one she already knew. It was a known fact she'd already been married to one homosexual man.

'He rubs us the wrong way,' I said, hoping she'd accept that.

She looked at me. 'I guess I understand that. I've heard the same from other friends of mine. But I've made up my own mind about Mark. I'm going to marry him.'

'Well,' I said, 'after this is all over and we all return to our everyday lives, the wedding can go on.'

Jerry grabbed another lobster tail. 'These are better than anythin' I've had in Sheepshead Bay,' he announced.

'Only the best for the Sands,' I said, cutting into my steak.

Sixty-Five

After dinner, Jerry played gin with Judy while I got on the phone. Jack wasn't in his office this late, so I called his suite.

'Where are you?' he asked.

'Judy's room.'

'And Frank?'

'He had somethin' to do,' I said. 'He's goin' back to Tahoe in the morning . . . unless I ask him not to.'

'And why would you do that?'

'I might want to talk to Momo, Jack.'

'Momo? About what? Oh, wait. You're not thinkin' he put this hit out on you, are you?'

'I don't know,' I said, 'but I think I'd like to ask him. That is, unless you already have?'

'I don't have those kind of balls, Eddie,' Jack said. 'I've asked around, but nobody seems to know anything.'

'All the more reason for me to ask him,' I said. 'Frank said he'd arrange it.'

'Eddie . . . Sam Giancana is . . . unpredictable.'

'Tell me somethin' I don't know.'

'If he put out this contract, he had a reason. And if you confront him, he might kill you on the spot.'

'Well, at least I'd know why.'

'But if he didn't commission this contract, he's gonna be pissed that somebody did.'

'And maybe he can find out who.'

'And you think all you have to do is ask him?'

'I think,' I said, 'I don't have any other choice.'

After talking with Jack, I tried Danny's office.

'I'm sorry, Eddie,' he said, sounding sadder than I'd ever heard him. 'I'm just comin' up empty. Somebody put the lid down on this contract.'

'That's OK, Danny,' I said. 'I've pretty much decided what I have to do.'

'You goin' straight to the horse's mouth?' he asked.

'Yep,' I said. 'Giancana.'

'Want me to go with you?'

'Thanks, but no. Frank's gonna arrange it.'

'You takin' Jerry?'

'That depends,' I said. 'I might want to leave him here with Judy.'

'Well, if you decide to take 'im, I can look after her.'

'Now that offer is one I might take you up on. I'll call you tomorrow, when I know more.'

'I'm sorry again, Eddie.'

'Hey, man, you did your best,' I said. 'The info's just not out there.'

'Gimme a call, Eddie,' Danny said. 'I'll do whatever I can to help.'

'Stay by a phone,' I said, and hung up.

I looked over to where Judy was laughing at Jerry because she'd schneided him. The big man was frowning. I picked up the phone and dialed the front desk.

'Hey, Eddie, what can I do for you?' a desk clerk named Brandon asked.

'I have to leave a message for Mr Sinatra,' I said, 'and he needs to get it before he checks out.'

'OK. What's the message?'

'Just have it say "I'll take you up on the offer of your plane",' I said. 'He'll know what it means.'

'And where will you be?'

'I'll be stayin' over,' I said. 'He'll find me in the building.'

'OK, Eddie. I'll make sure he gets it.'

'Thanks, Brandon.'

I hung up, looked over at Judy and Jerry. Now they were both laughing. I couldn't remember the last time I'd seen Jerry laugh like that. I caught his eye and beckoned him over to me.

'Judy, would you like some coffee?' I asked.

She collected the cards and said, 'I think I'd like some tea.'

'I'll take coffee,' Jerry said, 'and some pie.'

'In a minute,' I said, lowering my voice. 'I'm

gonna have Frank arrange a meet with Giancana. His plane will take me there.'

'Will Mr S. go with you?'

'I doubt it,' I said. 'I don't want him stickin' his neck out.'

'I'll go with you, then,' Jerry said. 'But what about Miss Garland?'

'Danny offered to sit with her.'

He shrugged. 'Suits me. When do you wanna go?'

'As soon as Frank can arrange it.'

'OK.'

'Jerry . . . are you sure you wanna go with me?'

'Sure I'm sure, Mr G.,' he said. 'Why would you ask?'

'It's possible Momo put the contract out on me,' I said. 'I wouldn't want to put you in a . . . bad position.'

Jerry frowned. 'Are you sayin' you think I'd pick up that contract?' he asked.

'That's not what I'm sayin', at all,' I replied. 'I just . . . I know who you work for, Jerry. I don't want to get you into trouble.'

'I may work for Mr Giancana, Mr G.,' Jerry said, 'but you're my friend.'

I stared at him, looked into his eyes, then touched him on the arm. 'Apple or cherry?'

Sixty-Six

When the phone rang the next morning, I checked the time before answering it. It was six a.m.

'Yeah?' I held the receiver in my right hand. I sat up gingerly, because my new bandages were pulling on my skin.

'Be in the lobby at eight,' Frank said. 'Momo is expecting you.'

'Frank—'

'I won't be going with you.'

'I didn't think you would.'

'Will someone?'

'Jerry.'

There was some hesitation, then Frank asked, 'Do you trust him?'

'Completely.'

'You know who pays him.'

'Yes.'

'I hope you know what you're doing, Eddie.'

I sat up in bed and rubbed my other hand over my face vigorously. 'So do I, Frank.'

I woke Jerry and he made it down to the lobby before I did.

'How do you do that?' I asked.

'Do what?' he asked.

'Look awake at this time of the morning.'

'Awake ain't a problem,' he said. 'I'm hungry. Do we get to eat?'

'On the way,' I said, starting through the lobby to the front door.

'On the way where?' he asked, rushing to catch up.

Before I could answer the question, things started to happen. I didn't see the beginning, but Jerry did . . .

* * *

240

I was heading for the door. Jerry was coming up behind and saw a man across the lobby raising a gun. Some other people saw him, too, and hit the floor, but Jerry started running. He dove for me, hit me in the small of the back and took me down as the man started firing. The shots went over us, I heard glass breaking and then I got a good bump on the head when it came in contact with the floor . . .

'Mr G.? Hey, come on, wake up!'

Somebody was slapping me on the cheek – hard. I opened my eyes.

'Jerry? What happened?'

'I'll tell you later,' he said. 'We gotta get out of here.'

'Wha—' He grabbed me by the front of my jacket and pulled me to my feet. I looked around at the hotel lobby, which was in a state of disarray. 'What the fuck?'

'Somebody took a shot at you, Mr G.,' he said. 'In fact, more than one shot.'

I looked around. 'Who? Where?'

'He's gone.'

'Did you see him?'

He shook his head. 'I didn't get a good look. I was too busy takin' you down.'

'You – you saved my life?'

'I dunno,' Jerry said. 'He was a pretty bad shot. Not a pro.'

'Anybody get hurt? I thought I heard glass—'

'Yeah, he broke some windows, but nobody got hit. Look, we gotta get outta here before the cops show up. Where were we goin'?'

'To the airport,' I said. 'We're takin' Frank's plane to see Sam Giancana.'

'Then we better hurry, or the only thing we're gonna see over the next few hours is the inside of a police station.'

I opened my mouth to speak, but he practically carried me through the front doors.

Sixty-Seven

Frank's plane had taken us to O'Hare, where he had a car pick us up and take us to Oak Park, where Sam Giancana had lived with his wife in a two-story brick house, raised their three daughters, and still lived since her passing.

'Mr Sinatra said I should wait,' the driver said, as we pulled up in front.

'Then you should,' I said, opening the door.

'How long?'

I had one foot out, turned to look at him again. 'Until we come out,' I said, 'or until you hear shooting.'

'Shooting?' he said as we got out of the car.

We walked up to the front door and knocked. Two torpedoes opened it. I don't know if they and Jerry knew each other, but they recognized each other for what they were and nodded.

'Sorry,' one of them said to Jerry, not me, 'got to pat you both down.'

'No problem,' Jerry assured him.

The speaker checked Jerry while his partner

242

patted me down thoroughly. All they came up with was Jerry's .45.

'Get it back when you leave,' the first one said, tucking it into his belt.

'Right,' Jerry said.

'OK, this way.'

They led us through the house to Giancana's den, where the man known as Sam Gold, Mooney and Momo – among other names – waited, wearing his trademark dark glasses and a suit. He had a drink in his hand and turned to face us as we entered.

'Eddie,' he said, and nodded at the big guy. 'Hello, Jerry.'

'Mr Giancana,' Jerry said.

'Momo,' I said, trying to establish us as friends from the beginning.

'OK, boys,' he said to his men, 'you can a-go.'

'But sir—' one of them started. Momo cut him off with a wave of his hand.

'I am very safe with these two gents,' Giancana said, 'especially Jerry, who I know carries a very big forty-five.'

'They took it away from me,' Jerry said.

'Did they?' He stared at his men. 'Who's got-a his gun?'

'I do,' the first gunsel said.

'Give it back to him.'

'But—'

'Give-a him his gun, *stronzo*!'

The man lowered his head, removed Jerry's gun from his belt and handed it over. Jerry ejected the cylinder to check the loads and then stuck it in his belt.

'Now get out!' Giancana snapped.

The two men slunk out.

'*Testa di cazzo!*' Giancana swore, for good measure. Jerry told me later it meant 'dickhead'.

'You guys wanna drink?' he asked us. 'Jerry, you know where the bar is.'

'Yes, sir. Bourbon, Mr G.?' he asked me.

'Sure.'

As Jerry walked to the bar to make the drink, Giancana took off his jacket and put it on the back of a chair. He had his sleeves rolled up by the time Jerry handed me my drink, and stood next to me holding his own.

'Frank says-a you need to talk to me, Eddie,' Giancana said. 'So talk.'

I figured he knew why I was there, but wanted to hear it from me, so I told him about the attempts on my life and how word had gone out that there was a contract.

'Somebody tried for you right in the Sands?' he asked.

'The lobby,' I said, 'this morning.'

'*Pezzo di merda,*' he said. That one I'd heard before in my youth, from my father. Piece of shit.

'I don't know who wants me dead that badly – except maybe a cop.'

'What cop?'

'This Vegas detective named Hargrove.'

'That one! He is *cagacazzo*. So dumb! And no balls.'

'That's what I thought,' I said. 'And the only other one I could think of was . . .'

244

'Who?'

'Jimmy Roselli.'

'Now that *cretino* – he's-a just idiot enough to do it.'

'You haven't heard anything about it?' I asked.

'It was-a not cleared through me, Eddie,' he said tightly. 'I'll check on Jimmy Roselli. If it was-a him, I'll have-a his balls.' You knew Momo was getting agitated when his accent thickened.

'And if it wasn't?'

'Do you want me to find out who it is?' Giancana asked. 'Is that what-a you askin' me?'

I knew that if I said yes, I was asking Momo for a favor, and I'd owe him one in return.

'Yes, Mr Giancana, that's what I'm asking you.'

'*Menache!*' he said. Oh, hell. 'Of course I will help you, Eddie.' He waved his arms in a magnanimous gesture. 'What are friends-a for? Besides, Frank already asked me to help. How could I ever tell-a him no, eh?' He stood up. 'So, you stay to eat? We're having spaghetti and-a meatballs.'

'Oh, we can't,' I said. 'Frank's plane is waiting to take us back. He needs it—'

'*Ah,* never mind. Come, I walk-a you to the door.'

He didn't quite go all the way to the door. He'd never expose himself that way. He stopped in the entry foyer, where his two torpedoes were waiting. Once there, he put his hand on my shoulder and gave Jerry a curt nod goodbye.

'You'll hear from me, Eddie,' he said. 'Soon. Until then, stay low, eh? Don't get-a your head shot off.'

245

'I'll do my best, Momo,' I said. 'My very best.'

I had considered briefly asking him if he knew a man named Amico, but decided against it. If Amico worked for him, he probably wouldn't say. Then he'd have to explain why he pretended not to know about the contract.

Or would he?

When we got in the car, I asked Jerry, 'What was that thing he said?' Most of my Italian had gone the way of my youth. '*Ti voglio un mondo di bene.*'

'He said he wishes us a world of good,' Jerry said. 'He likes you, Mr G.'

'*Us*, Jerry,' I said, 'he likes us . . . and thank God for that.'

Sixty-Eight

The driver took us straight back to the airport, and Frank's plane had us back in Vegas before daylight. We went to our rooms to get some sleep, agreeing to meet in the Garden Café for breakfast in a few hours. When I got to my room, I checked for messages. There was one from Frank, asking me to call him when I got in. I decided to give him a break, let him sleep and call him in the morning. Judy was asleep in her room, with Danny looking out for her.

I tossed and turned a while, going over everything that had been happening since someone first tried to run me down. I also replayed the conversation Jerry and I had in the plane on the way to Chicago . . .

'We haven't talked about what happened at the Sands,' I said. 'You saved me.'

'Again,' he reminded me.

'Yes, again,' I said, 'but you dragged me out of there before the cops arrived.'

'I thought it was a good idea,' Jerry said. 'We never would've been able to go and see Mr Giancana with them there.'

'You're probably right,' I said, 'but somebody's gonna want to talk to us when we get back.'

'Maybe not. Maybe when the cops got there, nobody told them about you or me.'

'No offense, Jerry, but you're not exactly hard to miss.'

'Yeah, but, Mr G., by the time the cops get there – got there – a lot of the witnesses might have been gone. The ones who don't work there, anyway.'

'You're right, and maybe the employees would keep quiet until they hear from me, or Jack.'

'Maybe . . .'

'And maybe the cops'll be waitin' for us at the airport, in the person of Hargrove.'

But they weren't.

I finally fell asleep. When I woke, I called Frank's suite and invited him to have breakfast with Jerry and me at ten.

'I'll be there,' he promised.

Next, I dialed Jack Entratter's office.

'What the fuck?' he said when he heard my voice.

'What the hell happened yesterday? The local news covered the "shooting in a local casino".'

'Somebody took a couple of shots at me in the lobby.'

'That's what I figured, but where'd you go?'

'To the airport,' I said. 'I had to see Momo. If I'd stayed, Hargrove would have kept me on ice for hours. In fact, he still might.'

'Well, you don't have to worry, so far,' he said. 'He was here, but he didn't find any witnesses. Players and guests who might have seen you took off before he arrived, and I managed to muzzle the employees. But he definitely wants to talk to both of you.'

'Was anybody else hurt?'

'No, just some shattered glass. But when I told him you were out of town, I don't think he believed me.'

'Well, I was, technically.'

'After the fact.'

'He can't prove I was there.'

'He might be able to find one customer who saw you, or Jerry.'

'Until then he can't prove a thing.'

'That won't stop him from questioning you.'

'I'll be ready.'

'What happened with Momo?'

'It wasn't him.'

'Are you sure?'

'Fairly sure.'

'And he didn't know who it was?'

'No, but I think he was pretty pissed off about it,' I said. 'He'll probably find out. He'll let me know if he does.'

'Or he'll take care of them himself.'

'Either way,' I said, 'I'll be off the hit list . . . but I'd really like to know who put the contract out on me. And what I did to deserve it.'

'I'm kind of curious about that myself, Eddie,' he said. 'What's on your agenda today?'

'Breakfast,' I said, 'with Jerry and Frank, and then I'll go and talk to Judy.'

'What's happening there?'

'I think I've got some answers for her,' I said. 'I just don't think she's gonna like 'em.'

'Poor kid's got enough problems,' Jack said. 'Maybe a little truth from you wouldn't hurt.'

'We could all use a little truth, Jack.'

'Amen,' he said. 'Personally, I'd like to see you get back to work without having to look over your shoulder, so do what you gotta do, Eddie.'

'That's the plan,' I said, and hung up.

Sixty-Nine

When I got to the café, Jerry and Frank were already drinking coffee. I slid into the booth next to Frank, who scooted over.

'You fellas order yet?'

'No,' Frank said, 'Jerry wanted to wait for you.'

The waitress spotted me and hurried over. Her name tag said 'Betty'. I'd never seen her before.

'The gang's all here, then?' she asked. Her accent was British.

'Yep,' Jerry said, 'we're ready to order.'

249

Frank and I ordered bacon and eggs – scrambled for me, sunny side up for him. Jerry ordered ham-and-eggs and a stack of pancakes. We all wanted toast.

'Be back in a jiff,' she said, and hurried away, her dark ponytail bouncing.

'She's cute,' Frank said. 'I love that accent.'

There was a pot of coffee on the table and I poured myself a cup.

'So, OK,' Frank said, 'what happened with Momo?'

I looked at Jerry.

'I didn't say nothin',' he said. 'Figured it was up to you.'

I told Frank what I had told Jack: that Momo wasn't behind the contract, didn't know who was, but said he would find out.

'He will, too,' Frank said. 'I wouldn't wanna be the guy when he does. When was the last attempt?'

'Yesterday morning, when we were on our way to the airport,' I said.

'Guy made a clumsy try in the lobby,' Jerry said, 'fired a couple of wild shots.'

'Doesn't sound like a pro,' Frank observed.

'As a matter of fact,' Jerry said, looking at me, 'none of 'em have been by a pro. Even the bomb in the car was clumsy.'

Frank pointed his finger at Jerry. 'Say you're a button man. You hear about an open contract, but you know it hasn't been cleared through San Giancana, and it should be. What do you do?'

'I stay away from it,' Jerry said. 'Don't want no part of it.'

'So no pro would pick it up,' I said.

'Not unless he wanted to stick his neck way out,' Frank said.

'So far a buncha amateurs have tried to cash in,' Jerry observed, 'but it would only take one pro lookin' for a big payoff.'

'So most pros might be staying away from it,' Frank said. 'You're not out of the woods yet, though.'

'But your odds just got better,' Jerry said, as Betty appeared with a bunch of plates.

We sat back and allowed her to set them down.

'Anything else?' she asked.

'We're good,' I said.

She smiled brightly. 'Just let me know.'

As she walked away, we quickly moved the plates around the table – she had gotten the placement all wrong.

'Still cute,' Frank said, 'but a bad waitress.'

'Just new,' Jerry offered. 'She'll learn.'

We started to eat, but kept talking.

'What about Judy's problem?' Frank asked.

'I think we've got that beat,' I said. 'It's just a matter of getting her to understand.'

'You need me for that?' he asked.

'No,' I said, 'I think I've got it. Danny's been with her since we left.'

'She's vulnerable, Eddie—' Frank started, but I cut him off.

'Danny wouldn't try anything, Frank,' I said.

'No,' Frank said, 'of course not. Sorry. So, is there any reason I shouldn't go back to Tahoe?'

'No,' I said, 'none that I can see. Judy's safe here. Momo's gonna come up with the answer on the contract thing—'

251

'Just for fun,' Frank said, interrupting me, 'what if he doesn't?'

'What?' Jerry asked.

'What if Giancana comes up empty?'

'But—' Jerry said.

'If someone out there has a contract out on me,' I said, 'and Sam Giancana can't find out who it is, I guess I'd be in real trouble.'

'As opposed to the trouble you're in now.'

'It would be worse, though,' Jerry said.

'Could there be somebody in organized crime who's not afraid of Sam Giancana?' I asked.

'The new breed,' Frank said. 'Idiots like Johnny Roselli.'

'Roselli,' I said. 'He doesn't like me.'

'Do you want me to talk to Johnny?' Frank asked.

'If it's him,' I said, 'that would be the same as warnin' him that we know. Let's just see what Momo can come up with – for now.'

'OK,' Frank said, 'then it's back to Tahoe for me.'

We finished eating and waited while Betty cleared the table, then we all had more coffee. When we were done, Frank wanted out, so I moved to allow him to stand. He grabbed my hand.

'Thanks for helping Judy, Eddie. In spite of having your own problem to solve.'

'Sure, Frank.'

'Let me know when you take Judy back home,' he said. 'And what the final outcome is.'

'Sure,' I said, again.

'Big Jerry,' Frank said, with a nod.

252

'Mr S.'

Frank turned and left the café. I sat back down, shook the coffee pot to see if there was any left. I managed another half cup.

Jerry looked around for Betty. 'I think I'll have a chocolate shake.'

'Then I'll get another pot of coffee,' I said, as Betty came over.

By the time Jerry's shake was gone I'd gone through half the pot. I pushed the rest of it away from me.

'What now?' he asked.

'I'm not sure,' I said. 'I'm guessin' we're gonna have to talk to Hargrove sooner or later about the shootin'.'

'We could avoid him for a while,' Jerry said.

'That'd just piss him off even more,' I said. 'I'm not sayin' we go in and see him or anythin', I'm just sayin' we don't hide out. Jack says he's lookin' for us.'

'So what do we do until he finds us?'

'Let's start with seein' how Judy's doin',' I said. 'Maybe give Danny a break.'

I called Betty over, told her to let me have the check.

'That's OK, Mr Gianelli,' she said. 'Mr Sinatra already took care of it.'

'Well,' I said, 'that's good for you, because he's a much bigger tipper than I am.'

'You said it!' she said, then her face fell as she thought she might have insulted me. 'I mean, not that you're a bad tipper – I mean, I don't know how you tip—'

253

'That's OK, kid,' I said. 'Relax. You better get back to work.'

'Yes, sir.'

As we left the café, Jerry said, 'I think she's gonna last.'

'The waitresses here come and go more than the showgirls do.'

As we headed for the lobby, I saw Jack's new girl hurrying in our direction. When she spotted us, her mouth opened and she quickened her pace.

'Oh, Mr Gianelli,' she said. 'Mr Entratter said I'd find you in the Garden Café.'

'As a matter of fact we just left there,' I said. 'What's up?'

'Mr Entratter sent me to tell you,' she said, 'or warn you, that the police are in his office, asking about you.'

'The police? Or Detective Hargrove?'

'I believe that's what he said his name was,' she said. 'He's there with another man.'

'No uniforms?'

'No, sir,' she said, 'just the two men in suits.'

I looked at Jerry, who said, 'If he was lookin' to take us in, he'd have more help with him.'

'Agreed,' I said. I looked at the girl. 'Why don't we go up and see if those guys are still there?'

'Mr Entratter told me that you might want to . . . avoid them?'

'He was right,' I said. 'We might have wanted to avoid them, but we've pretty much changed our minds. And they're probably givin' Jack a hard time right now. Whataya say we go up and rescue him?'

'Yes, sir,' she said, 'whatever you say.'

254

Seventy

It was noon by the time we got to Jack's office. Hargrove and his partner were still with Jack. We could hear his big mouth out in the hall.

'. . . tell him he's gonna be in big trouble if he doesn't come and see me,' Hargrove was bellowing.

'Lower your voice, Detective,' Jack shot back. 'I don't appreciate bein' yelled at in my own office.'

'Let me tell you something—' Hargrove was saying as we entered.

'You lookin' for us, Hargrove?' I said. 'That why you're yellin' at my boss?'

Hargrove turned and glared at me. His partner, Holliday, looked at us, too, but with a lot less animosity.

'You two!'

'In the flesh,' I said, spreading my arms.

'Where the hell have you been?'

'Here and there,' I said. 'Mostly there. Why?'

'Why? Your own hotel lobby got shot up yesterday morning. Are you gonna try to tell me you weren't the target?'

'I don't know,' I said. 'Do you have any witnesses that saw me – us – there?'

'No.'

'Then I guess we weren't there.'

'I've got something better.'

'Oh? What's that?'

Hargrove smiled tightly. 'I've got the shooter in custody.'

I stared at him for a few seconds, then asked, 'Well, why didn't you say that before?'

Jerry and I accompanied Hargrove and his partner to the police station where they were holding the shooter.

'His name is Delving,' Hargrove said. He turned to look at us in the back seat, while his partner drove. 'Do either of you know that name?'

'No,' I said.

'Never heard of him.'

'No, well, he's not a pro,' Hargrove said, 'just an amateur tryin' for a big pay day.'

'All the more reason to believe this was not a creditable, sanctioned contract,' Holliday said, glancing at us in the rear-view mirror. 'I'd bet all the attempts on you – the ones we know about and the ones we don't – were sloppy.'

'No bet,' I said.

When we got to the station, they showed us Delving through a window as he sat in an interrogation room.

'Can he see us?' I asked.

'No,' Hargrove said, 'not unless we turn a light on in here.'

'Do either of you know him?' Holliday asked. 'Or have seen him before?'

'No,' I said.

'Yes,' Jerry said. 'He's the one who took the shots at Mr G. yesterday.'

Jerry had just admitted that we were in the

256

hotel lobby when the shots were fired. But so what? He had a point. Were they going to arrest us for getting shot at?

I looked at Hargrove.

'What have you gotten out of him so far?' I was hoping he wasn't thinking of acting on what Jerry had just said.

'He's been sittin' in that room for almost twenty-four hours,' Holliday said, jabbing at the air with his forefinger. 'We've got nothin'.'

'And he's not a pro?' Jerry asked.

'Not a pro shooter,' Hargrove said. 'But he's an insider. We're sure of it.'

'OK, then . . .' Jerry said.

'OK, then . . . what?' Hargrove asked.

'He means,' I said, 'let us talk to him.'

'You think you can break him when we couldn't in twenty-four hours?' Holliday asked.

'I think you came lookin' for us for a reason.'

'Yeah,' Hargrove said, 'to lock your asses up.'

'For what?' Jerry asked. 'Gettin' shot at?'

'You want to find out who put that contract out on me before some innocent bystanders get hurt,' I said. 'Am I right?'

Hargrove didn't answer, so Holliday said, 'Well, that's our job.'

'This is the first time we got somebody who tried to cash in on that contract,' I pointed out. 'Let us talk to him.'

Holliday looked at Hargrove, who was probably the senior man of the two. 'What can it hurt?' he asked.

'Crap,' Hargrove said, waving his hand in disgust. 'Put them in with him.'

257

'Hands up,' Holliday said. 'I've gotta search you first.'

I expected him to come up with Jerry's .45, which would have meant trouble, but he didn't. We'd gone there in their car. Had he stashed it there? If he had, it could still come back to bite us on the ass.

'This way,' Holliday said.

Seventy-One

When the door opened, the guy looked up at us. He didn't flinch when he saw me, but as Jerry came in behind me, he pushed his chair back a few inches. Jerry closed the door and Delving realized it was just the three of us in the room – which smelled like a room someone had been sweating in for twenty-four hours.

'Hey,' he said, 'what—'

'What's the problem, Delving?' I asked. 'Don't wanna be in the same room with the two guys you shot at yesterday?'

'I–I wasn't sh–shootin' at him!' he exclaimed, pointing a shaky finger at Jerry. 'I was shootin' at you!'

'And why was that?' I asked. 'What did I ever do to you?'

'Nothin',' he said. 'It wasn't personal.'

'Just business, huh?' I asked.

'That's right,' he said, nodding, 'business.'

'Guess that ten grand looked like easy money

when I came walkin' across the lobby of the Sands, huh?'

'Yeah,' he said, sourly, 'too easy.'

'You ain't a pro, Delving,' Jerry said. 'You may be a hard guy, but you rushed your shots.'

'Figures,' he mumbled.

'Why's that?' I asked.

'I ain't never had the luck,' he complained. 'I get all the shit jobs. This was my chance to . . .' He trailed off, shaking his head.

'To what?' I asked. 'Move up?'

'Yeah,' he said, 'move up.'

'Well, you blew it,' Jerry said, 'but you still got a chance for some luck.'

'Oh, yeah?' he asked. 'How's that?'

'Tell us who put the hit out on me, and maybe you can walk out of here,' I said, fully aware of the fact that I didn't have the authority to let him walk anywhere.

'Look,' he said, 'I'll tell you what I been tellin' the cops. I don't know who put it out.'

'Then how did you expect to get paid?'

He clammed up.

Jerry moved forward, pointed his thick fore-finger at Delving, just a few inches from the man's nose.

'Now listen,' he said, 'you may think you're a hard guy, but by the time I'm done with ya, you ain't gonna be so sure.'

'I tol' ya,' Delving complained, 'I wasn't shootin' at you!'

'Wait a minute,' I said, pointing to Jerry. 'You know who he is?'

'I seen him around.'

Jerry and I exchanged a glance.

'Where?' I asked.

'In Brooklyn.'

'You from Brooklyn?' Jerry asked.

'Yeah,' the man said, 'so what?'

'You heard about this contract in Brooklyn?' Jerry said.

'Yeah, so?'

'Where? From who?'

'Same place you heard about it, probably,' Delving said. 'On the street.'

'And you flew here to collect?'

Delving nodded and said, 'On my last dime.'

I looked at Jerry again, then back at Delving.

'What's your first name?' I asked.

'Mickey.'

'Mickey,' I said, 'how would you like a shower, a steak and a suite at the Sands?'

His eyebrows shot up. 'Yer kiddin'.'

'No, I'm not,' I said, 'but before you get any of those things, we're gonna have to get you somethin' else.'

'What's that?'

'A good lawyer.'

'What are you tryin' to pull?' Hargrove asked when we came out.

'We need him cooperative,' I said. 'I set him up at the Sands and I'm gonna be his best friend.'

'And what do you think you'll get out of him?' Holliday asked.

'Names,' I said, 'just names.'

'You think he knows who put the hit out on you?'

'Probably not,' I said. 'Jerry heard about it, but he doesn't know where it came from.'

Hargrove looked at Jerry. 'How'd you hear?'

'A street source,' Jerry said. 'A guy who knew I knew Mr G. He sold me the info for a double sawbuck.'

'And where did he get the info?' Holliday asked.

'Heard it in a bar in East New York,' Jerry said.

'Did you check it out?' Hargrove asked.

'Yeah, but not real well. I needed to hop on a plane and get out here. The bartender said the guy heard it from a guy who knew a guy.'

'And what makes you think you'll get more out of this mug by putting him up in the lap of luxury?'

'It can't be any worse than you've done keepin' him here,' I said. 'Whataya say?'

Hargrove thought it over, then said, 'OK, you can have him, but Holliday goes with you.' He pointed at his partner, who apparently had no say in the matter.

Seventy-Two

Holliday drove us all in his unmarked car, heading to the Sands. We had to drive with the windows open because of the stench coming off Mickey Delving. My bandage was itching and I was sure Jerry's was, too. It'd be four by the time we got back to the hotel, and maybe we could all have a shower.

261

'Do you know anything about the FBI bein' in town?' I asked. I was in front with Holliday, while Jerry rode in back with Delving.

'No, why?'

'Because we met one. An agent, I mean. Don't they have to check in with the local cops when they come to town?'

'Man,' Holliday said, 'the Feds do what they want, make their own rules. What was this fella's name?'

'Seagrave.'

'Never heard of him. What'd he want?'

'It doesn't have anythin' to do with the contract,' I said. 'It has somethin' to do with why we were in LA.'

'Nothin' to do with me, then.'

'No.'

He shrugged. 'Suits me. I hate the Feds.'

'You see that car?' Jerry called out.

'What car?' Holliday asked.

Before Jerry could answer, we got slammed hard from behind.

'That one!' Jerry called out.

'What the—' Holliday said as we got hit again.

I turned in my seat to look behind us. As I did, another car came up alongside us, on the driver's side.

'Watch it—' I started to say, but the window next to Holliday's head shattered and something wet hit me in the face. It took me a moment to realize it was Holliday's blood.

'Get the wheel, Mr G.!' Jerry shouted. I saw that he had his .45 in his hand. Later, I realized he really had hidden the gun in the back seat of the police car.

I reached out for the wheel, but Holliday's hands were locked on it. I couldn't tell if he was alive or dead, but I couldn't get his paws off the wheel.

We got another hit from behind, and Delving yelled, 'Holy crap!'

We were on a residential street, and as we came to a lane of parked cars the shooter's car couldn't stay next to us. It dropped back, and now we had two cars behind us, but only one at a time could bump us.

Holliday's foot was also jammed down on the gas pedal, and we were picking up speed, careening out of control.

'Mr G.!' Jerry yelled.

'I'm tryin'!'

The rear windshield shattered – from how many bullets I couldn't say. I knew one whizzed by my head and poked a hole in the front windshield.

I finally got Holliday's hands off the wheel as I heard the report of Jerry's .45. He fired three times, but I had no way of knowing what effect they had.

Up ahead of us I saw a parking lot coming up and figured that was our best bet. We couldn't outrun our pursuers with Holliday stuck behind the wheel, and I couldn't get the driver's side door open to dump him out – not that I would have done that even if I could.

'The parking lot!' Jerry shouted.

'I see it!'

He fired again, but my ears were already ringing from his first shots. I jerked the wheel to the right and we catapulted over a curb into the parking lot at high speed. I reached across Holliday's leg with my left foot, feeling for the brake pedal. As I stomped down on it, his foot came off the gas and our tires screeched as we headed for a strip mall. The car started to swerve to the left, so I yanked the wheel in that direction. We spun around a few times and came to a stop with the rear bumper practically up against a storefront. I didn't know what damage we had done, but at least we hadn't gone through the display window.

'Out! Out!' Jerry yelled. 'They're comin'.'

Delving opened his door and fell out of the car, sprawling on to the asphalt lot. Jerry slammed his open and got out in a more deliberate manner.

I wasn't out yet, and Jerry yelled my name.

'In a minute!'

I frisked Holliday, found his gun on his belt and jerked it free, then opened my door and tumbled out gracelessly.

'Take cover!' Jerry yelled, crouching behind his open door and reloading.

Delving panicked and ran. He had got part of the way across the parking lot when a volley of shots made him dance and then fall.

Suddenly, it was quiet.

'How many?' I asked Jerry.

'Looks like four of 'em,' he called back, 'two from each car.'

'I got Holliday's gun,' I said.

264

'Good. We're gonna need to keep 'em off us until the cops get here.'

'And what makes you think they're gonna get here?' I asked.

''Cause you're gonna call 'em on the car radio.'

Shit! Why hadn't I thought of that?

Seventy-Three

I slipped back into the front seat, grabbed the radio mike, figured out how to use it and froze.

'What do I say?' I yelled to Jerry.

'Man down,' Jerry said. 'Tell 'em you got a cop shot in the parking lot at . . . Merchandise King.'

I keyed the handset and started shouting into it in what I hoped was a coherent voice.

'Hey, wait,' someone said, 'who is this?'

'What does it matter who this is?' I demanded, 'You've got an officer down out here. Tell Detective Hargrove his partner is dow—'

I might not have gotten the message across because the shooting started again right at that moment. I dropped the handset and ducked down as far as I could go. When the volley was over, I slid out of the car again, crouched down behind my door.

'Jerry, you OK?' I asked.

'I'm fine,' he said. 'Is Holliday dead?'

'I can't tell,' I said. 'I think so. I've got his blood on me.'

'And Delving?'

I looked over at the fallen man. 'He's down – hasn't moved.'

'Well,' Jerry said, 'if they were after him, I guess they'd be gone by now. That means they're after you, and this time they mean business. This looks like a pro hit team.'

'Oh, great,' I said. 'That's all I need.'

'No, Mr G.,' he said, 'that *is* what we need. If we can take one of these guys alive, he might know somethin'.'

'If we can take one of them alive?' I asked. 'How about we concentrate on gettin' ourselves out of here alive?'

'What kind of store is this Merchandise King?'

'I'm not sure,' I said. 'Lots of furniture, I think.' It wasn't five yet. Either it had closed early or it was closed up, out of business.

'If we can get inside, there'll be lots of places to hide until the cops show up. And maybe if they come in after us, I can grab one of 'em.'

'Jerry—'

'Come on, Mr G.,' he said. 'All we gotta do is kick out some glass.'

At that point I figured it might have been a good thing after all if the car had gone through the front window.

'They'll hear it and know we went inside.'

'I know,' he said. 'That's what I want. You still got Holliday's gun?'

'I've got it.' I gripped it tightly in my sweaty hand.

'What is it?'

'Looks like a thirty-eight, with five shots.'

'OK,' he said, 'don't fire unless you know you got a good shot, OK?'

Hell, I'd have to be in somebody's lap to get a good shot, but I said, 'Yeah, OK.'

'Now,' he said, 'when I say go, make for the window. I'll kick it in.'

I heard him fire two shots, then yell, 'Go!' By the time I got to the window, he was there. One swift kick and the thing shattered. He rolled inside and I felt a shard of glass still in the frame gash my right calf.

'Ow!' I shouted as we came to a stop.

'What is it?'

'I cut myself,' I said.

'Bad?'

'I don't know.' I looked down. 'I'm gonna leave a trail, though.'

'Good,' he said, 'we can use that.' He grabbed me by the jacket, pulled and said, 'Come on!'

We left a trail of blood leading to a living-room set-up, and then Jerry used his handkerchief and mine to bind my leg.

'Ain't too bad,' he said. 'Might need a few stitches.'

'A few more,' I said. 'It's the same damn leg. How's your shoulder?'

'It's OK.'

'Now what?' We kept our voices down.

'They're in here already,' he said. 'They'll probably split up. Your blood trail leads to that sofa. You hide behind that chair over there.' He pointed.

'And you?'

267

'I'll be over here,' he said. 'If they do split up, I may be able to take them one at a time.'

'And if not?'

He slapped me on the shoulder. 'Then we'll take 'em out together.'

'Great,' I said.

We heard somebody cry out then, sounding as if they'd walked into something.

'Go,' he said. 'Go!'

I dragged myself over behind the large armchair he'd indicated. The makeshift bandage felt tight on my leg, and I was no longer leaving a trail.

I peered around to see where Jerry had gone, but for a big man he moved quick and was nowhere in sight. I listened intently, still heard somebody moving around.

I slipped Holliday's .38 from my pocket, wondering if the detective was alive or dead.

Seventy-Four

'There,' I heard somebody say.

'We gotta get outta here before the cops come,' another voice said.

'I ain't walkin' away from ten grand,' the first voice said. 'Not when I'm this close to it. And I don't hear no sirens. Look, the blood goes there.'

'You guys are gonna hear more than sirens,' I heard Jerry say. 'More like little birdies.'

I peered around just in time to see the two men

turn to see Jerry standing behind them, towering over them.

'What the—' one of the said, but Jerry cut him off with a right that put him down and out. In fact, I would have been surprised if the guy wasn't eating through a straw for months.

As he went down, the other one reached for his belt. I could see Jerry's .45 was not in his hand.

'Don't,' Jerry advised him. 'We only need one of you alive.'

'Yeah, fuck you,' the guy said, and made a move for his belt.

Jerry drew his .45 and shot the guy once. I felt as if I was at an old Saturday morning matinee, watching Tom Mix.

'Billy!' a voice called from somewhere else in the store. 'You get 'im?'

'Billy?' another voice called.

'Billy can't answer right now,' Jerry called back.

I stood up as I heard one man curse and another say, 'Let's get the hell out of here.'

We heard them run, and then we heard the sirens.

'Mr G.?' Jerry said. 'Do we run?'

'We can't, Jerry,' I said. 'We got a dead man in here, maybe two outside, and one of them is a cop. We can't talk our way out of this one.'

'Well,' he said, sticking his gun back in his belt and gesturing to the man on the floor, 'at least we got this one alive.'

I looked down at the unconscious man. He had blood coming from his mouth. He might have bitten his tongue, and given it was Jerry who hit him, he might even have bitten it clean through.

'If he can even talk,' I said. I looked down at Holliday's gun in my hand and dropped it to the floor.

'He'll talk,' Jerry said. 'He'll sing like a canary, even if he has to write his answers down.'

'You said these guys were pros.'

'They acted like it.'

'Then if we couldn't get Delving to talk, what makes you think this one will tell us anything?'

'Because he'll be smart enough to be afraid,' Jerry said, 'once he finds out Mr Giancana didn't sanction this hit.'

Seventy-Five

Holliday was dead.

Turns out I didn't only have his blood on me, but his brains, too.

They stuck me into one interrogation room and Jerry into another. I thought I was in the same one Delving had been in, judging by the smell.

I was surprised when a doctor came in to have a look at me. He had me remove my trousers, and applied fresh bandages to both wounds.

'You've been mistreating this leg,' he said.

'Not deliberately,' I said. 'How's my friend? Did you look at him?'

'The big guy? He tore a stitch or two. I fixed him up.'

'I'm surprised Hargrove let you do that.'

'Oh,' the doctor said, as I slid my pants back on gingerly, 'he wants the both of you nice and healthy.'

'So he can put us away.'

'He really doesn't like you very much,' the doctor said. 'He says he thinks he has you this time.'

'For getting shot at?'

The doctor shrugged and left.

When Hargrove finally came in two hours later, he was alone. He sat across from me, opened a notebook and asked, 'What happened?'

'That's it?' I asked. 'No gloating? No threats?'

'I need a statement,' he said. 'That's what I want right now.'

'All right,' I said, and told him exactly what had happened since we left him earlier, in the company of his partner, Holliday.

When I was done, he closed his notebook.

'I'll have this typed up,' he said, standing.

'Hargrove, I'm sorry about Holliday.'

He didn't reply, just left, slamming the door behind him.

I could see how controlled his anger was. He was vibrating with it; for some reason, though, he was keeping it in check.

I didn't know if that was a good thing or a bad.

When the door opened again, I expected to see Hargrove. I'd been cooling my heels for another two hours. They were either questioning Jerry first or making us both wait.

But it wasn't Hargrove.

It was Amico. 'Let's go,' he said. 'You're out of here.'

'What?'

'You want to stay?'

'Hell, no!'

'Then hurry up, before Hargrove finds a reason to keep you.'

I stood up and rushed to the door.

I signed my statement and then we went outside. Amico had a car there, and Jerry was already in it.

'How'd you get us out?' I asked. 'Who are you?'

'A friend,' he said.

'Is Amico your real name?' I asked. 'It means "friend".'

'I think we should talk about this somewhere else,' he suggested.

I looked up at the police station, then said, 'Yeah, OK, let's get out of here.'

Seventy-Six

We went to the Sands. Amico waited while Jerry and I both showered in Jerry's suite.

'The first thing I wanna ask you is, are you working for Jack Entratter? Because if you are, I'll get him up here,' I said.

Jerry wasn't in the room yet, and Amico studied me for a minute.

'Not working for Entratter,' he finally said.

'Who are you workin' for, then?'

Jerry walked in and said, 'I'd like to know the answer to that, myself.'

'Well, at the moment I'm working for you two, trying to keep you out of jail – which is not easy, given what Jerry did with his forty-five.'

'He defended us,' I pointed out, 'and tried to save Detective Holliday.'

'A point I made myself,' Amico said.

'So, you're . . . what?' I asked. 'A lawyer instead of a hitman?'

Amico frowned. 'When did you think I was a hitman?'

'The thought occurred to me when we first met.'

'Maybe that's flattering,' Amico said. 'I don't know, but no, I'm not a hitman. I do, however, happen to be a lawyer . . . among other things.'

'Like what?'

'I'm a little like you, Eddie,' he said. 'I guess you could say I'm a fixer, only my arena is a little bigger than yours.'

'Well, if you can fix this,' I said, 'I'll bow to your superior abilities, believe me.'

'Wait,' Jerry said, 'what are we talkin' about? Fixin' it with the cops? Or takin' care of this open contract?'

'Both,' Amico said. 'Actually, the open contract isn't even the tricky part.'

'How's that?' I asked.

'It's gone,' he said, 'done. You don't have to worry about it anymore.'

'Did the guy we grabbed talk?' I asked.

'He didn't have to,' Amico said. 'You should be getting a phone call about it later on. No, what we have to worry about is the local law. They're pretty upset about their man getting killed.'

'Not our fault,' Jerry said.

'Well, Hargrove is holding Eddie responsible,' Amico said. 'He says if it wasn't for you, Detective Holliday would still be alive.'

'He's probably right about that,' I said.

'Nah, he ain't,' Jerry argued.

'It doesn't matter,' Amico said. 'I got you out of there. It remains to be seen if they want you back for an investigation, or if they'll simply bring charges. Personally, I don't think they'll do either.'

'And how involved will you stay?' I asked.

He smiled and said, 'I'm in till the end, Eddie.'

I didn't know who was paying the freight on Amico, but I was glad they were.

After Amico left, Jerry and I hit the bar to try to decompress.

'I don't know where this guy came from,' Jerry said, 'but I'm glad he did.'

'I'd still like to know who he works for,' I said, 'and who put up that contract.'

'He said you'd be gettin' a phone call,' Jerry said. 'Maybe we should check for messages.'

'Why not?'

Jerry picked up the phone and called down to the desk. 'Yeah,' he said, 'I got it.' He hung up. 'The only message is for you, from Danny.' He pushed the phone over to me. 'Says to call him in Judy's room.'

274

I dialed the number. He picked up on the first ring.

'Where've you been?' he demanded.

'It's a long story,' I said. 'Let's just say things heated up, and have since cooled down.'

'You mean . . .'

'The contract has been lifted,' I said, 'or so I've been told. Apparently, I'm waiting for a phone call to confirm it.'

'Well, that's good news.'

'Have you got something for me?'

'Yeah,' he said, 'and I think you're gonna like this. I tracked down the owner of the house where you found Jacks and the girl.'

'Make it easy on me,' I said.

'I had to wade through a bunch of dummy companies, but finally found the one that owns it.'

'It's owned by a company?'

'A real estate company with several partners.'

'And they would be?'

'Only one should concern you,' Danny said.

'OK,' I said, 'don't milk it. Let me have it.'

'One of the partners is David Begelman.'

Seventy-Seven

Danny let us into Judy's suite.

'Have you told her?' I asked.

'No,' he said, 'I figured I'd leave that to you.'

'Good.'

'I've already said goodnight,' he told me. 'I'm going home to take a shower and get some sleep.'

I shook his hand and said, 'Thanks, Danny.'

Jerry slapped him on the back as he went past us into the hall. We found Judy sitting on the sofa, her hands clasped in her lap. As usual, she wore a white blouse, black pants and slippers. She looked for all the world as if she was going to a dance rehearsal.

'Judy.'

'Are you both all right?' she asked. 'I was so worried.'

'We're fine,' I said. I sat next to her, Jerry across from her.

'But you have some news for me,' she said. 'Bad news?'

'News,' I said.

She looked at Jerry, then back at me.

'Judy, I don't believe anyone has been watching you, or following you, or breaking into your house.'

'You . . . you think I'm paranoid, then? Like everyone else?'

'No,' I said, 'you and Sid are right about one thing.'

'David and Freddie?'

'Well . . . David,' I said. 'He's definitely not on the up-and-up. I think you should go ahead with your lawsuit. Fire them as your managers.'

'I knew it!' she said. 'H–How much have they stolen?'

'Not sure,' I said.

'That Bagel-Man is driving a Caddy that should've been yours,' Jerry said.

'What about the blackmail?'

'We believe Begelman set that up and kept the money,' I said.

'And the people who were killed?' she asked. 'That private detective and the girl?'

'That's for the cops to solve,' I said, 'but we found out one thing we can pass on to them. Begelman is a partner in a real estate company that owned that house.'

'Oh my God.'

I touched her arm. 'That doesn't mean he's involved in their death. Like I said, that's gonna be for the cops to find out. All you have to do is sue him and get what's comin' to you.'

'I can go back home?'

'Yes.'

'But, what about the . . . hitman?'

'That's been taken care of,' I assured her. 'There's no longer any danger.'

'I'll call Sid,' she said.

'And,' I said, 'now you can go ahead and marry Mark Herron.'

'If you still want to,' Jerry added.

She looked at both of us and asked, 'Is there something you found out about Mark?'

'No,' I said.

'We just don't like him,' Jerry said.

She covered her face with both hands, then dropped them into her lap and sat back. 'I've been making more problems for myself,' she said. 'In my head. I have been paranoid.'

I was about to tell her she was wrong, but believing it actually seemed to make her feel better.

'All because of David,' she finished.

277

'Yes,' I said, 'because of David.'

Jerry leaned forward and said, 'Sue his ass off.'

Seventy-Eight

Jerry and I went back to his room. Mine was not a suite and was too small for us.

'I'm starved,' he said.

'Order room service.'

'Anything?'

'Anything.'

While he called down, I got two cans of beer from the refrigerator.

'Steaks. I ordered steak dinners.'

'Fine.' I sipped my beer.

'What's botherin' ya, Mr G.?'

'Jimmy Jacks.'

'You wanna find out who killed him?'

'No,' I said, 'it bothers me that I don't care who killed him.'

Jerry shrugged. 'Me, neither.'

'And you don't wonder why?'

'No,' Jerry said. 'It ain't our job. Let the cops find out who did it.'

'And the girl?'

'That's too bad,' he said.

After we ate, I decided to head back to my room. No amount of discussion made me feel any better. I let Jerry eat both desserts himself.

'It ain't such a bad thing, Mr G.,' he told me

at the door. 'Sometimes it's just better if you don't feel nothin'.'

'Goodnight, Jerry.'

I was lying awake in my bed when the phone rang. 'Hello?'

'Gianelli?'

'That's right.'

'This is Agent Seagrave.'

'What the hell do you want?'

'I have instructions to call you.'

'Instructions from who?'

'Never mind. I assume you've told Miss Garland about her manager?'

'She's gonna sue his ass,' I said.

'That's good,' he said. 'Maybe we'll get to him after that.'

'Is that what you called to tell me?'

'No,' he said, 'I was told you'd be expecting my call.'

'Expectin' your—' I sat up in bed. 'Wait. You mean . . .?'

'You're aware that the contract on you has been lifted?'

'Yes,' I said, 'but by who? Giancana?'

'I'm sure Mr Giancana has passed the word,' he said, but it sounded as if it wasn't Momo who lifted it.

'Was it lifted by the same person who put it out on me?'

He hesitated, then said, 'Yes. It came from the source.'

'Who?' I asked. 'Who was it?'

'Are you familiar with the name Maheu?'

279

Epilogue

I settled into my seat in the second row, the band tuning up practically in front of me. As people were milling about around me, finding their seats, the seat to my right remained empty. I still didn't know who had sent me the ticket to the Judy Garland tribute show. I was looking forward to finding out, though.

To this day I'm convinced that the open contract on my life had come either from Howard Hughes, because I'd kept him from moving in on Las Vegas a few months earlier during Edward G. Robinson's stay in town, or from his man Robert Maheu, who might have taken the decision upon himself to try to appease his boss.

Whichever it was, though, there was no danger from that day forward, after my short conversation with FBI Agent Seagrave.

Hargrove was never able to bring charges against me and Jerry for what happened to Detective Holliday that night. They put away the guy we caught, and he gave up his other two partners.

Judy and Sid Luft sued David Begelman for royalties she had coming to her. Freddie Fields was kept out of it. As far as I know, the FBI never got to Begelman. He and Fields went on to bigger and better careers – separately – in

280

Hollywood. Maybe they all deserved each other. The murders of Jimmy Jacks and his girlfriend were never solved. I never saw or heard from Agent Seagrave or the man I knew as Amico again. Never found out who they actually reported to.

Judy performed a few concerts after returning home, including a triumphant appearance at New York's Carnegie Hall – twenty-six songs in two and a half hours. It was amazing. She never made another film, though. She was cast in the movie version of Jackie Susann's *Valley of the Dolls*, but was replaced soon after shooting began by Susan Hayward. The complaints were that she was difficult and constantly late to the set.

She called me a few times over those last years, usually late at night. Sometimes she slurred her words, sometimes not. Usually it was just to talk, not about anything in particular. She did marry Mark Heron, but they separated six months later. He went back to his actor lover. On June twenty-second, 1969, her fifth husband, Mickey Deans, found her dead in their bathroom of a drug overdose. It was ruled an 'incautious self-overdose'. The medical examiner's opinion was that there was no intent on her part to commit suicide; nevertheless, Judy Garland's sad story was over.

As for Howard Hughes, he eventually came back to Las Vegas with his wallet in 1966 . . . but that's a story for another time.

The appearance of someone on my right brought me back to the present. She settled into her seat and, just as the lights were going down for the show to start, leaned over and whispered into my ear, 'Hello, Eddie, my darling.'

I took her hand in mine and said, 'Hello, Liza.'